Colour

Colour of My Heart

Kavita Comar

YOUCAXTON PUBLICATIONS
OXFORD & SHREWSBURY

Dedication

To My Parents...

You've shaped the person I am today with
your love, laughter, courage and guidance.
I've not made it easy for you, but this story
could not have been written from the heart,
without you being present in my heart.

To My Readers...

I hope that you have at least half as much joy
in reading this book as I've had in writing it.

To 'Chris'...

Thankyou.

Contents

PART ONE

Chapter One

*"Those who are too fussy will never find anyone.
They'll be left on the shelf.".**...Dad***

Some people would describe their life as an open book. I wish that I could say the same about mine, except I'd describe my life as a secret diary which has a locked key. Searching for that key would prove futile because it lies deep rooted; buried inside a tiny pocket of my heart. And so for that reason alone, unless *I* want to reveal it, it'll always remain hidden.

I have no recollection of how, why or even when my life became complicated. But it is there's no doubt about it. At my relatively young age of thirty – and I say relatively young, because when you're Indian, or British Indian in my case, and a daughter belonging to fairly traditional Hindu parents and large extended family, then reaching thirty and not even close to getting married is a recipe for suspicious Indian minds.

I'm "sitting on the shelf" according to my father, who believes I'm getting far too old and worries that I'll remain a spinster my entire life.

"You're too fussy about what you want," he proclaims often. "And those who are too fussy will never find anyone. They'll be left on the shelf."

So as I grow older, I'm gathering dust apparently, due to my lack of ability to find my perfect partner.

"I just want to be able to click with him," I tell my parents. "It's not just about his family background and what job he does and whether he's financially stable. There's so much more you have to consider."

They don't always understand me though.

My parents' marriage wasn't exactly arranged, but they were introduced to one another.

Dad was born in India and moved to England at the age of nine. Sixteen years later, he and my grandparents returned to India in search of a suitable wife, and after only a handful of "meetings" Mum and Dad literally tied the knot.

They never dated one another, to see if there was a spark, any chemistry, compatibility or even some common interests that they shared. And if I let that thought last longer than a fleeting moment, then a sudden bout of shivers travels through my body uninvited. Occasionally my heart begins to do somersaults in my throat and I find myself struggling to catch my breath; so I force myself to reason with it.

Since they're coming up to thirty-one years of marriage, I can only assume that it hasn't been such an ordeal for either of them.

"I don't know what you mean by this clicking, *shicking*," Mum often admits, who is equally worried like Dad, that time is ticking on and there's still no hint of a potential suitor on the horizon.

Both of them truly believe that they'll have fulfilled their biggest duty in life, as parents, by getting their two daughters married to "suitable" men.

My granddad moved from Amritsar in Punjab to the North West of England in the early Sixties, having lived within walking distance of one of the most stunning, monumental wonders of the world, the Golden Temple.

I've heard the story dozens of times of how my granddad first arrived in England, yet still, even today it never ceases to amaze me that he embarked on that journey alone, with only a few coins in his pocket.

Like most people of my grandparents' generation, Granddad took that step with hopes of making a better life for his family. He worked tirelessly for three years before saving enough money to call Grandma, my dad and his brothers and sisters over.

So for someone like my dad - who's been brought up in England most of his life - I thought, or rather hoped, that he'd be quite savvy about the world and what goes on in it, but he can still be mighty traditional and strict when he wants, holding some unusual ethics and firm beliefs.

When you're fifteen, sadly you don't have a choice but to accept your parents' decisions about your life, but as a fully grown adult, it's painfully hard to comprehend unreasonable explanations, simply because they don't like something, or just because you're living under their roof with their set of rules.

What they fail to accept is because I was born and bred here I have an entirely different point of view on most things and opinions that I'm not afraid to express. It's often the reason why I land myself in hot water - because of my inability to control a condition called verbal diarrhoea!

I can move out if I want to. It's not that I'm not allowed to get my own place. I mean, no one could physically stop me, but it's the mental stress I'd endure from everyone if I voiced my thoughts - that I want my own place, my own space with nobody stopping me or questioning me about my life.

Culturally and traditionally an Indian daughter is seen as a 'child on loan,' so to speak. Eventually she's going to be part of another family, and her parents are bringing her up for that other family. You see, marriage itself isn't just about the union of two people or two souls in the Hindu religion, it's about the joining together of two families.

Many Indian parents would be of the same opinion - that there are more pressures with daughters, because as soon as she reaches a marriageable age, they don't want her going astray and getting into pre-marital relationships. Broadly speaking, it's not morally accepted in the Indian culture.

Perhaps it's a bit harsh, arguably cruel to think of an unmarried daughter as a 'child on loan,' but I do understand the concept behind it. It's actually quite endearing. I love the fact that my parents want the very best for me and my future, because there are many out there who don't care at all. I just wish they didn't hold unsavoury views about me at times. I'm often told,

'You just want to be like your English friends; go out drinking, clubbing, out till all hours.'

'You don't have any respect for us.' 'You answer back.' 'You've lost your culture and identity.'

'Indian girls don't stay out till all hours. They shouldn't behave like that!'

How exactly should they behave? That's what I want to know.

It's almost as if my parents are clueless on what goes on in the real world. Or, maybe they do know but they don't like what they see. Thirty years on and perhaps they're still trying to hide me away from a lifestyle they think is ugly - believe is too western and not 'Indian' enough.

I mean I'm no angel, but nor have I been a trouble-maker either. I never hung around in gangs drinking and swearing, or being a general nuisance to law abiding citizens. I never dabbled in drugs, even when cannabis became widely available at university; easy as picking it up over the counter. In fact I've never picked up a cigarette in my life. But that's only because it doesn't intrigue me the way alcohol does.

And if I do drink a little more admittedly, than I should at times, it's only because I need it, not because I want it. I don't particularly like drinking, but it does help me to unleash my inner self and release my inhibitions; unwind and become the real me - British born Anushka Lamba - true to myself; because most of the time I feel like a caged up animal biting at the bars with my teeth, roaring to be let out.

Hindu's aren't too dissimilar to traditional Catholics, in the sense that they don't believe in having children out of wedlock. But having children hasn't even entertained my mind, unlike my cousin Sarika, who is quite vocal about telling the family that she wants a baby, but doesn't want to get married or want the father to go with her baby!

I'm frightened of the whole pregnancy process if I'm being honest. Watching and feeling a human being grow inside you right in front of your eyes is a concept I still haven't grasped; though everywhere I turn I find another one of my friends telling me they're having a baby.

Some tell me that pregnancy is the most natural and beautiful thing a woman will experience in her life; but I don't see it. Becoming more fat and frumpy each day is psychologically a depressing thought, not to mention the countless hours of birthing pains, and the prospect of being in labour for hours on end - gassed and goodness knows what else with doctors and nurses prodding and pinching you. Well frankly it frightens the life out of me.

According to my cousins I have no broody bones in my body, just a heart made of stone, they'd joke. They think I lack the love that's needed to nurture a baby, because I get irritated at the slightest of things.

I'm not hesitant in disclosing to Mum that I'm not fussed about having children; but she often drops subtle hints into conversations.

"By the time I celebrated my twenty first birthday Anushka, I'd been married eight months you know, and I was expecting you. By thirty I'd already had you, Sanya and your brother Krish. Look at you, you're thirty and there's not even a man yet."

Sadness glides over her face momentarily and a glint of disappointment fills her eyes. I can almost see the game of self blame she plays in her mind. Questioning herself if this is an inauspicious sign – if whether she's failed somewhere along the years as a mother - in her duty of my upbringing and nurturing.

During my early teens, conversations with my cousins usually revolved around boys and marriage. I can still vividly remember a time when we compiled a list with the names of eleven of my cousins, in ascending order of who would get hitched.

Arjun, the eldest of my cousins was naturally the first on the list. Rohini featured next to him, because she's the eldest out of all the girls. Jaya and Sarika are a little older to me, but I sat in between them both, half way down.

"Let's reserve Ritu now with babysitting duties for Anu's kids," Jaya said to the rest of my cousins one evening at a family get together.

"Six months after it's born she'll be handing the baby on to you Ritu." Jaya laughed out loud, looking in my direction.

"Six months? You're joking aren't you?" I replied a little too quickly. "That's a bit long, Jaya. More like one month, I reckon. I'll leave the little thing at Ritu's house in the morning, and then the dad can come and collect it in the evening!"

Without giving it an extra thought I referred to my made up, unborn child as an 'it,' and a 'thing', but I'm sure I half meant it at the time.

Mum walked in just when I was vocalising my thoughts a tad too loudly and gave me her disapproving look, like she couldn't quite believe that at fourteen I could possibly know anything about having children.

Unlike my school friends who were fortunate enough to openly discuss sex and puberty with their parents', I learnt everything I needed to in Biology classes and amongst my peers.

There's two and a half years between me and my sister Sanya, and exactly a decade between my brother Krish - the youngest, doted on only son - and me - the eldest, rebellious and opinionated daughter.

Within twelve months of Mum getting married and living in a *'foreign'* country, adjusting to a lifestyle that was totally alien to her, her father passed away whilst she was expecting me. To make matters worse, her pregnancy was horrendously difficult to cope with, and that too for the whole eight months before I popped out prematurely. For that reason, Dad half jokingly and half seriously reminds me that because of Mum's tough pregnancy, it's no wonder I've been a difficult daughter to manage.

Mum has always lived with her in-laws since the day she got married; even today we all live with my grandmother, my *Dadi*.

When I was seventeen, my granddad (dad's dad) passed away. I was heartbroken beyond belief, because Granddad was another father figure in my life from the moment I was born. His untimely and unexpected death left a gaping hole in my heart and an incomprehensible void in my life which could never be filled again.

My nanni (mum's mum) lives in a joint house, in South Delhi with her two sons and their families. She's one of the sweetest people I have ever met. I've been to India about six or seven times since I was born, and each time I see Nanni I'm pleasantly surprised to see how gracefully she is growing old. Although the last time I visited, she had started to look quite frail, as if all the Hindu God's had finally got round to making up for lost time with my nanni.

She's petite in height at only four foot ten and extremely thin with long, wiry grey hair; she always dresses modestly in her Indian attire. I've never seen her wear makeup or accessories, and her hair is usually always braided in a plait. Nanni is a woman of few words and as far as I can remember I've never heard her raise her voice with anyone.

Nanni has never been flamboyant in either character or appearance - unlike Dadi who is larger than life, and has a voice and demeanour to match.

At also four foot ten, Dadi's Indian attire is always colour coordinated. Every outfit will be complimented with a cardigan which she matches to perfection. She pays particular attention to the detail on her cardigan's embroidery, material and texture before making any purchase.

Dadi is eighty-four years old, and always manages to keep her hair looking immaculate. She dyes her hair black; uses hairspray to ensure her hair is set properly and that no strand is out of place. She puts on face powder, doesn't walk out of the house without a hint of lipstick, and likes to pose for a photograph (without wearing her glasses). It must be where I get my genes from!

I accept that some cultural ideologies have changed as the world has evolved, but I don't truly believe mindsets have. Some may have – but only for those who haven't got tangled up in a web of notion that they're an 'Indian living in Britain.'

Every year I grew older I thought I could do it; really change my parents mindset, their way of thinking and how they interpreted my world. But even now at thirty, I lose on the battlefield to my parents who have swallowed the, *'We-know-what's-best-for-our-children- until-they-get-married'* book, and then try to dispense their wise words on us.

I can still remember my younger, rebellious days – where I tried so hard to be like my English friends. But I always got a nauseating feeling, where my heart was about to jump out of my mouth each time I uttered a lie. I was going to get caught out. There were so many questions, so many lies to remember - each one becoming grander than the previous. I was convinced I was going to trip up.

But I just wanted to be like my friends; no questions asked, no barriers, no limits, just freedom.

From a young age I always knew what I wanted to be when I grew up. I wanted to become a Journalist and write stories about people and events; travel outside of my home town to meet interesting people that had a different life to mine, a more fascinating and colourful one.

It was when I left college and went on to further my studies in a field I was passionate about that Dad said to me, "If I'm sending you away to university Anushka, then you're not going to come back with that diploma, what's it called – a H.N.D. You know what that qualification stands for? It stands for Have No Degree! No. If I'm letting you go all that way then you're going to get a proper degree - an Honours degree!"

That moment was the only time I didn't argue with them. I'd have been foolish to do so. I wasn't about to turn down an extra year of freedom to live *my* life the way *I* wanted to, so I wisely accepted their condition whilst fighting hard to contain the euphoric feeling which had consumed me that day.

I wanted practical hands on experience in TV, film and radio production and post production; to explore the medium of each and be creative in my thinking, behaving, and living. But it wasn't really the course an Indian girl should be thinking of pursuing at university.

"Become a Radiologist," Mum said to me when I was exploring my options.

"Do you even know what a Radiologist is, Mum?" I asked her, sarcastically.

I was never good at science subjects and she knew that. I later learned though that she really liked the sound of a Radiologist. She knew it had something to do with the medical world, so that of course meant that I should become one; because when it came to getting married, surely I'd stand a better chance of meeting someone. After all who'd want to marry a Camera Operator, a Journalist or an Editor?

"And what are you going to do once you complete your Media Studies course?" she'd repeatedly ask.

In my irritable tone of voice, I'd remind her that it wasn't a Media Studies course; but she never did understand what essentially it was that I was studying.

When I brought home videos, short films, newspaper articles, script ideas, storyboards and photographs to show them my work, Mum pretended to understand what I was doing, but her facial expressions made it so easy to read her thoughts. Dad on the other hand, attempted at displaying a little more enthusiasm.

Following countless hours of heated debates and floods of tears, eventually they both agreed to let me go to university, down south. A five hour journey door to door via two trains, to study a subject they were neither happy with nor knew a great deal about.

My freedom and independence was waiting for me in anticipation and abundance.

A bittersweet wave of nostalgia always hits me in the face whenever I think about it now - a loss at the freedom in every sense that I lived.

Those days and nights passed me by like a flash in the pan, but a time that will remain with me in my heart forever.

Chapter Two

"I went to the pub after class with some friends.
I only had a bit, but I think it's gone to my head."...Anu

"Do I need a passport?" I ask innocently; shamefully unaware that I've made myself an object of ridicule in front of my friends, whilst hanging out in Stuart and Christian's room.

A chorus of laughter erupts within the four walls, which is quickly followed by a light hearted comment from my roommate Jess.

"Awww bless her, that's so cute Anu," she says, in between bursts of chuckles at me.

Christian turns his face to meet my eyes and instantly I'm locked into his gaze. My heart melts bit by bit with the coy smile I give him - thanks to those mesmerising sea green eyes which stare deeply into mine.

"No babe," he begins, with a straight face. "We're not going out of the UK; we're only getting on board a ferry which will take us to the island." He then looks away and joins in with the entertainment I have unknowingly provided.

But it's in the English Channel, I want to say out loud; *across the sea, surely you need a passport.* I daren't say it though in case I further ridicule myself in front of them.

Sitting here, making plans for a trip across the mainland to the Isle of Wight, I feel more like the independent girl I've dreamt of being for so long; learning to stand on my own two feet, without the stabilisers propped up on my bicycle by my parents, who refuse to push me down the street on my own, in fear that I'll ride away and never come back.

Yet here, my friends can see my naivety and vulnerability from a mile away.

After a few moments of laughter at my expense, we decide to call it a night. Most of us are slightly suffering the effects of a hangover from last night, when all drinks were a pound during 'Happy Hour' at the Students' Union.

'Ladies Night,' courtesy of a male stripper was undeniably a happy hour for all the over excited female students, who were far more interested in abs than labs and pecs than specs!

The moment the stripper, named by the girls as, 'Sexy Pecs' appeared on stage, I found myself carefully studying his perfectly shaped body. Not an ounce of skin or a strand of hair stood out of place; and when he stepped out from behind the curtain, I immediately felt my cheeks flush. The screams around the room quickly rose in pitch and tone, whilst the guys had decided that this was also their moment to showcase their manliness in front of the ladies.

I followed Sexy Pecs' sharp eyes around the room until they suddenly paused. His piercing blue eyes rested on my sapphire coloured contact lenses that I'd decided to wear.

My heart battered in excitement as he swaggered towards me. For the minutes that followed, I somehow became the centre of attention, resulting in screams of delight from Jess, Maya, Teresa, Vani and Ella who all watched in awe as Sexy Pecs approached our table and extended his hand out towards mine. Naturally, I held it at once and allowed myself to be led astray by him.

I was already feeling slightly tipsy having downed shots back in the room with the girls, so inevitably feeling even more excitable at the thought of what I was about to be subjected to. I draped an elongated smile across my face when he whisked me away from my friends and pulled me up onto a platform, sitting me down on a chair in the middle of the stage.

The lights went dim and apt music played loudly in the background. I watched him attentively as he started to grind his perfect, eight pack body in front of me. He slowly opened the palm of my hands and began to pour a generous amount of baby oil into them. With every drop, I quivered with delight.

Teasingly, he then moved his hands to the fastening of his tight fit leather pants. My eyes gulped in astonishment and a dark colour of pink flushed my cheeks out of embarrassment. But with a welcomed look of surprise on my face, he pulled out a blind fold, placing it sensuously in between his teeth, teasing me and the crowd with his slit eyed look. Gently he tied the blindfold around my eyes and once again more screams arose. Using both his hands he travelled down my arm, intertwining my fingers with his. He lifted my hands up against his body and guided them around his torso, making me rub oil on to him.

A minute or so later he then placed my hands over the fastening of his pants. Still blindfolded, I shifted nervously in my seat, and in surround sound all I could hear was, "Sexy Pecs! Take them off!" When I felt the closeness of his warm breath and voice in my ear, my heart almost rushed into my mouth.

I vaguely remember Chris standing directly in front of me even with my eyes covered. I could sense him watching my every move and it made my hands tremble with unusual apprehension. Sexy Pecs must have sensed my reluctance when I didn't respond to his instructions to pull down his leather pants, following his third attempt; so instead he untied the blind fold and pulled me up from the chair.

"I'm sorry," I shouted in his ear loudly, trying to drown out the music. "My boyfriend is stood opposite."

"Don't worry about it sweetheart," he muttered back, grinding his body against mine for a few seconds before hugging me and escorting me off the stage.

"Right little minx you are, aren't you, Miss Lamba?" Jess says to me, interrupting my flashbacks from last night. "We've got the photos to prove it as well."

"Just a bit of fun, that's all it was," I say defensively, observing Chris' reaction.

"Uh huh?" she grins. "I desperately need some sleep. I had to make it in for a lecture on the History of TV broadcast for nine this morning with Lois. God, her voice grates on me at the best of times, but when you can still taste and smell vodka red bull and vile shots on your breath, and feel like you're going to vomit just as you open your mouth, then Lois really isn't the person you want to be listening to first thing, let alone be making conversation with."

Surprisingly I'm not feeling too bad even though I did have quite a lot to drink last night, from what I can remember. I've never really been able to handle my drinks too well. I don't always know how to drink moderately or responsibly, and with whichever other warnings that come with drinking alcohol.

It doesn't serve its purpose to me if I don't feel the buzz of being under the influence whilst forgetting my senses. That doesn't mean to say that I go out to get wasted all the time, but it's not far off! I just haven't figured out what my tipping point is. I've let myself climb over the fence without realising, and without a moment's notice the ladders have been taken away from right under my feet. By that time it's been impossible to climb back over without taking the long way round.

I experienced my first alcoholic drink at the age of seventeen. A bit of a late starter by some people's account, but nonetheless it was a memorable one.

We'd all decided to call it a day in college one afternoon after we'd worked hard all week, preparing for a line-up of 'live' TV broadcasts that were to be transmitted around college.

Each one of us got the opportunity to take on a specific role each day of live broadcasts; from director, floor manager, camera operator, sound operator, lighting operator, VT operator, runner and presenter. My favourite was being director - sitting in the gallery and in charge of calling the shots. Talking in the headsets of camera operators, telling them how wide or how tight I wanted the frame to look - deciding which shot to cut to next to make it look artistic and more creative. It was the one role where I was sat in the driving seat with the power to make all the decisions; unlike at home where there were rules and regulations. Here I was my own boss.

We'd spent days painting and building our own set to use as a backdrop in the impressive, purpose built studio in the media block, when out of nowhere Ben said to me, "Anu, I bet I can drink you under the table."

"Err, yeah whatever," I said, waving a paint brush in my hand, blue and orange paint dotted all over my overalls.

He shouted out across the room to everyone within earshot, "Does anyone want to go to The Nelson for a few?" About a handful decided to go.

I'd never been into a pub up until that point. I was excited at the prospect of tasting my first alcoholic drink but a little apprehensive at what I was letting myself in for.

Girls drinking alcohol, is another thing which many Indian parents frown upon - mine included. Dad drinks. In fact we have a large bar cabinet in our house which is always stocked with almost everything you'd find in an off license; from Johnny Walker Black Label (a popular Indian man's drink), Bacardi, Vodka and Bombay Sapphire Gin, to Chivas Regal, and everything in between.

We arrived in The Nelson a few minutes later, leaving tins of paint, brushes and large backdrop boards strewn across the classroom floor. Ben walked up to the bar and ordered a pint of Stella.

"What are you having, Anu?" he asked me.

Suddenly I froze. I had no idea what to order. My thoughts raced back to all the bottles I'd seen in Dad's cabinet at home, but I couldn't remember the names of any at that precise moment.

"Surprise me," I replied evasively, trying hard to hide the fact that this was my first time in a pub and the first drink I was about to taste.

"Down, down, down, down," chanted Laura, Rob, Louise, Mark, Sarah, Teresa and Martin, just after I accepted a challenge to play a drinking competition with Ben. I had no desire to play drinking games but I wasn't someone who failed to rise to a challenge.

I had no idea that a pint of Guinness would taste so bitter! I struggled to sip the pint, let alone down it in one.

Like a typical guy, Ben smiled like the cat that got the cream. "Ha ha, I won!" he grinned.

"Let's do it again," I insisted, with the pint glass still a quarter full in my hand and a horrible taste of beer on my tongue. I was determined not to let him beat me.

"Are you sure, Anu?" Laura asked me, sitting next to Ben and doing her best to flirt with him in front of me, to let me know that he was her man.

I liked Ben. He had a shaved, ginger head, with a cheeky smile and an infectious personality. We always got on well, but he was with Laura and I was cool with that. I did fancy him but I wouldn't have done anything about it; though I always felt Laura had a problem with us being friends as if I was some sort of threat.

"If you say so," said Ben. "But you're going to lose Anu; you may as well face it now."

"We'll see," I said, feeling stupidly confident.

Once again, on the count of three we both brought our pint glasses to our lips, and poured the foul tasting liquid into our mouths. This time I closed my eyes, trying to hold my breath as I downed it, having no desire to taste any of it.

"Well done Anu," Louise said to me as I slammed down my empty pint glass on the table before Ben.

Ben looked up, pleasantly surprised. "One all. Well done Miss Lamba."

He seemed impressed, because I don't believe he thought for a second I was the type of person who'd let a pint of beer pass my lips.

I'm petite in height; unfortunately falling one inch short of five foot and without a doubt, the girliest looking girl on my male dominated Media Production course.

But from that day onwards, I honestly felt that I was worthy of fitting in with the rest of my class mates.

It was only when I got up to use the toilets that I felt the alcohol hit me. It was a surreal feeling which I'd never experienced before; almost like I was flying in the air free as a bird. My head was buzzing and my senses felt numb. I felt the urge to pinch myself and it was weird when I didn't feel myself hurt. The room started to spin. It was the most unusual sensation, filled with emptiness but at the same time, full of everything. I liked this feeling, I felt relaxed for the first time ever.

When I checked my watch - having made out the time in double vision, I realised it was about time I was heading home; so I said my goodbyes and made my excuses quickly to avoid any awkward questions. The truth was that I was also feeling slightly apprehensive about my mum and dad seeing me like this.

"See you on Monday, you two," Louise said to Teresa and I as we walked out together. Ben winked and gave me his cheeky smile.

Teresa was shouting in my ear, "Anu, your stop's here." But I had my head on her shoulder and my eyes half closed. This time she started shaking me. "Your stop's here hun. Come on I'll drop you half way."

Somehow I managed to stagger off the bus. Teresa linked arms with me helping me to walk in the direction of home. I was still slightly buzzing and on a high, but the cold air hitting my face was doing me good. As we got half way to my house, I told her I'd go on myself.

"Are you sure? I don't mind walking you all the way up."

"Honestly it's ok," I replied. I gave her a hug and told her I'd see her in college on Monday.

"Have you been drinking, Anu?" Sanya asked me, in a shocked tone of voice, when she opened the door to find me standing there reeking of alcohol.

I held my index finger to my mouth in a bid to stop her from announcing to whoever was home that I'd spent the entire afternoon with a pint of beer in my hand instead of a camera and tripod.

"Sssshh I went to the pub after class with some friends. I only had a bit, but I think it's gone to my head."

"Don't let anyone see you like this," she said sternly, displaying only a hint of compassion in her voice.

"I can smell it on you. Mum and Dad are on their way home from work and Dadi is inside, so just go straight upstairs and brush your teeth. I'll make some coffee and bring it up to you."

§

One by one, most of my friends vacate Chris and Stu's room, until there's only me, Maya and Simon left with them both. The three guys are childhood friends from the island. We finalise our plans for the next day and the boys decide which one of them is going to drive down to Southampton ferry port.

Chapter Three

*"My folks are the most chilled out people in the world,
they'll be glad to see you bossing me around!"*...**Chris**

As I look up in front of me, an overwhelming feeling flows through my body. The enormous vessel is standing tall and proud in a brilliant white colour, shining brightly in the winter sunshine.

My stomach knots in nervous anticipation. A gradual build up of excitement is evident across my face and I can feel my eyes twinkle like an excitable child. Chris turns to smile at me and I blush with embarrassment as I sense him feel my over excitement.

"We're just going to park up, get the tickets and walk onboard, sweet cheeks," he tells me, as I gather my jacket and hand bag, ready to make my first ever ferry crossing.

Stepping out of the toilets, Maya and I look round for the others and notice that they are stood by the bar ordering drinks.

I settle for a hot chocolate as the rest order hot beverages too. Simon gets straight onto the beer, much to Maya's dismay. The poor girl tries to hide her disgust at him drinking so early in the morning. It's only ten o' clock.

Maya is the first girl I met when I arrived onto the university campus. She moved in to the room next to me. To save ourselves some money, Jess and I opted for a sharing room with twin beds. Jess was on the same course as me at college but at university she'd decided to study the 'Have No Degree' course instead!

I arrived on campus before Jess, because my family and I caught the train down early that Sunday morning. Mum helped me pack most of my essential clothes and belongings that I'd need for university one week before moving. She had it parcelled up and sent via courier to my new address.

I remember sitting on the train, praying that the two huge boxes I'd helped pack with such eagerness had reached its destination. I breathed a huge sigh of relief when I unlocked the front door to the room I'd be living my new life in, and saw the boxes sitting there in anticipation to be unpacked.

It was a surreal atmosphere, because at every entrance to the building students and their parents were lugging suitcases and boxes down corridors and into their rooms. I finally felt like a grown up; like the first exciting chapter in my life was only just beginning.

Some of the rooms on the corridor were single occupancy ones and there was even a dormitory which five boys shared. But on my corridor most of them were twin rooms, like mine. Yuvani, (who liked to be called Vani), a Sri Lankan girl - even more petite than me, and looked as though she'd not been fed a decent meal in her life she was that skeletal looking, moved in on one side with a girl called Ella. Maya moved in with Teresa on the other side.

My college friend Teresa was also studying the same degree as me. Mum and Dad felt a little relieved knowing that I wasn't completely alone, half way across the country with strangers. However, saying that Dad didn't think much of Teresa. After every occasion he was lucky enough to meet her, he always said that she drove him potty.

"She gives me an earache and I can't understand what she says half the time."

Teresa is how some would describe 'common as muck.' She has a heart of gold, and a very broad, northern accent. It's significantly different to the way I speak considering we live literally ten minutes away from each other. When people listen to us both talk, they're under the impression that we live tens of miles apart.

Dad constantly joked with me when he found out Teresa was coming to the same university. "I feel sorry for the poor person who has to share a room with her, Anushka. She's such a chatterbox."

That poor person was Maya. Although they're a match made in heaven because they both never stop talking!

We're sat chatting amongst ourselves enjoying our journey across the English Channel when I ask Chris to show me around the ferry. He takes my hand immediately and pulls me up to follow him. He happily becomes my tour guide, telling me how he's made this trip numerous times in the past.

We walk on to the upper deck, in to the open air. Chris finds a perfect spot where we stand and watch the stretch of sea ahead of us glisten in the sunshine. It's a clear, crisp winter morning. Spring is just around the corner, yet a slight February chill can be felt in the air. My body shudders in the cold and Chris' eyes glance to the side of my face where I can feel the light hairs on either side stand up. He takes me into his arms, giving me a warm hug.

"I'm a bit nervous about meeting your parents Chris," I confess, pressing my lips together, looking out as far as my eyes can see into the horizon. He turns my body all the way round, encircling his arms around my waist from behind me to let my head rest on his chest.

"Why babe? There's nothing to worry about. My folks are the most chilled out people in the world, they'll be glad to see you bossing me around!"

A nervous laugh passes my lips. I know he's trying to put my mind at ease, but this isn't a minor thing to me, it's a major one. I've never met a guy's parents before - well not in that way anyway.

What will they make of me? Will they treat me differently? Talk to me differently? Like the way some people do who have never seen a brown face before; speaking slowly perhaps, emphasising words and talking with their hands?

It sounds ridiculous even when I think about it, but I can't tell him that, he'll think I'm insane. There's not a chance in hell I can even contemplate bringing Chris home to meet my parents. The thought of it for a mere second makes me shiver.

Fifteen minutes later, following Chris' best attempt at making me feel relaxed about this weekend, we head back down to join the others.

When I bring up the conversation about things to see and do on the island, Simon isn't backwards in coming forwards with his response.

"Fuck all!" he replies with a wry laugh. "There aren't many Black or Asian people who live on the island, unless you count the Indian take-away owners and corner shop owners," he says, matter-of-factly. "They're mostly White people and even they're all inbred!"

Stu slightly agrees with Simon. He continues to tell me that there are mainly old or retired people living on the island and there's not much to do for youngsters, compared to the mainland.

Chris adds that there are beautiful beaches with stretches of sand.

"The island is approximately twenty- three miles by thirteen miles, and it represents a diamond shape." I look up and listen with interest. "It boasts coastal scenery and beautiful landscapes, and is home to the famous Isle of Wight Music Festival." He sounds like a travel agent trying his hardest to sell me a holiday.

"Which dictionary have you swallowed that from Jamieson?" Simon asks Chris, and then mimics sarcastically, "boasts coastal scenery!"

"My parents live more or less on the beach," Chris goes on, ignoring Simon.

Well that's it. It's sold. I'm buying this holiday from him now. I absolutely love the beach, the sea, the waves and the sand. There's something so calming and soothing about the sound of waves hitting the shore, and the wind gently or even frantically blowing.

As a child, on some of our family days out to Blackpool, I loved to sit on the beach with my bucket and spade, and walk bare feet on the sand, feeling the grains spread over my feet whilst making sand castles. Dad used to pick me and Sanya up in his arms and run into the sea with us. I loved to watch the water rise up my little legs. Sanya was frightened of the water and she used to cry when the tide came in. The water felt icy, but even then there was something so tranquil about standing bare feet in cold water.

I'm beginning to feel excited.

Simon's house is the first to arrive on the way to Chris,' so we drop him and Maya off and Chris tells them that we'll meet up with them later.

Maya is Muslim, but not a strict one in the slightest. Although she doesn't drink, she'll happily go into a pub or a bar and order non-alcoholic drinks. She doesn't even pray five times a day – in fact I don't think I've seen her pray once. She doesn't wear a *burka* or a *hijab* and certainly doesn't cover up everything. Ironically, she's in a relationship with Simon, who's White and more than makes up for those that don't drink.

Maya's parents pretty much disowned her not so long ago. I don't know if it was bravery or stupidity, but she told them she was seeing Simon. They hit the roof - totally lost it, telling her that she'd shamed the family by not only getting into a relationship, but that too with a White guy - a *gora*. Her brother and sister cut off ties with her for a while on their dad's say so.

She's the eldest in her family - the one who should have been setting an example, according to her father. She confided in Teresa and me, telling us that her younger siblings secretly rang her because they missed her. Maya was hoping, rather praying that her parents would learn to accept her relationship and Simon, but I had my reservations. I wasn't being pessimistic, just pragmatic.

To my eyes, Simon isn't the type of guy you would want your parents to meet. In fact I have no idea what she sees in him. His big, crooked, yellow stained teeth stick out in an obvious manner, accentuated even more so by the number of cigarettes he inhales a day. His hair falls just below his ears in a floppy mess, and he wears a back-to-front cap on his head. He swears too much, burps even more and talks to Maya like she's his servant rather than his girlfriend.

His parents are surprisingly wealthy, but you wouldn't think so looking at Simon's untidy appearance. He scrounges off Maya, always telling her that he has no money, and yet miraculously, never fails to find cash to indulge his smoking and drinking student lifestyle.

I can't tell her what I think of him (much as I'd like to) because it's not my place to. She loves him, and so I put up with his antics for her sake.

A few minutes later Chris's car pulls in at Stu's place and we drive up the sloping driveway. The first thing I notice are two cats sitting in the bay window. They peer at me, following my stare with their menacing, sharp eyes.

"Why don't you both come in and meet Mum?" says Stu, picking up his bag from the boot of the car. "She'll be really happy to see you, and meet Anu."

Chris looks over to me. "If you want babe," I tell him. "It's up to you."

"Alright, we'll come in for a few minutes," says Chris, looking at his watch. "But not for long. I want to get home and see the folks. They're eagerly waiting for us!"

We walk through the front door into a tiny hallway that leads us to the living room. Stu's mum is sat on the sofa, taking up two seats because of her noticeable large size. One cat lies snuggled up beside her, looking quite content watching TV. I turn to look at the other two cats in the window - they haven't moved an inch.

"Hello Christian," says Stu's mum, in a broad southern accent.

"Hello Myra." He bends down to plant a kiss on her cheeks, then points to me. "This is Anu, Anu this is Myra."

"Nice to meet you," I say, extending out my hand to shake hers.

But instead she looks me up and down making no attempt to stand up from the sofa. I can feel her eyes dissecting me from top to bottom.

"She's tiny Chris; skinny and small. I thought Indian food made you fat, all that oil and butter. But she looks like she doesn't eat anything. There's no meat on her bones."

I force myself to smile. She doesn't make conversation with me, instead she directs all her questions about me to Chris, as if I'm an illegal immigrant who's just landed in the country and can't speak a word of English.

I want to put on my best Indian accent for her just to hear another ridiculous comment fall out of her mouth. Chris can tell by the expression on my face that I'm unimpressed, so he exchanges a few quick pleasantries and tells her we have to leave.

I can't help but start to feel even more apprehensive about my imminent introduction with Chris' parents.

Stu is one of Chris' closest friends. I like him. He always has time for me, and his cheekiness is always something that I've been fond of.

For Stu, going to university on the mainland has been quite an accomplishment. He was a home-bird from what I gathered off Chris and Simon - someone who never left the island. When Chris told me that Stu had never been on a plane before, I was gob smacked. I thought I'd lived a sheltered life, but compared to him and his mum, I'd seen most of the world.

We say our goodbyes, and Chris tells Stu we'll meet him later on in the pub, with the others.

Chapter Four

"You southerner's take about ten minutes to say one word."...Anu

"Hello son!"

A small, handsome gentleman with an olive complexion and dark hair is standing in front of me, beaming from ear to ear.

"Hey Dad," Chris responds, in an equally energetic manner.

I look on with growing fascination at the remarkable resemblance between them both. Although there's a subtle difference in height, Chris has unquestionably inherited his good looks from his dad.

Just as they pull away from a father and son bonding moment, I hear a female voice in the distance coming from inside the house. "Rick, is that Christian and Anu?"

"Yes it is Sally," replies Rick, ushering us in.

I step inside the doorway and the first thing I notice is that it's much bigger than Stu's house; there's a large L shaped hallway, and from what I can make out so far the house looks immaculate and well maintained. I'm pleasantly surprised with my first impression.

"It's nice to finally meet you Anu," Chris' dad tells me, moving closer to put his arms around my shoulder and a peck on my cheek. "I have pronounced that correctly, haven't I?" he asks, with a worried look on his face.

"Yes you have, Mr Jamieson."

"Oh there's no need to be so formal Anu, just call me Rick."

But I have this urge to call him, uncle Rick!

Young, Asian people have always been taught to address their elders or people they don't know well as 'uncle' or 'auntie.' It's a cultural custom we've grown up with, considered to be more polite and respectful than calling someone we don't know well by their first name. But if I call Chris' dad, uncle I'll sound like an idiot!

"Ok Rick," I reply, feeling oddly embarrassed.

I take my shoes off and leave them sitting in the hallway, then proceed to follow Chris into the living room. Sally walks in moments later wearing an apron over her clothes, covered in a dusting of flour.

"Hi Chris, hi Anu," she says excitedly, wiping her hands on the apron and untying it from behind her back. "Sorry about the messy look," she says, flinging it onto the dining table behind her. She hugs Chris first and then gives me a warm, tight hug. "I've been testing out my new bread maker. You can't beat the smell and taste of fresh bread."

I smile tentatively.

"I'm only a domestic goddess in the kitchen when it comes to bread making! Everything else I let Rick take charge; he's the cook in this house!"

"I don't have a choice Sal!" says Rick, shrugging his shoulders.

"Well it's so nice to finally meet you," Sally tells me. "We've heard lots about you."

"All good I hope?" I say cheekily, glancing over at Chris.

"Well actually, one thing Christian forgot to mention is how beautiful you are!"

I look at her shyly. "Thank you."

"Honestly, you are; perfectly petite and well groomed," she continues.

Sally doesn't sound patronising or sarcastic. There's sincerity in her voice and it makes me feel warm on the inside. The insecurities

I was feeling a few minutes earlier instantly vanish and I start to believe that things are going to be just fine.

I'm comfortably perched on the sofa next to Chris, enjoying a glass of wine with his parents, having polished off nearly two thirds of the bottle to myself.

We've just finished watching back to back episodes of *Only Fools and Horses*. It's obvious by looking at the box set lying next to the TV that this traditional, British comedy is a firm favourite in the Jamieson household. When each pause requires an explosion of laughter the Jamieson's have impeccable timing and do not disappoint.

Chris' mum asks us how the journey over on the ferry was and whether we have any plans for the rest of the day. Chris looks at me and without either of us saying another word to one another, we both burst out laughing.

His parents exchange confused looks.

"Mum, what you don't know about Anu is that she's quite naïve, bless her; very innocent indeed. Can I tell them, sweet cheeks?" He smiles sweetly at me, in the hope that I'll say yes.

"Go ahead," I gesture.

The very first time Chris discovered my simplicity, which is often mistaken with naivety and innocence, was during the first few days of Freshers' week.

A group of us were walking back to halls from the Students' Union; actually I was being carried by Max – the six foot three friendly giant who lives in my halls, and is in most of my lectures.

I'd been dancing all night because it was my kind of music. For once it wasn't the same cheesy pop music that'd been churned out on repeat all week. It was R&B and I loved almost every tune that played.

It wasn't me it was the music - admittedly with the aid of alcohol, which made me follow my feet to the dance floor. I had no control over them so I stayed there all night.

Walking back to campus in the early hours of the morning, I clung off Max's shoulders, holding my six inch heels in my hand with dear life. But he dropped me to the floor when we came across a burger van parked half way along the main road.

Usually Maya and I are the two who end up making food for our entire hall after night outs. Our specialty is cheese and sweet corn toasted sandwiches with black pepper. I butter the slices of bread whilst Maya fills the sandwiches generously with whichever supermarket's own brand value cheese and sweet corn we have. I then toast them in the sandwich maker and dish them out.

That's how I first met Chris. After a drunken night out when we all returned to campus, I enticed him with my culinary skills!

Chris is exactly six feet tall and muscular, with broad shoulders. He has dark brown, thick hair which is spiked up most of the time with enough wax that could light a room full of candles; and his cute dimples become more evident than usual when he smiles. I'd never looked into a man's eyes so intently before, the way I did with Chris'. I fell in love with those sparkling sea green eyes from the moment I saw him.

Everyone was taking their time ordering food - as if it was a sit down restaurant meal we were having, so I told the Asian man behind the counter what I wanted.

"Can I have the chicken burger, without the beef please?"

Just as I said it, everyone creased with laughter, over exaggerated by their intake of alcohol, presumably.

"It's a chicken *or* beef burger," said the Asian man serving, in his thick, South Asian accent.

"But the menu on your board says, chicken and beef burger, two pounds fifty," I stated.

"Yeah but it's a chicken burger, or a beef burger that's two fifty Anu," explained Chris.

Up until that point the flirtation between Chris and I was hugely obvious to everyone around us, and it had unmistakably intensified. Our friends could see that we'd eventually get together, so I felt mortified at my moment of drunken naivety. Naturally because we were all intoxicated, I ended up blaming the drink.

"Oh right, well just a chicken burger with chips then," I said to the man, laughing off my silly mistake. I turned around and joined into a conversation two others were having, hoping that no one was going to take my innocent mistake any further!

But as it happened, I was put in the spotlight the very next day during a lecture, when Max decided to tell everyone my 'chicken without beef burger' story!

I felt my cheeks burn as all eyes around the lecture hall became locked on me. Max recreated the scene outside the burger van, adding his own special effects and dialogues to make me sound even more stupid than I already felt. Sniggers could be heard around the room.

After class I decided to add a few special effects of my own and brought on the waterworks in front of Max. He felt so bad he began to apologise profusely, until I felt I'd made him sweat enough, and told him that I was just as good as him at being a drama queen!

"Anu thought you needed a passport to come over to the island," Chris tells his parents.

His mum lets out a snigger, but his dad bursts into a fit of laughter. Watching him roar with laughter in his loud and eccentric manner sets us all off into giggles, including me. None of us felt that we needed an ice breaker, but it certainly helped to lighten the mood even more.

"Ok, you can leave her alone now you two. Stop laughing, it's not that funny," says Sally, wiping away tears that have filled her eyes. "She's never been to the island before so how's she supposed to know?"

"He's going to show me around the island," I say, changing the topic. "And first stop is the beach."

"Good idea," she says. "It's a nice day today too; the weather's been lovely on the island over the last few days. We've had quite a bit of sunshine so hopefully it'll hold up a little while longer."

"We're lucky enough to have beaches on our doorstep here," Rick chips in. "Just make sure you wrap up warm Anu, it gets cold out there."

"I will, thanks Rick."

His dad is right. They literally do live on the doorstep of the beach. Chris and I walk hand in hand down the steps which take us towards the cliffs and sandy beach. I immediately take off my trainers and socks and let my bare feet touch the softness of the brown sand.

"Where she go, where she go?!" Chris jokes, placing his arms around my shoulders and looking over my head towards the sea.

"Ha ha," I reply, sarcastically.

My height and my cheekiness is one of the first things that attracted him to me, or so he says. And the fact that I make a mean toasted sandwich!

Chris is studying Sports Science, and is hoping to become a sports injury therapist, or a personal trainer.

There's always been chemistry between us, everyone could see it. In conversations we both tried to outdo each other's witty comments. I'd always make fun of his accent.

"You southerner's take about ten minutes to say one word."

"And us southerners need to be more careful with our property around you northerner's," he'd retaliate, in a flirty manner. I became a northern monkey, and he became a southern fairy. I used to tease him by telling him I'd rather be a monkey any day over a fairy.

He agreed.

I let go of my hand from his and run out towards the sea, which is glittering in the sunlight. But a chill can be felt even more fiercely as I stand in front of the waves - my body shivers and my fingers feel numb.

Chris walks towards me. He takes my hand and intertwines it with his. We walk further along the sandy beach, taking in the sea air and peaceful sound of waves. He catches me off guard when I look the other way for a split second - sweeping me up into his arms and running into the water. I half laugh and scream like a girl, telling him to put me down, but he finds pleasure in twirling me round and round until I tire him out.

He picks up a stick lying a few yards away and begins to draw something in the sand. I watch as the lines begin to shape and I can read the writing.

"You softie, Christian Jamieson."

'Anu for Chris,' he writes, inside the heart shaped sand.

Chapter Five

"We've invited two hundred and fifty people to the wedding, what difference will another two make?"...uncle Danesh.

Almost five weeks have elapsed and I haven't been home to see my family. I don't know if it's a blessing in disguise or just pure luck that my studies have been quite intense recently that I haven't had the chance to make a visit.

But without fail I'm made to have a telephone conversation with my parents every evening. Most of my friends, including Jess will go days, sometimes a week without speaking to her parents; but not me.

Once when I called up in the evening, having had the usual conversation which consisted of the same repetitive questions and answers from everyone, turn by turn, I said to Dad, "I'll ring you in a few days."

"A few days?!" he repeated, as if having to confirm what he'd just heard me say.

"Yeah Dad, nothing's changed since yesterday when I spoke to you. Uni's fine, work's going good. I tell you what I've eaten for dinner. I've asked how everyone is, it's the same stuff. I'll ring you when I've got something new to tell you."

I wish I hadn't opened my mouth, because he chewed my ear off, telling me I couldn't care less about the family.

"Fine, I tell you what you don't need to ring me at all if you don't want to. It's not like I don't pay your phone bills or anything, is it? I mean, I'm the one paying for you to speak to me right now."

He was going ballistic. I hadn't meant it or even said it in a malicious way, but he didn't see it like that or give me chance to explain. I'm sure Jess could hear everything Dad was saying. She was only sat on her bed opposite me, playing with her phone.

"Ok forget about me, don't you want to know how your dadi is?" He was trying to give me the guilt trip. And it was working. For a second I felt as though I'd failed in my duty as a caring and considerate granddaughter.

I'm sitting on the first of two trains heading back home but I'm not looking forward to the Spanish inquisition when I get in.

It's been a week since I spent a weekend on the island with Chris and his parents.

I thoroughly enjoyed myself. Chris' parents welcomed me with open arms and even told me to visit them again soon. I got the impression that they were happy that Chris had met me at university, and that in turn made me happy.

Sally made a Sunday roast before we left, and even cooked a special one for me - with chicken rather than beef. I felt a little embarrassed that she'd gone out of her way to cook an alternative meal for me, and so I thanked her profusely.

I enjoyed the night we met up at the local pub with the others. As usual, Simon walked in half cut smelling and looking like he'd not had a wash in about a week.

"Was I right or was I right then?" he shouted across the room, in the packed pub as he walked in with Maya.

"What about?" I replied.

"The island. Inbred! Boring! Do you want me to carry on?"

"I wouldn't say it was boring Si. I really enjoyed it. There's some quaint little shops, cafes and quirky coffee places right on the beach front. And the cliffs are amazing. You won't find scenic sights like this up north where I'm from." I tried to sound convincing, like I was promoting his own home town to him.

I did enjoy myself on the island, but I couldn't imagine myself living on it. I'm happy in my own city where I don't get stared at twice for being a darker shade of colour. There I blend in with the diverse culture I live in. On the island, I felt like an exotic but rare delicacy; a golden colour star fruit placed amongst a bowl of bananas, apples and oranges - admired from afar but afraid of being picked up to savour.

"Guess what I had today?" I said excitedly to Maya. "A battered mars bar from the chip shop."

"What, have you never tasted a battered mars bar before?" she asked, looking surprised.

"Tasted one? I've never even heard of one until tonight. There's a fish and chips mobile van, called The Jolly Fryer which drives around the island on a Friday night. It looks almost like an ice-cream van. It parked up literally next door to Chris' house. There was a queue going down the road!"

I sounded like it was the most amazing thing I'd witnessed my whole life. But I didn't care. I was having fun and on my third Malibu and pineapple drink.

The business of the train station overwhelms me. When the train grinds to a halt, people are running around frantically as I walk onto the main concourse area. I tune my ears into a tannoy announcement which is informing passengers of an electrical fault with the main line train travelling up north. As a result passengers from that train are expected to pile on to the train I'm catching.

A sea of people congregates in front of me. When I near closer they are pushing and shoving and shouting in loud, angry voices. I've missed my last lecture of the day in order to catch this train and to make it home at a reasonable time. It's only Ged's, World Cinema lecture I'm missing. I don't feel too bad about skipping it because he'll only bore all the female students in class, by spending the first half hour of the lecture talking about some attractive lady he's seen somewhere and then proceed to tell us what assets she had. Or he'll start on his usual topic of porn once again. But even by Ged's standards there's no way he can pigeonhole porn into a genre within World Cinema!

I weave in and out of disgruntled passengers until I reach the front. Two platform attendants are stood unsympathetically telling people there's no more room on the train.

"Excuse me, I've got a ticket for this train," I chip in as politely as I can to an attendant, holding out my ticket to show him.

"You and everyone else on the platform, love," the fat, middle aged man replies coldly.

"I can't miss this train," I tell him crossly. I look up and notice a pregnant young woman covering her belly with her hands, stepping on to the train. "My sister has just gone into labour," I say boldly. "I need to be with her." I'm not bothered in the slightest that I've just fabricated a story to try and get on the train. "There's no one with her right now. I've got to get on it."

"I'm sorry love but there's no more room on here, you're going to have to catch the later one."

"Please, I just told you that I have to catch this one. My sister is having a baby, like right now. I can't wait for the next one. Surely you can give me priority?"

My facial expression tells him I'm not about to back down.

The man looks round to his colleague, who gives him the nod to let me on.

I let out a "thank you," as he checks my ticket and allows me to pass him. I hurry on to the train before giving him a chance to change his mind.

Every compartment is full. Literally seconds after I've boarded, the doors close and we depart the platform.

I stand in the aisle of the 'quiet' zone, squeezed in amongst other passengers and their luggage, hearing the odd grunt from irritable people. I hold my bag in between my legs and my handbag close to my chest.

That was quick thinking on your feet Anushka; clever girl.

There's no way Sanya would have been able to do what I just did. Her mind isn't devious like mine!

Sanya is only two and half years younger than me but we're not really alike; not in appearance or personality. She's petite like me, at five foot, a little slimmer than me and has a fairer complexion to mine.

For some illogical reason, many older Indian people still have this bizarre notion about skin colour. It's perceived that the fairer the skin colour, the prettier and more socially acceptable you are within the Asian community. In some extreme cases being dark in complexion can be like having a disease. People can look at you differently, treat your differently, as if you're inferior to them.

So the whiter you are, the prettier you are - that's the general consensus. It's so ironic when I think about some of the differences between South Asian and White people. I mean White people spend hundreds of pounds using sun beds, or travelling thousands of miles into the sunset, just to end up like fried tomatoes. And on the opposite spectrum, Asian people waste so much money buying whitening products, in the hope that their skin will go shades lighter and they'll fit in with the rest of the crazy society living by the same notion.

No thanks to social conditioning and misguided expectations, Sanya is often seen as more superior to me, whether she'd agree with me or not.

Based on my experiences, many Asian people are prejudiced within their own societies and half of them are too blinded or brainwashed to even notice it. Apart from the standard dialogues many youngsters are polluted with, such as:

'Don't even think about marrying someone who is not Indian, and especially not Black or Muslim; don't put shame on our family', there are deeper, hidden meanings lying in the roots of my religion and culture.

'They aren't the same caste as us.' 'Their status in society is lower than ours.' 'The boy hasn't even got a degree.' 'Have you seen how dark she is? How fat she is?'

The list is endless and pointless. As far as I can make out, my parents generation is always busy trying to conform to social grooming because they're more concerned with what their next door neighbour and people in their social circle are going to think, rather than find out what makes their own child happy.

For as long as I can remember, there hasn't been that sisterly love between Sanya and I like there should be. I always used to feel pangs of jealousy whenever I saw my cousins Ritu and Rohini getting on.

They're a little older than us, and also have a couple of years between them; but they look out for each other and have that special bond, unlike anything that Sanya and I share. I longed for that so much when I was growing up. But instead we were always at each other's throats, blaming one another and trying to get each other into trouble. I've lost count the amount of times we've made up and fallen out since kids.

I pass the second to last stop before mine so I call home and speak to Mum, telling her I'll be arriving in fifteen minutes.

Walking out of the exit from the station, I spot Dad's car in the distance. I notice he's parked up in the disabled bay with the hazard lights flashing. I stride towards the car, throw my bags in the back, dive on to the front seat and signal to him to move on, in case we get into trouble for taking up a disabled spot.

"Oh don't worry, it was only for a few minutes, it won't matter," Dad says, using his Indian mentality to try and justify it.

I make general chit chat with him, but try not to make too much conversation. I know I'm only going to have to repeat it all again when I get in. So instead I tell him about the drama at the train station this afternoon.

"Oh really? Is that what you said? I can't believe it," Dad says, sounding impressed with my quick thinking.

"How did you think of a story like that on the spot?"

I start off saying, "Well it just came into my head…" and then I tail off. I suddenly realise that if I tell him I'm good at making things up on the spot, then he may just think I'm a pretty good liar, which could get me into more trouble than it's worth. That's the last thing I want him to think.

"I looked up and there was a pregnant woman trying to get on the train, so I said my sister had gone in to labour and I had to get home straight away."

Well I wasn't technically lying!

And he buys it. In fact he thinks it's so hilarious that as soon as we get home, he can't wait to tell Mum.

I walk up the drive way, taking in a long, deep breath, with hopes of a pleasant and smooth weekend ahead, free from any arguments and shouting between me and my parents. I ring the doorbell and Mum arrives to open the door. For a second I feel like nothing has changed since my last visit; she stands there clutching her rolling pin in one hand. I take a moment to inhale the smell of freshly made chapatis wafting through the air and the pungent smell of various dishes being cooked in the kitchen.

"Sita, Sita, guess what Anu did at the station when she was waiting for her train this afternoon?"

"Hi Mum," I say, before I let Dad ramble on in excitement.

Mum gives me a hug. "Hi Anu. So what did you do at the station then?"

"Oh I'll let Dad tell you." He's far keener on telling the story and I wouldn't want to ruin it for him. He has this knack of making things sound so much more dramatic and exciting than they actually are.

Dadi is sat on the sofa, cross legged in her favourite spot watching one of her Indian soaps when I enter the living room and Krish is too interested in a game he's playing, that I'm lucky to receive a "hi" when he glances up in my direction.

"Only you Anu," says Mum, when I return to the kitchen. "Only you can do something like that."

It's Friday night and everyone is sat downstairs on the sofa watching one of their regular Indian soaps. I roll my eyes in despair and grind my teeth as soon as the cheesy music starts. It's my cue to make a sharp exit, before I get cornered into sitting down and watching their soaps all evening.

But it's too late.

"You'll learn something about our culture and our religion watching these dramas," Mum starts, just as I motion out of my seat.

"Not like your stupid Eastenders and Coronation Street," adds Dad. "Your soaps are so cheap. At least they teach you some values and morals in ours."

I have no intention of getting into a debate about soaps, especially on a Friday night. I can think of much better ways of spending my time. This time last week I was on the Isle of Wight in a pub getting drunk and having fun - staggering out at closing time. But before I know it, words just slip out of my mouth and I can't help getting into a rant.

"What are you talking about?" I shout. "These soaps are so stupid and unrealistic, it's unbelievable. All these female actresses, no matter whether they're young or old, are glammed up in so much make-up, extravagant clothes and accessories. They go to sleep looking like they're ready for a night out on the town, with all that slap caked on their faces. And when they wake up, there's not a smudge of lipstick or mascara, or a strand of hair out of place. It's so unreal."

I get more irate as I go on, having firmly taken my seat back on the sofa again.

"There's always at least one evil relative in every soap. Someone who's out to kill or ruin a marriage and an even more evil mother-in-law who hates her daughter-in-law so much she tries to make her life hell, by poisoning her or by convincing another woman to try it on with her son! Is that how you want to culture us? Are these the values you want us to adopt? At least I know where to go if I want some tips on how to kill off my in-laws."

I say it jokingly but Mum's face is a picture. "I wouldn't put it past you Anu!"

"But the best bit is when someone dies in your soaps," I carry on, really getting into it now. "You think yes, that's that character out of it for good. But no that would be far too realistic. These characters are invincible. They come back to life again, in some shape or form to take revenge."

After I've finished verbally abusing the entire cast and production team of most Indian TV programmes I decide to go upstairs and watch something else, in Dadi's room. It gives me the opportunity to ring Chris and catch up with him.

"Say hi to Dadi from me," he tells me sneakily, accentuating the word 'Dadi' in his best Indian accent. I smile inwardly.

"Yeah I will," I joke. "But right now she's too engrossed in watching her soaps, she won't hear anything."

We talk for a few minutes but when I hear someone walking up the stairs I tell him I have to go. He gets pissed off at me, as he often does when I tell him I can't speak because someone is around.

"What difference does it make that you're on the phone, Anu? You are allowed to have friends you know."

"I know I am; that's not the point. It's just... I'll get twenty questions; you know what they're like."

He understands, I think. Well he does a pretty good job at convincing me he does anyway. He hears the same story each time I go home.

There aren't many people I know that take the time and effort to be genuinely interested in me, my life, my family and my culture.

But Chris does. He's always interested in what festival is going on in my religion or what cultural event is taking place. When I went home for Diwali a couple of months after we started seeing each other I even brought him back a box of Indian sweets. And he rang me on Diwali, just as we'd finished with the prayers. He regularly asks me to teach him Hindi words just so that he can greet Dadi properly one day.

But just when I think he gets me, he disappoints me. I know he only does it because he's frustrated that he can't speak to me whenever he wants to, and sometimes I feel he blames me for it. I don't blame him though. I'm sure I'd get pissed off if I was in his shoes.

I end the conversation on a high note, telling him that I can't wait to see him on Sunday and that I'm bringing back lots of delicious, homemade Indian food.

The weekend seems to fly by. My cousin Arjun's wedding is fast approaching so I decide to go over to his house with Mum to see him. All his family is home; his two sisters Ritu and Rohini, and my auntie Beena and uncle Danesh.

Out of all my cousins – and I do have lots of them – I've always got on with Rohini the most. When I was younger I idolised her and wanted to be just like her; so pretty, with her long and silky, dyed brown hair which fell down her neck in cute ringlets.

We love the same type of music and both have a passion for Bhangra music. Whenever we're at parties together, Rohini is my dancing partner. We'll be the first ones on the dance floor and the last ones to leave. When dinner is being served we never eat. Our parents give us evil looks from afar; looks that shout

out 'ok enough of shaking your hips and bodies, and bopping up and down in front of all the boys, because they're all looking at you two.' Rohini and I pretend we don't see them shoot us with that look in their eyes. We stay glued to the dance floor instead. We'd both get told off later on though, on the way home by our parents.

"How are the wedding arrangements going Arj?" I ask him.

"Getting there slowly; Mum and Dad are freaking out at the little time that we've got left and all the things that need to be done."

"Just leave it to them, you just relax and look forward to your big day. You know what our parents are like, they stress over everything and anything. It's an Indian thing?!" Ritu agrees with me.

"It's a good job it's not Rohini getting married yet," I say. "If they're freaking out with you, imagine what they'll be like when it's her turn."

"I'm going to have my wedding simple and low key," Rohini states. "None of this over the top malachi."

Mum looks over at us, "Just wait until it's your turn. We'll find you all nice Indian boys and get you married off all at the same time; lined up together in a row. And that's it we'll all have done our job in one go!" Mum looks at auntie Beena who is smiling gleefully, and agreeing with Mum's fantastic idea.

"Yeah right," I say. "Like that's going to happen."

"Of course it will. It'll be their responsibility to look after you from then on."

"You can try Mum, but I don't think there's an Indian boy made for me, and I certainly don't need looking after. I don't think that's entirely what being married is about."

I don't remember how we get onto the topic of English people, and how they love Indian weddings, but before I know it I'm talking about my roommate Jess and my 'friend' Chris, and telling everyone how they've never seen an Indian wedding before. Uncle Danesh says, "Well why don't you invite them to Arjun's wedding then and they can see for themselves how we Punjabi's put on a wedding?" I dismiss his comment as a joke. He always jokes about everything. But he persists with it.

"I'm being serious, if you want to invite a couple of your friends, then you can. Where we've invited two hundred and fifty people to the wedding, what difference will another two make?"

Out of those two hundred and fifty people, I wonder how many of them Arj actually knows.

I look at Mum, who is smiling at uncle, telling him there's no need for his polite invitation.

But inside I'm feeling ecstatic.

Oh my God, it'll be fantastic if I can invite Chris to Arj's wedding. He can meet all the family. Obviously I'll introduce him as my 'friend', and that will give him the chance to get to know them.

"It's fine with us, but just don't tell all the other girls in the family, Anu," auntie Beena warns me. "I don't want everyone else saying they want to bring their friends to the wedding. We haven't got space for anyone else."

Mum looks over at me, and in turn I look at Arj who says it's ok with him; after all it is his wedding!

So it's settled. I can't wait to get back to tell Chris the good news.

I'm shattered after making the same five hour journey back to campus on Sunday afternoon.

Mum has packed containers full of my favourite dishes. Every tub is wrapped ten-fold in a polythene bag before being placed into another large carrier bag. She has this very Indian habit of tightening carrier after carrier around everything so that when it comes to unwrapping, it's like going in to battle.

Even though breakfast and dinner is catered for in halls, I always crave my Punjabi food. There's only so much that someone who's been accustomed to the culinary delights of Indian spices and cuisine my entire life, by the two best cooks in the world – my mum and my dadi – can take of the bland, tasteless food that gets served up day after day in the campus dinner hall.

I'm getting tired and fed up of the crunchy cauliflower cheese dumped in lumpy sauce, accompanied with fat, greasy chips that always remind me of my school days.

If you decide to come a little late into the dining hall you may as well not bother; or starve for the rest of the evening because you'll only get the left over scraps scraped from the bottom of the serving dish.

Once a week, there's a chicken curry dish served with basmati rice. It's usually the one night of the week where most people look forward to; but not me. The chicken always tastes half cooked in a dull and flavourless curry, as if a few tins of tomatoes and onions have been thrown into a pan, along with an ungenerous amount of chilli powder to give it only a slight colour, rather than the pungent taste it deserves.

The best thing about going back home is that Mum knows exactly what food I like to eat. Before I'd even arrived on Friday evening, she'd already bought the chicken and vegetables for my three favourite dishes to take back: Desi chicken curry: boneless chicken cooked in an infusion of strong and colourful spices and green chillies; with each spice having its own distinctive aroma.

My second favourite, *bhindi*: okra soaked in spices and fried in juicy plum tomatoes and onions. And my all time favourite Punjabi dish, *maa di daal* – by far the best lentils in the pulses world - also known as the brown *daal* because of its colour.

It's early evening and I've arrived just in time to get dressed into my uniform and start my three hour shift at the hotel restaurant.

Not long after I moved down south and started uni, I felt I needed a job to earn a few extra pounds to fund my unprecedented social life. But after a few late nights out – on more than one occasion, where I'd drunk in excess of my limit, I struggled to get up on time for a six am breakfast shift. Somehow I'd gotten away with it so far, sneaking in without anyone noticing.

My shifts alternate around breakfast, dinner and bar duties depending on my lectures, assignments and after uni activities, which usually involve the Students' Union and alcohol in some form or another.

There's just another hour to go before I finish work. I light a candle and finish setting up a table for two by the corner of the restaurant, close to the window.

I sent Chris a text when I was sat on the train, telling him I had some exciting news for him, but would tell him when I finished work. Typical bloke though he was, with no patience. He kept ringing me and probing me into telling him what my news was. But I wanted to do it face to face to see his reaction. "I'll tell you when I get back from work," I told him.

When I return to halls I'm ready to collapse into bed. There's no way I can handle making a start on the radio scriptwriting project, it can wait until tomorrow. I want to see Chris. Jess isn't back from work, so I change into my pyjamas, walk down the corridor and knock on Chris and Stu's door.

"What food has mummy Lamba sent me then?" Stu asks, as soon as he opens his door. He never makes small talk, just gets straight to the point. "Mummy Lamba has sent *me* lots of nice Indian food," I say teasingly.

"Where's Chris?"

"Inside, playing on his guitar. Can't you hear the puff singing?" he asks. "He thinks he's going to be the next Robbie Williams," he goes on, with sarcasm seeping through his veins. "His ego's definitely the size of Robbie's!"

Although Stu and Chris share a room, it's better laid out than mine and Jess'. They each have their own space, with an adjoining door that separates them both. I open his door and walk inside without knocking. Chris is sat on the edge of his bed, guitar in hand, singing softly to my favourite Robbie Williams track, *Angels*. I stand there for a minute, watching him lost in his own little world - his fingers hovering over the strings of his guitar. After a while, he notices me standing there and walks over towards me.

"How long have you been stood there listening?" he asks.

"Not long. You're really good, you know that?"

"I'm ok, I guess. I taught myself to play the guitar, I just do it for fun and it helps me to relax." He looks down at what I'm wearing. "You look so cute in your pyjamas, Anu. I've missed you this weekend." He then bends down to kiss me on my lips.

"I missed you too babe," I tell him.

He pulls me in by the waist, lowers his neck and face, and kisses my lips tenderly; letting our tongues dance more passionately now.

"What's this big news then?" he asks, pulling back briefly. "Don't tell me, you've told your parents about me and they're coming down here with a shotgun as we speak?" He smirks, whilst pretending to show me a gun.

"Forget the shotgun. Do you think I'd be stood here right now if I'd have told them about you? You'd probably never see me again! Anyway, forget that," I say, clearing my throat. "How do you fancy coming to my cousin's Indian wedding?"

He looks at me with a confused look on his face. "Who's getting married?"

"Don't you remember I mentioned a while ago that my cousin Arjun was getting hitched soon? Well its next month. And I thought you might want to come."

He looks at me with an even more perplexed look this time.

"Let me get this straight. You're asking your secret boyfriend to come to a family wedding? So the shotgun really will be out! Are you being serious babe?"

"Yeah, why?"

"Babe, you won't even speak to me on the phone at home without ducking and diving; how on earth are you going to get away with me being with you at a wedding? Isn't it a bit risky and a little foolish?"

For a brief moment my mind wanders to an uneasy thought.

What if he's not being cautious, but reluctant, because this is a big step? A little too serious and rushed perhaps for our relationship which is still in its infancy? He can't be thinking like that? If he is then surely he wouldn't have taken me to the island to meet his parents.

My plan is back firing.

"I have thought about it Chris and there is a way. By inviting Jess it won't look so suspicious."

Slowly I see him registering what I'm saying.

"Please don't tell me you're going to say that Jess is my girlfriend too?" He asks the question with an almost terrified look on his face.

I laugh. "No way, I wouldn't go as far as saying that to you."

I never let on to him that it was the very first thought I had as soon as uncle Danesh suggested the idea.

"It'll be a great opportunity to meet everyone; plus you've never seen an Indian wedding. You always said that you wanted to, well now's your chance."

His brain is ticking. He's still thinking about it far too carefully.

I on the other hand have already imagined the scene at the first function he'll attend.

I'll be inside the beautifully decorated marquee, sat amongst my cousins soaking up the wedding atmosphere, laughing and joking; feeling elegant and beautiful in one of my dazzling Indian outfits specially picked out with Chris in mind. He walks in and his gaze is fixated on me and only me. He comes towards me and I get up with uncontrollable elation to greet him. My cousins' mouths drop to the floor. They're wandering who this six foot White guy is walking towards me with a beaming smile on his face.

Chris will be looking sexy and stylish - well turned out in his tux. His hair perfectly styled; smelling gorgeous in that favourite aftershave I love to smell on him - the one that I bought him for his birthday. He bends down slightly to plant a kiss on my cheek and whispers gently in my ear that I look beautiful.

He's ruining the scene.

He watches the glow in my face disappear in a flicker. And as I look away disappointed, he asks, "How many outfits do I need then? You lot have weddings that go on for weeks, don't you?!"

"So you'll come then?" I ask, my face brightening up again.

"Damn right I will. Got to show your cousins the 'Jamo' snake hips on the dance floor haven't I? They'll never be able to resist my charm."

"Don't you go flirting with my cousins Christian Jamieson, I'm warning you," I say sternly.

"Or what? What exactly are you going to do Anushka Lamba? Tell them that I'm your boyfriend and to stay away? Now I'd pay money to hear you say that." He's teasing me. He knows only too well that I'll never be in a position to say that.

I let him keep up his pretence with an uninterested remark, "Ha ha. Fine, flirt with them if you like, I'm not bothered."

"We'll see," he says. "You'll have to teach me your cultural customs though. I'd hate to disrespect anyone."

"Relax, you won't disrespect anyone. Just don't swear and don't be affectionate in public - in fact don't be affectionate at any time or in any way and you'll be just fine!"

"I gathered that much," he says disappointingly.

"Great. Jess has already said she'd love to come."

"You've already asked her then?"

"I text her on the train and filled her in. She said she didn't mind if you didn't."

"Oh great. Well tell her there's to be no public displays of affection."

"Whatever. Sorry to burst your bubble Chris but she doesn't fancy you!"

My tiredness fades into an emotion of ecstasy and I'm unable to fall asleep.

§

The next morning the guys are in their element during Media in Society lecture, where we're analysing director and producer, Stanley Kubrick's work – in particular his controversial film, *A Clockwork Orange*.

The film is not foreign to me. On the contrary it's a familiar title in my newly formed collection of, *'Never before heard of titles to be dissected.'*

My second year at college was more or less dedicated to the works of this enigmatic director, so I'm more than aware of the violent and disturbing storyline this film depicts. The rest of the girls however, who are outnumbered by the guys in class, have never seen it - therefore unsuspecting of the treat, Frankie our eccentric lecturer has in store for us.

Some of the boys are sat on the back row sniggering. "Have you seen the sex scenes in this film?" I hear Dan says to someone in a whisper that is loud enough to be heard. They start discussing it in finer detail when Amanda turns around and tells them to stop being so disgusting. "You've obviously not seen it then Mand," Daniel shouts back.

Just before Frankie turns on the TV he warns everyone about the content of the clips.

"We'll talk more in depth about the film once you've seen the clips I've lined up, but I have to warn you that some of the images you're about to view are quite disturbing. There's a fair bit of nudity and a couple of rape scenes."

I'm sitting next to Kerry. We look around the room and notice the other girls exchanging nervous glances with each other.

Kerry is one of my closest friends. She lives in a different hall on campus; only about a five minute walk away. We became friends on the first day of university when we both ended up sitting next to one another when all seats in the class were occupied. We parked ourselves on the front row and waited for our lecturer, Lois to turn up.

Lois came in flying through the door ten minutes late, wearing a short denim skirt, black and white stripy tights, big black boots and the brightest yellow top she could find. Her hair looked like a birds nest. Her whole attire, including her hair set me and Kerry off into fits of giggles. We both agreed that Lois must have got changed in the dark that morning, which is why she was running late. And from that day onwards our friendship formed.

Frankie turns the lights out and presses play. The guys sit back, like boisterous teenagers on the back row of a cinema hall, about to watch their first certificate 18 showing.

A few minutes into the first clip, I look around the class and notice Cassie's face. If anyone has something to say about anything in class, it's usually her. She's never happy until she's had at least one moan per day.

This time though something seems to have stirred with her emotions because she gets up and walks out of the room before the lights are switched back on, and she doesn't return for the rest of the lecture.

The dinner hall seems busier than usual this evening. It's not even curry night. I walk in with Jess, pick up a tray and join the queue. "I wonder why it's heaving in here tonight," enquires Jess.

"I was just thinking the same thing. I hate this bit of the night. It's bad enough having to actually eat this food, but to waste an hour every day standing in a line to be served spoonfuls of it is even more crap."

"I know what you mean."

I consider abandoning my tray and going back to halls to heat up the *okra* dish I brought back from home, along with the *daal,* and toast a couple of slices of bread; but it's unfair to leave Jess on her own.

"Are you going to the Students' Union tonight?" I ask her. "It's that traffic light party isn't it?"

"Yeah maybe, I'm not sure yet," she says. "The whole thing just seems a little sleazy and desperate for my liking. I don't really want people knowing the status of my love life or knowing whether I'm up for it or not."

"Don't be daft. It'll be a laugh Jess. Why don't you wear all three colours, that way you can be the mystery woman and no one's the wiser?"

"Yeah I could do, I suppose. I will go but I'm not going early or anything. That's just got desperation written all over it."

"Don't think too much into it Jess, it's a party, loosen up. Let's see what time the others are planning on going... Hey, do you think I should wear a green light?!"

"Yeah I dare you. In fact I think you should do. I'd love to see Chris' face when you walk past him on the door flashing a green traffic light."

"You're on!"

The discussion in the dinner hall seems to be focused on tonight's traffic light party.

Ella and Vani knock on our door. They've brought with them a bottle of Lambrini; cheap and cheerful and just what we need to start off our night. Ten minutes later and there's another knock on the door. Wendy and Natalie from down the corridor have also joined us.

"Just knock it back," Ella says to Vani, who isn't a big drinker and makes curious faces whenever she drinks alcohol. Vani reminds me a lot of myself, especially the first few times I started drinking.

I hide my dislike of alcohol a lot better than she does though. If I don't like the taste of a drink, I force myself to gulp it, but I hold it in my mouth for a few seconds until I muster up enough courage to neck it down in one.

Vani is a pretty quiet person who seldom smiles or makes conversation with anyone; and only really speaks when asked a question. Her face is expressionless most of the time and sad, like she's carrying the weight of the world on her small bony shoulders. I often mistake her sadness as just Vani being miserable. But when she knocks back a few drinks, it's good to see her come out of her shell. There's even a hint of a smile on her face when someone cracks a joke. On a good day, you can hear her humming from the communal showers down the corridor. Tonight she is steadily showing signs of cheeriness.

Most of the time Vani wears black, which suits her personality. Even tonight she's wearing an entirely black outfit.

"What are you wearing Anu?" she asks me.

"Open my cupboard hun; it's hung up behind the door. It's a cut off shoulder black and electric blue top with a pair of skinny jeans and knee high boots." She picks it out and holds up the top, putting it against her chest. "It's really pretty."

"Thanks. You can borrow it whenever you like," I offer.

"Cheers m'dears!"

We arrive at the doors just gone eight thirty, to join a long queue of scantily clad girls and rowdy boys, standing in the freezing cold. Everyone is wearing flashing traffic lights around their necks. I've decided to go for all three.

Red, for 'I'm already taken'. Yellow for 'undecided - try me.' And green for 'single, I want to mingle.'

I shout to Jess who is a few people behind me talking to a friend. "I've gone for all three Jess!"

"You are so going to be in trouble tonight," she says.

"He'll be fine with it, it's only a laugh," I shout.

Chris seems far from impressed at the yellow and green traffic lights around my neck as he watches me walk in, whilst checking student I.D cards at the door.

"Hey, it's busy in here, isn't it?" I say. "How's work going?" I lean in to him to give him a kiss, but he pulls away. "What's wrong with you?" I ask, even though I'm fully aware of the reason for his unwelcoming response.

"Anu, are you trying to take the piss out of me or something? Most people here know that we're together, so what are you doing wearing all three traffic lights?"

"It was just a dare between me and Jess this afternoon. It's only a bit of fun. There's no need to get so serious about it Chris."

"Fine do what you want. It's cool with me. Anyway I've got work to do; I'll catch you in a bit." He turns his face away from me in disappointment.

I too decide to ignore him and walk off in the direction of the bar instead where Dan is getting the drinks in.

"Dan the man! Mine's a vodka redbull if you're buying," I say, cheekily.

"Because it's you Anu angel eyes, I suppose I can stretch to a drink for you."

"Ah thanks sweetie. So are you up for some fun tonight?"

"That depends, are you?"

"Cheeky, cheeky Daniel. Don't let Chris hear you say that."

"Let's see shall we," he says, rubbing his hands together excitedly. "It all depends on what the talent's like in here tonight."

He hands me my vodka. "Or how much you've had to drink, you mean!" I tell him.

I walk over to the table that Teresa and others have saved for us. I notice Chris looking at me from the corner of my eye, but when I turn my head to face him he quickly turns away to avoid any eye contact with me.

Most people are mingling. The guys are trying their luck with all the girls, regardless of what light they are wearing. A few girls are looking sheepish, making flirty eye contact with lads who are blatantly giving them the eye. There's some serious flirting going on in the room.

Maya scurries over to me with a worried look on her face. "What's up with you?" I ask.

"Jags is drunk and he's handing out ten pound notes to everyone upstairs. Well I think they're ten pound notes, anyway!"

"What, you're kidding me?! What is that bloke playing at?"

"I don't know, but you know what he's like. When he's had a few too many, he doesn't know how to handle himself or his money."

Jagdeep, Jags for short, is a Sikh guy from London who wears a turban. He also wears his heart on his sleeve and is a proud Punjabi guy.

It was Mum who saw him in the car park with his dad on that first Sunday when I arrived on campus. She noticed two brightly coloured turban wearers walking sprightly to and from the car park. She came back into my room, and in an excited fashion she told us all that a *Sardar* had moved in.

I remember smiling at Sanya and thinking, why Indian people did that. At the sight of other Indians, why do they feel this over powering sense of security and belonging, like everything will be fine now (as if it wasn't before) because the Indians are here?!

"It's nice to see there's another Punjabi person here, isn't it Anushka?" she said.

"If you say so Mum."

But as it happened Jags and I became very good friends. He had to settle for friendship because even though he blatantly told me all the time how much he fancied me he also knew that I wasn't interested in him in that way, because I was with Chris.

"What are you doing with a *gora* Anu? Why a White guy? What's wrong with one of our own?"

That's the question Jags often asks me, usually when he's tanked up on whisky and coke.

"What would your parents say if they knew you were with a *gora*?" he asked when he found out I was seeing Chris.

"Don't start getting all hypocritical on me Jags. You're a fine one to talk. You're on the prowl for any girl with a pulse when you're out. I've seen the way you're all over women. You're not bothered about what colour or religion they are. And you're asking me what I'm doing with a White guy. Your mum would be so proud of you too, wouldn't she?"

"You know what I mean Anu. You should stick to *apne*, our own."

"Listen Jags, let's not get into a stupid argument and ruin a perfectly good friendship, because you know I can get really pissed off and I'll probably say something to you which I might regret. So let's end this discussion now."

"OK, chill Anu. But you'll come to me yourself one day. By then, who knows if I'll be here waiting for you."

"I'll take my chances!" I replied with certainty.

Maya and I are just about to walk up the stairs to see Jags, but instead we watch in horror as he tumbles down the steps, literally falling down each one. Luckily a couple of guys are stood at the bottom and grab him before he falls to the floor.

The damage has already been done though. Not only has Jags flaunted a wad of ten and twenty pound notes and thrown them into the air for scavenging students to take advantage of in his inebriated state of mind, but the unthinkable has also occurred. His turban unravels around his head, letting loose his mane of long hair as he reaches the bottom of the stairs.

I can't believe my eyes. Jags doesn't have any control over his actions and falls into the arms of the two guys. I look over to Chris, who's also witnessed it - along with so many others - and is making his way over to Jags as quickly as he can. Students watch in disbelief - their eyes transfixed on Jags and his long hair, which has fallen just above his backside. They've never seen a Sikh man's turban come off.

I want to protect Jags - tell him that everything is going to be ok. But tears are sliding down his cheeks and he's shouting at

Chris to get him out of there.

"It's ok mate. Let's get you in the back."

Chris remains calm and tries to deflect the unwanted attention Jags is receiving. But Jags wants to get the hell out of the Students' Union, and fast.

Chapter Six

*"Namaste Dadi."...**Chris***

My heart races with nervous excitement and bubbling energy as soon as I awake. But time is ticking painfully slow, as if someone knows how much I'm looking forward to tonight; how long I've been waiting for it, and then cruelly decides to turn back all the clocks in the house to make me suffer. I've easily checked the clock at least a dozen times in the space of an hour.

It's late afternoon on the night of Arjun's pre-wedding function before his big day. I'm eagerly awaiting tonight because I'll be seeing Chris for the first time since coming home for Easter, and this will be the first function that he'll be attending.

Sweat gathers in the palm of my hands and my mind runs at lightning speed at the thought. Chris and I spoke fleetingly last night when he drove up from the island, having spent a couple of days at the start of the Easter break with his parents. He was making his way straight to Jess' parents' place.

Her parents have kindly offered to put him up for a few days, so that the both of them can come to the wedding functions together. It looks far more inconspicuous, than both of them arriving individually as guests of mine to my cousin's wedding.

My house is swarming with relatives and the atmosphere is buzzing. Arj is the eldest and the first of all my eleven cousins to be getting married.

This is a big, family occasion.

I knock on the door to my parents bedroom and wait until I hear Mum tell me to come in. She is standing by the window facing the long length mirror when I enter, carefully adjusting the pleats of her sari with precision, making sure that each pleat is folded correctly and that it's the right size and width apart before tucking it into the waist of her petticoat.

"You're not ready yet Anu?" she asks, with an unsurprised look on her face. "We've only got an hour before we have to go to Arjun's house. I know how long you take getting ready. Hurry up."

"I can't find anywhere to get changed," I say in frustration. "Every room is taken."

Mum holds out a safety pin and asks me to help her fasten the drape of her sari over her left shoulder so that the sari is firmly pinned into place.

"Get dressed in here," she says. "Sanya has just finished getting ready here too."

I walk back out and knock on the door to my own bedroom which has been invaded by my relatives from London. My cousins Sarika and Amber are both stood facing the mirror. Sarika is skilfully applying black eye liner onto her eye lids. Amber has sections of her hair pinned up whilst straightening it and Rishi is adjusting the tie on his white shirt in the corner of my bedroom, facing a smaller mirror.

I pick up my clothes, jewellery, make-up and shoes that I neatly put into a pile in my cupboard last night. I let out a, "you all look great by the way," before walking back out and into Mum's room again, to start looking my best for Chris tonight.

§

I'm meeting and greeting guests, doing the usual formalities with my relatives, whilst in between darting a glance or three in the direction of the marquee entrance. Each time a guest enters I have a charming mixture of glum and glee across my face. Patience is getting the better of me and I start to wonder when Chris is going to arrive. I consider phoning him to find out where they are, but decide against it. I don't want to arouse any suspicions in the room.

This is to be the first time that my entire family will be in the same room as my secret boyfriend. I'm petrified, yet feeling surprisingly brave.

Dadi has found a place to sit, taking up two chairs so she can put her feet up, cross her legs comfortably and give herself a good view of everyone and of everything going on around her.

She's the head of the family, ever since my granddad passed away, and is honoured with the utmost respect by family and friends alike.

Arj's wedding has been the hot topic of conversation on everyone's lips for months, and I found out that over the last few months auntie Beena was either on the phone or at our house discussing the wedding ceremonies with Dadi; because if anyone knows about the finer details of Indian wedding ceremonies, then she does.

The starters are being served. I queue up with the other guests to fill a plate of food for Dadi. None of the immediate family is eating yet and they don't look like they're in a hurry too by the looks of it.

"It's rude to eat first at your own party," said Dadi last week, when I dived into the canopies being served at Arj's Sangeet party. "You have to feed your guests before yourself. What will everyone think if you're eating before them?"

This time I'm picking food for her so that makes me exempt from receiving any evil looks or snooty comments from anyone. Frankly I don't care what anyone thinks anyway, because my hunger isn't dictated by my relationship to the groom.

I pick up a couple of *aloo* cutlets, *bengan pakoras* and a few chilli *paneers*. I drop a spoonful of tangy tamarind sauce on to the plate to accompany them. Just as I finish piling some salad on to the plate, I hear a familiar voice that sets my heart beat racing.

"Hi sweet cheeks."

I'm holding on to the plate with such force that I realise it may break in my hands. I compose myself quickly before turning around to face the person I've been so desperate to see since this morning.

"I see you're the first one in the queue for food. Good to see some things never change!" Chris jokes.

"You know me so well don't you," I reply, trying hard to contain my excitement. "You took your bloody time didn't you?"

I'm completely engrossed in him standing in front of me that I forget about Jess, who's stood to the side of him. "Hi hun. Good to see you," I say quickly, trying to recover myself.

I follow her curious face around the room.

"I can't believe how many cars are parked outside. I wasn't expecting quite so many people," she says with surprise.

"This is nothing Jess. You just watch tomorrow at the wedding. You're going to love it, I promise. Just prepare yourself for a long day though."

"What's going on tonight then?" asks Chris.

But before I have chance to explain, Mum and Dad appear behind me. Dad pulls his arm forward to meet Chris'.

"You must be Anu's friends?" he asks, looking at them both. Chris replies with a stern handshake.

"Nice to meet you, Mr Lamba, and Mrs Lamba. I'm Christian, but people call me Chris."

"It's nice to meet you, Chris," replies Dad.

"Hi Mr and Mrs Lamba. I'm Jess. We met that first day you came to drop Anu off. "

"Yes, yes of course I remember you Jess," Mum tells her. "How are you finding your course? Are you glad you chose this university?"

"Oh yeah, absolutely. It's very well recognised, especially in the field that Anu and I are trying to get in to."

"Well I hope so," says Dad. "This is why you are so far away after all. We hope you both get a job out of it, that's the main thing, right?"

"Yep, I guess so" replies Jess.

Dad turns to Chris. "So Anu tells us that you haven't attended an Indian wedding before? Is this your first one?"

"That's right," replies Chris. "I've never been to one, so it's going to be a real eye opener. We're really looking forward to it."

I look over at Dadi who seems impatient, waiting for her food. I swop the *pakoras* I have on my plate with some fresh, hot ones that have just arrived. "Be back in a minute," I say, walking over to the other side of the marquee.

"Have your friends arrived?" Dadi asks, looking at them from afar.

"Yes, I'll introduce you to them in a minute."

This isn't the scene I had in mind when I envisaged Chris walking in. I wanted it to be perfect, just how I had imagined.

Mum, Dad, Chris and Jess appear to be locked in deep conversation about something when I return.

"It's yellow turmeric paste mixed with mustard oil and barley," Mum says. She smears pretend mixture from her hands onto her face to show Chris and Jess where exactly you rub it on to the groom.

"Relatives of the groom rub a bit of the yellow turmeric paste on to his arms, legs and face. This is what's called the *Vatna* ceremony. The bride's side of the family does it too, but because it's a Punjabi tradition it probably won't be happening on their side."

Chris and Jess' expression is one of fascination and confusion.

"Are you telling me that Arj is going to be sat there naked while you all cover him in paste?" Chris asks Mum. We all start laughing.

"Have I said something really dumb?" asks Chris, with a confused smile on his face.

"No no," Mum says. "He'll be wearing old clothes tonight, ones that he can just throw away once he's worn them, because they're bound to get dirty."

"And what does it signify?" asks Jess.

"Well the paste is applied to cleanse and purify the bodies of both the bride and the groom so that they are ready for their married life together. It's supposed to give them a positively glowing look on their wedding day."

She then goes on to tell them what else is going to be happening tonight. "Because it's the night before the wedding we're singing and dancing to traditional wedding songs. It's called a *Sangeet.*" They continue to look completely engrossed in what Mum is telling them, but I'm not sure if they fully understand. "Although we had the official *Sangeet* function last week, this is a smaller one, since all the family is together, and because it's the last of the functions before the big day tomorrow. They had their civil ceremony two days ago, so technically in the eyes of English law they're already married. But for us, it's the Indian wedding we are mostly looking forward to. The one that is most important to us."

After her short but sweet insight into tonight's events, I tell Mum I'm going to introduce Chris and Jess to Dadi. I sense at least half a dozen pairs of eyes wandering in my direction as we walk over to her.

"Dadi, this is Jess and this is Chris, my friends from university."

"Hello," Dadi says, nodding at them.

"Hello," Jess replies. "Nice to meet you."

"*Namaste* Dadi," says Chris.

I watch in astonishment as he places his hands together to symbolise the greeting of his gesture.

It dawns on me that the night I told Chris about Arj's wedding - when I'd been so excited about finishing my shift at the hotel so I could invite him, he asked me that evening how he should greet Dadi and my parents. I remember showing him what to do with his hands and how to pronounce the words.

But no words can describe the emotion I'm feeling at this exact moment, witnessing him saying *Namaste* to her. I feel humble and so proud of him. Dadi seems equally impressed with his accentuated pronunciation because she puts her hands together and greets him in the same manner.

This is good, this is definitely good. He's got off on the right foot with Dadi.

"So are you going to introduce us to your friends then Anu?" asks Jaya.

One by one I introduce Chris and Jess to all of my cousins, knowing full well that they'll never remember any of their names in about ten minutes time.

As the evening unfolds so do the ceremonies. Arj is sat on a stool in the middle of the marquee and all the guests and family surround him. For nearly one hour of the evening he doesn't look like a groom about to get married tomorrow. He's dressed in an old white shirt covered with blotches of paint. He's wearing three quarter length tracksuit bottoms and a battered pair of flip flops.

I feel relieved that Mum had that little discussion with Chris and Jess and pre-warned them about this part of the ceremony. If she hadn't I dread to think what they'd be thinking right now; probably something along the lines of, the groom has turned up to his own party looking like a vagrant!

Arj knocked on at most of his neighbours' houses to warn them of the noise levels this week. Even if anyone objected, it wouldn't have stopped the *shor-sharaba* – the combination of over excited and loud voices of Indian people, drinking and dancing in both a provocative and embarrassing manner whilst singing in high pitched voices to traditional wedding songs.

Most of them know that there's a wedding in the family, or that something big is going on - from the size of the marquee at the side of Arj's house, and by the number of guests and cars that have been turning up over the last few days. Luckily they've been extremely accommodating and haven't objected to the late night noise pollution and free entertainment on offer. Most of them have joined in with the celebrations.

Once all my close relatives have been up to see Arj and have smudged paste onto any visible spot on his body they can find, all my cousins go up and follow suit. Chris and Jess look fascinated at the goings on. Chris is stood beside me, but takes me by surprise when he whispers in my ear, "Is this what your cousins will have to do to me if I marry you?"

I can feel myself going crimson in the face. For a second I'm unsure whether he's actually said that to me or whether my mind has played tricks on me because it's what I want to hear. I look up at him, thinking that he's brave to even utter such words in front of all my family. He winks and gives me his sexy smile.

I wonder whether Mum has overheard what Chris has said, as she stands on the opposite side to me. She looks over and signals something. Then I realise that she's telling me to take Chris and Jess to the front, up to Arj. I take them both over to Arj, who is sat on a small stool in the middle of the marquee looking helpless. I choose a small spot on his cheek. Chris and Jess each find an un-yellow marked space on his leg and fill it. Mum walks over to us and tells us to pose for the camera. She thinks that Jess and Chris might want a memory of their experience at the *Vatna* ceremony. I smile at her for the kind gesture and nod a 'thank you', to her.

Just as we get up to leave, Arj introduces himself to my friends. "Hi, I'm the groom, although you wouldn't think so. I hope seeing me like this hasn't put you off coming to the wedding tomorrow? I promise I'll be looking more human later once I've had a shower, taken this muck off my face and put on some clean clothes."

"I've certainly not seen anything like this before," says Chris. "It looks like your cousins are having the last laugh with you tonight, mate!"

"I think you're right."

The party is in full swing. Drinks are flowing, food is being consumed. The music is playing and aunties are singing dreadfully in their screeching voices to some popular traditional wedding songs. All of them are getting highly emotional. I'm sure I even hear Arj's mum reminiscing about the night before her own wedding. Everyone seems to be having a good time; even *my* guests. And I am on an amazing high, soaking up all the atmosphere and energy in the room.

Dad on the other hand appears a little on edge tonight. I've noticed him paying more attention to me and my friends, than with anyone else in the room. He might be on the other side mingling with guests, but his eyes are firmly placed on me at all times.

I notice him walking towards me but I avoid any eye contact with him; I turn my head to face Jess instead.

"So what are you drinking?" Dad asks casually, appearing at the side of Chris.

"Coke. Smell it if you don't believe me," I say, defensively, with both my friends standing beside me and oblivious to the fact that they're giving me Dutch courage. I know that there's no way Dad will pick up my drink and smell it in front of my friends. But I suspect that it's not just the contents of my glass he has come to inspect; it's my company too - in particular, the male company.

Uncle Ashok appears seconds later. He too, I imagine has turned up to check on what all the girls are drinking.

It doesn't really matter to either of them that most of us are over the age limit, and legally allowed to drink alcohol without having to seek their permission. I want to shout out that if they knew what sort of state I got into at university then their eyeballs would pop out of their sockets. But this is neither the time nor the place to be getting into a debate on the morals of Indian girls drinking alcohol. The issue is more trivial.

The room is full of guests; respectable people from their social circle - friends of our family. For any of the girls to openly stroll over to the homemade bar area - where alcohol is freely available like tap water, isn't a clever idea.

There is an awkward silence between us. Dad doesn't know what to say after I offer him a whiff of my glass. I'm praying that he doesn't take up my offer.

"No, no. I believe you," he says, unconvincingly. But I haven't given him any choice to interrogate me further.

Chris finds it all amusing, because he very quickly arrives at the conclusion that a few of my cousins are a lot like me - quite conscious about how they are perceived amongst relatives and close family friends.

"It's less hassle if you just get it for us," Jaya said to Chris, when she unashamedly asked him outright to get her a drink earlier on. I did wonder whether Arj's dad - who became barman for a while - thought that my friends were taking the piss with the whole 'free bar' as they'd already made several trips in a short space of time.

Dad walks off in embarrassment and I feel a moment of guilt override me for my childish behaviour.

Arj has showered and changed into something more respectable and presentable. His yellow stained shirt, mixed with old, multi-coloured paint stains has been replaced by a baby pink, striped, short sleeve shirt and black trousers. His tired looking flip flops have been swapped with some shiny black shoes. He's starting to look almost human again, without the yellow gunk stuck like glue to his face.

I wonder whether I will be in high spirits on my wedding like Arj must be feeling. Although I'm almost certain it's a different feeling for a girl. I know I'm only eighteen but I can't help thinking what my own wedding will be like.

I don't know who the groom will be and what he'll look like; or even what ethnicity he'll be. All I can visualize is me in a beautiful, deep red and gold Indian bridal outfit and he sat next to me at the mandap, in his traditional head dress, with garlands covering his face.

With the nuptial knot tied between us, we walk around the fire seven times; each circle representing a step, a promise that we have made to one another in the name of love, marriage and commitment. Our close family and friends are watching whilst the priest recites our marriage vows in Hindi, and then translates them in English for those that can't understand the Sanskrit language.

Suddenly I'm snapped out of my beautiful dream by the lyrics of a Punjabi song that catches my attention.

The effects of alcohol are slowly seeping through my body and taking over total control of my senses. I have to be careful not to make it obvious to everyone that I'm a bit too merry on a little coke. The truth is that I'm also on a natural high in the presence of my secret boyfriend.

I don't hold back either when Arj's sister Rohini pulls my arm and drags me on to the dance floor with her. Chris and Jess sit and look on, observing their surroundings and embracing the colourful craziness.

A short while later auntie Simmy makes her grand entrance on to the dance floor. She isn't a blood relative; she's a close family friend who I've known since childhood, so therefore she more than qualifies as my auntie.

She's one of the few, glamorous and entertaining people in our families' circle of friends, who often becomes our host entertainer - catering for everyone's taste.

Auntie Simmy is really going for it; moving those hips from side to side, waving her hands up in the air. The sari blouse she's wearing reveals a daring cleavage and is certainly sending a few shockwaves through the guests; both men and women, but for wholly different reasons. Not everyone can pull the look off, but auntie Simmy can. She is bold and beautiful and I admire her self confidence.

I don't anticipate her next move though. She continues to shake her hips, dancing her way off the floor and towards Chris - staring at him as she moves closer to him.

Meanwhile, he is sitting on his chair nervously, twitching from side to side, wondering what the hell this crazy woman walking up to him is doing shimmying her hips in his direction. Before he has time to grasp what's going on, she grabs him by the hand and tells him to get up because she wants to dance with him. Jess lets out a snigger. "Go on Chris," she tells him.

He looks a little bewildered.

"I don't know how to dance to Indian music," he admits.

"It's ok, I will teach you," auntie Simmy says. She doesn't give him a chance to respond. She pulls him up by his arm, dragging him to the dance floor; and he helplessly follows her like a little lost puppy.

She's showing him the light bulb move. She puts one hand on her hip to show him what to do. He stands at a slight angle and his other hand is in the air twisting it backwards and forwards to the music, imitating the manoeuvre of changing a light bulb. He has completely immersed himself into it.

The singing, drinking and dancing continues until just after midnight, until we can no longer feel our legs anymore. Thanks to auntie Simmy, Chris seems to have had a blast tonight. I'm not so sure about Jess on the other hand.

On the surface she appears to look happy about being here, but Jess always keeps her emotions under wraps. Even though I know she likes Chris, I often think that she tolerates him for my sake. After all, we're roommates so she doesn't have much choice but to get on with my boyfriend.

But Chris and Jess have had their moments. One afternoon when Jess arrived back to our room - after finishing early from lectures - she tried to put her key in the door, when she noticed that it'd been pushed ajar a little, and the lock slightly broken. She stepped into the room cautiously because her first instinct told her that someone had broken in. But nothing had been taken. Not that we had much in our room to take anyway, unless you counted my stereo system, our hair straighteners and both our CD collections.

On closer inspection, her eyes were drawn to half a dozen or so pairs of knickers and bras which looked familiar to her. They belonged to her and had been strategically hung in various places around the room.

Later that evening, in the dinner hall Chris and Stu came to sit next to us. Jess hadn't mentioned anything to me about what happened that afternoon. Perhaps because she was embarrassed that someone - a complete stranger whose identity was unknown had rifled through her knicker drawer.

Half way through eating our evening meal, Stu said out loud, "So Chris, are you going to get some sexy lingerie for Anu on Valentine's Day next year?"

I looked at Stu, and then at Chris who both giggled like naughty school boys.

"What's so funny?" I asked.

"Nothing babe. I don't have any problem with looking at women's underwear," Chris said unusually loud and then erupted into laughter with Stu. I looked at Jess, who didn't seem to find any of it funny. She remained quiet. I carried on eating, blissfully unaware of what was going on at the table.

Suddenly Jess put down her knife and fork, picked up her glass of water and mine - stood up and threw both glasses over Chris and Stu's face.

"I don't know which one of you it was that pulled that stunt in my room, but it's obvious that you're both in it together." she shouted angrily. "I didn't find it amusing at all. In fact it was completely childish; but then that's you two all over isn't it? And whoever broke the lock to the front door can fix it too."

She was fuming. I'd never seen her look so angry. But then as soon as she said her piece, she sat down and carried on with her dinner, as if nothing happened. The dinner hall was only half full, but everyone in there watched what happened. When the show was over she even got a round of applause from some of the lads sitting on the next table.

Chapter Seven

*"My cousin has just got married and it's time to dance
like a true Punjabi, Christian Jamieson.
It's my turn to show you some Indian moves!"...Anu*

At first I can hear a faint, continuing sound grating in my ear. It gets louder and louder. I'm in a semi conscious state, but it's deafening me all the same. I switch over to my side, feeling the vibrations from underneath my pillow touching my cheek. I slide my hand underneath it and press the first key my finger hits, to turn off the irritating alarm on my mobile phone. It's six thirty am.

My feet ache from all the dancing last night and the tossing and turning in the make shift bed on the living room floor hasn't helped either. Soon everyone in the house will be scrambling to get into the bathroom to start getting ready.

There are already loud voices coming from upstairs. It has to be Dadi's voice. She's an early riser, and a loud talker. No one usually gets more than an extra hour of sleep the moment Dadi wakes up, because by the time she's fully come round, with her usual morning cup of tea brought to her in bed by Mum, and the ear deafening volume on her TV blasted up to the highest decibel, she operates like an energizer bunny, rearing to go with her powerful and masterful voice.

She never quite believes us when we tell her that she listens to the TV too loud. Her excuse is, "With all the background music they play I can't hear the words or what the characters are saying!"

We have literally two hours for eleven people to get showered, dressed and out of the house to make it to Arj's for nine o' clock sharp - to get on the coach to Newcastle.

I'm already exhausted just thinking about it.

We're back at Arj's house in less than seven hours after leaving last night. His mum looks tense. I go over to her and ask her if she needs any help with anything.

She squeezes my hand tightly. "Anushka, you'll be helping me greatly dear, if you and some of the others can look after the guests. The *chai* and coffee needs to be served, and there's the breakfast snacks too. Everyone is arriving, so they need to eat a little something before we set off. Please can you help out?"

I stand with my cousin Tina behind a long folding table which is covered in a red and white organza crunched up table cloth from last night's party. We lay out polystyrene disposable cups, filling them half way with jugs of tea and coffee, which are being prepared in the kitchen by my mum and auntie Lalita. Auntie Renu brings out trays of hot, fresh *pakoras* and *samosas* from the kitchen.

"How can anyone eat this food so early in the morning?" Tina says to me.

"I know. The smell of it is making me nauseous. It's not bothering any of this lot though is it?" I say, pointing to people. "Look at them. Anyone would think they haven't eaten in days. Have you seen the way they're piling the food onto their plates?" We snigger lightly, under our breath.

I check the time on my phone; it's nine am.

Right on cue, Chis and Jess walk in, sending my heartbeat racing through the roof again. I've worn a heavily embroidered peacock green and gold *Shalwar Kameez*; green and gold matching colour bangles on each wrist, and a pair of gold strappy heels. I've decided not to accessorise with a necklace or earrings because my outfit is fancy enough with all its intricate stitching. The last thing I want is to look like a dazzling Christmas tree covered in baubles.

Chris winks at me. He's looking dapper, dressed in a charcoal colour granddad collar suit and same style white shirt; his hair spiked up in the usual fashion. All I can think about is kissing him passionately on the lips, and running my hands through his sexy hair. But I look away in nervousness; afraid that everyone can read my mind.

The aim is to leave Arj's house at nine, but so far no one has taken their seat on the coach. Most of the parents are running around like headless chicken, but not actually doing anything other than flapping. The boys are the first to pile on, parking themselves on the back two rows - leaving the girls to take the seats just in front of them.

All the gifts that Arj's family have packed for the bride and her family lie carefully on the seats towards the front of the coach.

We eventually leave Arj's house at precisely nine twenty-five am.

"I had a really good time last night," Jess says, sitting next to me. "It was a lot of fun."

"Good I'm glad you did hun. To be honest I was wondering whether you were enjoying it. At times I thought you seemed a little out of your comfort zone."

"No it wasn't that Anu. I've not been feeling too great since the holidays started, that's all. My hay fever's come on a little with the change in weather that's all. I am having a good time, honest."

"Well, that's good to hear. Hey, is Chris behaving himself? I mean, at your house and with your parents?"

"He's a cheeky sod, but yeah he's being as good as gold."

"Who's a cheeky sod?" Chris' voice lurks from behind me. "Never you mind, big ears," she says. "We're talking about you, not to you."

Sarika gets up from her seat to occupy the vacant one next to Chris, when Neel gets up and heads to the front of the coach. She keeps him busy talking, bombarding him with question after question. I have no idea what they are talking about; I can just hear their voices intermittently behind me.

Before we left campus, I filled both Chris and Jess in about this weekend; giving them more things to remember so that they didn't put their foot in it. I wasn't worried about Jess, she didn't say much anyway. But Chris has a tendency to open his mouth before engaging his brain.

"I have very inquisitive cousins," I told them both in the Students' Union, the night before we broke up for the Easter break. It was probably not the best of places to be speaking to them though, as the likelihood of them remembering much the following day was pretty low. "If my cousins' minds are anything like mine, then they probably won't believe that we're just good friends. They'll keep stinging you like bees, after some honey. Something. Anything. No matter how much they flatter you, or appear simple and straight with their talking, believe me there's always a hidden agenda. There always is with my family, especially the girls."

Sarika is studying law and has the attributes of becoming a damn good lawyer, with her bold and fearless personality. She's the most opinionated and outspoken member in our family; who likes to bring up taboo subjects, which ordinarily would go down like a led balloon at the breakfast or dinner table. But she has this skill to just start talking about daring topics, like mixed race marriages, teenage pregnancies; homosexuality - just for the sake of it. She completely sucks everyone in to her controversial debates for hours because she knows that the mum's and dad's within our family have strong views on everything. I'm sure she gets some kind of sick pleasure in watching Dadi, or any of the parents wound up, of the possibility of something abnormal entering their lives.

At times debates around the table can become highly contentious; but that's her aim – to go above and beyond the norm of Indian family household discussions.

It doesn't take long for the Punjabi's to start the party. Not long after we hit the M62 motorway auntie Simmy brings out her *dholki* – a South Asian hand drum. Some of the aunties and uncles, including Ritu and Rohini gather in the aisle and around auntie Simmy's seat, to begin the entertainment for the day. Chris and Jess don't seem surprised at all with their latest instalment of unusual Punjabi entertainment. It's not even been a full twenty four hours since they were introduced to my world. They've only encountered one night of it so far, but they look like they've been used to it for longer. Chris in particular looks happy, and in turn that makes me happy.

"Come on, all of you girls and boys hiding at the back there," auntie Simmy bellows. "It's your cousin's wedding, we have to make more noise than the Gujrati's today; after all we are the *baraat,* and that too the Punjabi *baraat.* It's our job to be loud and jolly. Come down here and join in."

I look round to Amber, Tina and Sanya, who are hiding behind their seats, quietly mimicking auntie Simmy in her thick Asian accent. I stand up to make my way down the coach. Jess decides to stay in her seat and watch the entertainment from afar. Chris is still engaged in conversation with Sarika but his eyes are fleetingly met by auntie Simmy's, who sends him a flirty grin from her seat. I watch Chris as he responds politely with a friendly smile. But the smile is ammunition for auntie Simmy to corner him again, in public this time.

"You remember the steps I taught you last night, Christopher?" she yells at the top of her voice; hoping to provoke a reaction.

"It's Christian. And yes, how can I forget the light bulb dancing," he shouts back, re-enacting the moves with his hands. Some of the aunties, including Mum start laughing at his hand movement.

"Do it again for us all," she demands. "So we can see you. We will sing and you can dance for us. Ok?" She sounds as though she's doing him a favour.

"No, no no," he laughs. "It's fine. I'm quite happy sat down for now. But I promise I'll come and find you later on at the party." He gives her a wink, which sends auntie Simmy into a fit of giggles again.

I desperately want Sarika to offer me her seat so I can sit and talk to Chris, and listen to the assessment he's undoubtedly made of my family so far.

Does he think they're mad? That everyone is a nutcase and hard work. Does he think I have unusual cultural traditions?

Even though I'm stood metres away from him, in the same confined space as he's standing in, we're still so far apart. I need to find a way of sneaking off with him later without anyone noticing.

After three hours of nonstop, unadulterated Punjabi entertainment, including a twenty minute rest break at a service station, we finally arrive into Newcastle.

Dressed in a traditional white and gold *sherwani* and *sehra,* Arj looks like prince charming as he steps out of his car.

There are two *dhol* players dressed in traditional Indian outfits waiting in the hotel car park. Their drums are securely tied around their necks by a sturdy rope. As everyone steps off the coach, the *dhol* players, in sync bring two wooden sticks to both sides of their drums and begin beating it loudly. As they do, a beautiful white horse appears. The horse is decorated in a traditional red and gold embroidered cloth. The horse and its handler slowly walk towards us. All the uncles are helping Arj to mount the horse, so that he can begin to fulfil yet another Indian tradition - which normally takes place in India - that of a groom arriving on a horse on his wedding day to marry his bride.

Family and guests have quickly formed a circle in front of the horse and are dancing to the beats. I join in with them, leaving Chris and Jess to digest what they are witnessing.

Allowing around fifteen minutes of celebrations to continue, the procession has slowly moved its way to just outside the entrance of the hotel. Arj dismounts the horse with the help of the men, where he and all the rest of the wedding guests from the groom's side are welcomed into the venue, by Shreya's family.

Chris, Jess and I pick up a glass of champagne from a tray whilst watching a small orchestra play in the corner of the room. The captivating sound of a flute and piano floats sweetly in my ears; I begin to absorb all the joy and happiness that's filling the air around me.

After a short while, we're asked to make our way into the function room where the Hindu marriage ceremony is about to take place. I check on the time, and I'm pleasantly surprised to notice that we're no longer working to Indian timing. We're almost bang on cue with the running order of the day.

The bride's side of the family is sat on one side of the room whilst the groom's side is on the other. I take my place in between Chris and Jess.

Soft, instrumental Hindi music plays in the background as we sit, waiting for Shreya to make her entrance.

Suddenly the music falls silent for a few seconds, which is our cue to stand. It starts again once Shreya enters, escorted to the *mandap* by her uncle. Her brother and some of her male cousins are holding up a big white veil in front of her so she can't see Arj's face. I crinkle up my face and turn to my cousins, who also have curious looks on their faces.

Ritu is quietly explaining to Amber that in the Gujrati culture, on the day of the wedding ceremony the bride and groom aren't allowed to see each other's faces until the vows have taken place.

The priest tells Arj to place his hands underneath the veil that separates them both so that he can hold Shreya's hand once the wedding recitals begin.

The vows take about twenty minutes, after which the priest holds a steel plate and bangs it loudly to let everyone know that the couple are now married, and that the veil can be lifted. They then exchange garlands on each other.

Shreya's father then begins the next part of the ceremony – the *Kanya Daan* – where he washes Arj's feet and gives Shreya's hand to him, in faith and hope that he'll take good care of her. This is performed in front of the sacred fire.

§

Shreya delicately rises from her seat at the top table. The cameraman is pressed up against her face following her every move. She's acutely aware that the entire hall is watching her on big screen, and she looks a little anxious.

It's to be expected though. She's the most important woman in the room today; the reason why so many relatives and friends, young and old have travelled afar from all corners of the world to share her special day.

I can't help but imagine myself as a bride on my own wedding day - all eyes will be on me.

Every person in the room will be looking at my bridal outfit, my wedding make-up; the way my hair is pinned up and styled today. The bindi's which are stuck accurately and symmetrically across my forehead just above my brow; the dark and radiant colour of henna on my hands. The red and white bangles on my wrist, signifying not just that I'm a new bride, but also the commitment I've made as a married woman.

I'm entering into a lifelong bond with a man for the remainder of my life. There's no get out clause. It's not a rehearsal, to see what a taste of married life will feel like; be like. The priest won't be shouting 'cut', or 'take seven, scene two' when he blesses us with our marriage vows. I'll be nervous, anxious, apprehensive and excited all at the same time.

The master of ceremony is holding a mic and we all stand up to clap for the happy couple as he welcomes them on to the floor to take their first dance. Arj takes Shreya's hand into his, and makes his way slowly onto the stage. They both look magical - like a prince and princess made for each other.

But both of them have suffered ups and downs with their

respective parents - who were far from accepting of their relationship and marriage at the beginning. Even though they are both Hindu and in good jobs - from decent backgrounds and upbringings; Shreya, the daughter of a well respected doctor and Arjun, a technical computer genius. It still wasn't enough. They weren't the same caste.

Arjun is a Punjabi boy and Shreya, a Gujrati girl.

They have their unique identities, which aren't visible to the naked eye or to most people unless you really know them. But their difference in language, dressing style, eating habits, culture, and festivals - however microscopic and insignificant they seem in the grand scheme of things, became the main obstacle in their relationship with both sets of parents.

Arjun and Shreya's love really has conquered all. Both families look the happiest today, sitting proudly at the top table. They've allowed themselves to let down their guard, open the barriers and happily embrace their children's happiness.

Watching the newly married couple and Arj's mum and dad gives me a glimmer of hope. A hope that one day, I might also be stood like Shreya is today - the happiest girl in the world, with the man of my dreams.

The lights dim when everyone sits back down. The music begins. Already I'm humming the tune in my head; the perfect first wedding dance song, *Tujhe dekha to yeh jana sanam - I saw you and I knew.*

They hold each other closely by the waist, gliding across the dance floor looking into each other's eyes, talking and smiling. For a minute I wonder if they have forgotten that everyone in the hall is watching them. I watch their lips move on the big screen above where the DJ has set up. They seem oblivious and in their own little newly married world.

Everyone gives the couple about a minute together on the floor before the first guest descends on them with a crisp ten pound note, waving it in the air around the couple's head - blessing them both. He then places the money with the DJ before walking off the stage. More guests arrive and in turn do exactly the same. All that Shreya and Arj can do is politely wait for their guests to finish with this ritual - even if has eaten into their first dance.

Just as the next song kicks in my cousins and I look at each other in excitement. It's the song we've all been waiting for. Chris and Jess watch as one by one most of us disappear from the table and on to the dance floor. This time even our parents' can't help themselves but stand up and join in. The Dj is playing, *Dil le gaye kuri Gujrat di – the girl from Gujrat took his (Punjabi boy's) heart.*

We all cheer and dance, moving our hands, feet and every other part of our body to the rhythm, beats and lyrics. I glance over to Chris and mouth at him to come and join in with the dancing. But instead he begins to fidget with his jacket pocket and fishes out something, holding it up in the air. At first I can't see what it is, but when he waves a white plastic card in the air I realise it's a room key. He then signals to me with his hands - gesturing for to me to come outside.

My heart is beating fast in trepidation at his subtle intimation. I continue dancing to give myself thinking time to come up with a plausible excuse; to disappear without arousing any suspicion.

I look over at him again - a minute later but he's nowhere to be seen. Jess is sat talking to Sarika. I take a quick look around the hall to see what's going on. Mum and Dad are busy doing light bulb moves with Jaya's mum and dad. Some of my cousins including Arj's sisters have formed a circle around the happy couple and are watching Shreya as she dances shyly with Arj as the new Mrs Jaitley.

Rak, Neel and Sham are at the bar. Dadi looks engrossed in a conversation with an old looking auntie. Everyone is in vision and busy doing something to notice me. I make my quick exit while I have the chance.

Chris is stood by the side entrance to the men and ladies toilets.

"I've got the key to a room," he says, pulling it out of his pocket to show me.

"Put it away Chris, someone might see."

"Well let's go upstairs then before they do see. I only want to hug you, Anu. Do you know how hard it's been for me, not being able to touch you, hold your hand and kiss you, when you've been stood at arm's length from me the past two nights and wearing amazing, gorgeous Indian clothes?" I look up coyly, feeling slightly embarrassed.

He moves a little closer to grab my hand, but I stop him.

"No, not here."

"I know somewhere we can go," he tells me.

But I look at him with a fear in my eyes.

"We won't go into any room, don't worry. I explored this place earlier when we arrived, when all of you girls were getting ready. Me and all the lads were sitting in the bar waiting, so I told them I was going to take a look around. It's a big old hotel, you know."

The palms of my hands start to feel moist. He gives me verbal directions to a place, and tells me to meet him there. "Follow me in five minutes."

"Chris we can't be long or someone might suspect something. I'm scared."

"It'll be fine, don't worry. Five minutes, that's all."

He walks on towards the lift. I walk into the ladies to waste a couple of minutes; wiping my sweaty hands with some tissue paper. I look in the mirror, adjust my hair and pull the top of my *lengha* blouse down to stop it from gathering. I walk back out casually and in the direction Chris has walked in. I step into the lift and press the button which takes me to the eighteenth floor.

I almost trip over my *lengha* as I scurry out of the lifts. Turning to my immediate right, I try to remember Chris' directions. I walk on a bit further until I reach a set of double doors which lead me to a spiral staircase. When I reach the top of the stairs I open the black heavy doors facing me. Ahead of me I see Chris leaning by the edge of the building, his hands gripping the bars. I realise that I'm standing on the rooftop of the hotel, overlooking the city of Newcastle.

The view is breathtaking. Dusk is setting and there's a hint of bright gold seeping through behind the clouds. The beat of the music vibrates from seven floors below us. Chris holds out his hand indicating for me to walk over to him. I look around me, at the bright lights across the city, taking in the stunning view, so high up.

My heart beats faster and faster with every step I take towards him. I'm feeling nervous, with both excitement and in fear of getting caught.

He takes me into his arms holding me close to his chest. "I've wanted to do that since I saw you last night, Anu." He pulls away for a moment, inspecting me closely. "You look beautiful, golden girl," he says, staring deep into my eyes. "That shade of purple really suits your skin tone."

I look down at my change of clothes from earlier. I can make out the shadow of my face in his eyes. He cocks his head at an angle, slides his hand on my face gently and presses his lips against mine - kissing me tenderly and stroking my cheek, whilst brushing his other hand through my hair. We're locked in a passionate kiss for a few seconds until I hear a noise coming from the entrance of the doorway.

I pull back. "What's that?" I ask, in a whisper.

"It's nothing Anu. It was probably the wind or something." He leans forward to kiss me again, but I stop him.

"No, I think someone's coming up."

"No one's coming up sweet cheeks, there's no one around."

I glance around one last time. "Chris, are you having a good time?" I ask worriedly. "I mean, honestly you can tell me if you're not."

"I'm having an amazing time babe." He moves his face closer to mine again.

"We've not had chance to speak properly, not since you arrived last night. And even today on the coach, you were sat talking with Sarika most of the time."

"Do I detect a trace of jealousy?"

"You wish Mr! I just don't want all this to be so overwhelming for you, that's all."

"Are you kidding me? I'm feeling great. It's a really good wedding. I can't believe there's a free bar again! And the food, oh my God Anu, it's just out of this world. You know me; I can never turn down an Indian!"

I press my lips to smile.

"I could get used to all this. Everyone's been coming up to me and Jess, trying to feed us. It's crazy."

"Sorry about that. Don't take it personally. It's just Indian people have this god-awful habit of feeding people; especially if you're a non Indian looking guest. It's called being overly hospitable."

"Oh don't get me wrong, I'm not complaining."

"Didn't think you would be Jamo!"

"You know your cousins are funny. Now I know why you're so gullible and where you get it from."

"What do you mean by that?"

"Well your sister for example. She came over to me before and asked me to get her a drink. When I asked her what she wanted, she said anything that had alcohol in it. Anyway I ended up bringing back just a coke with a slice of lemon in it because one of your uncles hadn't moved from the bar since the last time I went up, so I didn't want to risk getting another drink in front of him. When I got back and gave her the drink, she sipped it and said that the vodka was quite strong!"

I smile at him with slight embarrassment.

"Come on babe we better go back. People might start talking if they notice we're not there."

"People are already talking, Anu."

"What? What do you mean, they're already talking? Has someone said something to you?" I ask worryingly.

"Well for a start your cousin Sarika, on the coach this morning asked me what was going on between us."

"For a start? You mean someone else as well as Sarika has said something?"

"Anu, don't worry. I told her there was nothing going on between us and that we're just very good friends. And that I wanted to see an Indian wedding, that's it, chill sweet cheeks."

"And do you think she believed you?"

"I don't think so to be honest but she didn't pursue it. She's a clever one though that girl."

"And who else said something?"

"Is it Rakesh? Rak? He asked me straight out what the score was with us two. Again I told him what I told Sarika. Don't worry about it Anu, everything's cool. As long as you don't have this worried look across your face the whole time, then no one will suspect anything or say anything."

He kisses me on the cheek. "Ok come on, we better go. I'll go first, and you follow a few minutes later. Let me get back inside first."

My heart is doing somersaults again when I step out of the lifts. I'm consumed with apprehension. I sense the fear of having gone much longer than anticipated, and my dad frantically looking for me, realising that Chris is nowhere to be seen either.

Dad thinking that he was right all along with his intuition; that there's more to this friendship than meets the eye. I have visions of him checking the hotel inch by inch, walking up and down on every level to find us together - somewhere we shouldn't be. I grip the skirt of my outfit with my sweaty hands to remain calm; trying my best to hide the panic that's drawn on my face - but looking more and more like a criminal who's just been caught out.

I enter the hall cautiously and the first thing I see is Chris talking to Dad. I fear the worst.

What is he talking to Chris about? Has Chris said anything to him about where we've been? Accidentally let something slip?

Dad doesn't appear to look uneasy, annoyed or even bothered. There are no signs of anger on his face. I saunter in, trying to look cool and sit down at the table next to Jess. She raises her eyebrows at me, giving me that, *I-know-what-you've-been-up-to* look.

"I won't ask where you disappeared to."

"Did anyone notice?" I ask anxiously.

"No I don't think so. Your dad came over once asking where you were. I told him that you'd gone to the toilet."

"Thanks," I say. "I wonder what my dad and Chris are talking about." I glance over nervously, wanting to know what deep conversation they could possibly be having. I'm afraid of finding out, but at the same time I want to race over. Instead I sit and wait for Chris to come back to the table.

Most of the seats are empty. Everyone seems to be on the dance floor. A few minutes later Chris appears next to me. "Did my dad interrogate you?" I ask, nervously.

"We were just generally talking. He was over at the bar when I came back in, so I thought I'd catch him on his own. Nothing to worry about, don't worry. We were only talking about the wedding."

"He didn't notice that we both disappeared together?"

He nods to say no. "Don't stress babe, there's nothing to worry about; trust me."

"Well in that case, come with me." I rise from the table, not knowing where this sudden burst of bravery has popped up from. "Let's get this party started properly."

I pour a little wine into an empty glass, from a bottle sitting on the table, and gulp a mouthful.

"My cousin has just got married," I declare, "and it's time to dance like a true Punjabi, Christian Jamieson. It's my turn to show you some Indian moves!"

Chris looks surprised at the change in me, but gives me his sexy smile in approval. I take hold of his and Jess' hands and whisk them to the dance floor with me. I squeeze into the circle that the girls have formed once again. Chris watches me as I immerse myself in dancing.

The men are starting to form a piggy back one on top of each other. Arj climbs onto their shoulders until he's lifted high up into the air. He waves his arms above his head - one hand holding on to a bottle of Johnny Walker Black Label whisky. He's dancing to the music re- enacting a scene from an old Bollywood film where the actor pretends to be drunk.

When he's brought down to his feet he continues to dance ecstatically like no one, and everyone is watching him.

Chapter Eight

*"From now until you go back to university
I want you to make chapatis every night in this house, until you
get them looking more like the shape of a moon rather than the
stars in the sky."...**Dad***

Being at home suffocates me. I feel as if I've left my independence and freedom behind, buried somewhere deep until it can be rescued and brought back to life again - a bit like me.

Only three weeks have passed of the summer break, but it feels like months. I've fallen into a routine of usual petty arguments with my parents about pointless and meaningless things. And there's still six more weeks of accepting further rules and regulations set out by them.

"You have to learn how to cook, Anu," Mum tells me frequently. "Just start with the basics so that you can at least make something on your own when you need to. You can't always rely on your mother's chapatis and tubs of curry when you go back to university."

"Why not? It's worked well so far."

Mum gives me her disapproving look, where she rolls her large eyes at me, and raises her eyebrows high.

"Because you're an adult Anushka and it's vital that you know how to cook. I think every university course should also teach students housekeeping skills and home economics, especially cooking. I tell you what, I'll teach you how to make the dough and the chapatis tonight. I'll show you how to make perfectly round chapatis - just the way mine are."

I spend an hour in the kitchen that evening learning how to make round chapatis, but no matter how hard I try I can't seem to roll a decent one that resembles a circular shape. When we all sit down together for evening meal Krish picks up one of my chapatis, holding it high in the air, inspecting it closely.

"Mum, you didn't make these tonight did you?" he asks deviously.

"How can you tell?" Dad responds craftily, looking over in my direction. He knows that Krish is having a sly dig at me, but he doesn't stop him from doing so.

"Because these aren't round like Mum's, they look like the map of India!"

So I'm the laughter on everyone's lips over dinner, as each person takes a bite out of my hand made chapati and comments on which continent or country they think I've managed to individually tailor for them. Mum tells me it wasn't bad for my first attempt, but Dad has other ideas.

"From now until you go back to university I want you to make chapatis every night in this house, until you get them looking more like the shape of a moon rather than the stars in the sky. You've got two months to get them looking perfect!"

When I'm not being harassed into behaving and acting more Indian, Chris occupies most of my waking thoughts for majority of the day.

I reminisce about our day trip to Southall a few weekends ago. Chris said he wanted to eat an Indian meal, and because I'd run out of Mum's tubs, I suggested a trip to the heart of the Indian population, down south.

His eyes lit up when I found a South Indian restaurant, down a narrow back alley. It was the first time anyone had introduced him to a *dosa;* a popular South Indian dish. The crepe was overflowing on his plate, with potato, mushrooms and black lentils smothered in spices, served with coconut chutney, vegetable and lentil broth.

There wasn't a crumb left on his plate.

Walking out of the restaurant, he took my hand; my arm locked in his as we strolled down the street. Minutes later a group of four Asian guys were walking towards us. Just as they passed us one of them deliberately spat on the floor and shouted, "Fucking Asian whore is doing a *gora*, man!"

I unlocked my arm from Chris' and turned around, ready to dish out some hand-picked, unsavoury words of my own too. But Chris stopped me, telling me that they weren't worth it.

"Babe, we're always going to find people like that wherever we go. If they're not Asian, they're going to be White. We're not going to please everyone, so forget it. We can't change people's low level minds so just rise above it. That'll wind them up even more."

At the time I got annoyed with him, and told him that he should be bothered by it. That we shouldn't let people get away with saying things like that.

I smile to myself as I think back. He was so calm about it all, so different to the way I'd reacted.

Now I worry that he's going to leave me. Dump me. Find someone else, because it's been three weeks since I last saw him, when he dropped me off at the train station. And because we've not seen each other I'm scared he'll think I'm not putting enough commitment into our relationship - the effort that is required to keep it going even with the long distance between us.

Chris is unquestionably the guy I've fallen for in a big way. His longing look makes me weak at the knees, and his touch makes every muscle in my body tremble. I'm totally and utterly besotted by him. And he knows it.

Whilst our friends continue to fall into and out of relationships every other month, it's been nearly ten months since Chris and I have been seeing each other.

Tom and Wendy were in a relationship for six solid months until one day they had a major argument and ended their relationship. Everyone on our corridor was shocked because they were the least likely couple to break up. They were always joined at the hip, spending every waking moment together.

The week after they split, Ella saw a girl that was clearly not Wendy creep out of Tom's room in the early hours of a Sunday morning. Wendy had gone home for the weekend, but when she returned that night, it didn't take long for the news to travel to her ears. She went ballistic. In a complete turnaround in personality, Wendy went from the sweetly spoken, butter-wouldn't-melt-in-her-mouth girl, to a raging bull; stood outside Tom's door, shouting and swearing at the top of her lungs, letting all the students of Wroath Hall know that Tom Connor lasted less than five minutes in bed, amongst other unsavoury revelations!

But living *my* double life can be hard work. I don't spend quality time with my family, according to my parents - even when I'm physically in the house. Dad comments, frequently.

"Where are you so lost all the time?" he asked me, a few days after I returned home for the summer.

I wondered where he was going with the question, so I hesitated for a second before answering. "Nowhere, you can't be lost within four walls of your house, can you Dad?"

"You don't sit with us, talk much or watch TV with us. You're always in your room, lost in your thoughts? What's wrong with you? What are you always thinking about?"

"There's nothing wrong with me Dad. I just like my own company, what can I say?"

How could I tell them I wanted to see my boyfriend so desperately? The one who they'd already met at Arj's wedding. I wanted to tell him that we were boyfriend and girlfriend and that I wanted to go and see him. But the sentences didn't form on my tongue. They couldn't. They never could. It was the one thing I was frightened of in the world - telling my parents that I was in love with a White man.

Would they let me stay at uni and study if they found out I had a boyfriend, and that too, a White boyfriend? What would Dadi say if she was to find out? What would happen to me and Chris?

Right now I'm not in a position, both mentally or physically to find out the answers to those inevitable questions; so I remain helpless, lonesome and subdued.

I have a large and loud family who insist on keeping me busy and involved in a family atmosphere, but I can't help feeling frustrated most of the time.

My heart never knew loneliness - until now that is - when I'm a few hundred miles away from Chris.

§

I've managed to find work as a Sales Assistant at the airport to keep myself occupied, sane and out of the house, until I can go back to my life.

I buy a sandwich on my lunch break and head up the escalators to grab a seat by the window, overlooking the runway. A Singapore Airlines plane is about to taxi and I look on with fascination at the enormity of it - failing to comprehend how the aircraft stays up in the air.

I pick up my phone and dial Chris' number. After three rings, he answers. "Hi babe."

"Hiya, how are you?" I ask.

"I'm not so bad, just in the house, doing some work on the computer. How's your day going?"

Chris has moved into our new house for second year at university. Seven of us are renting an old Victorian four bedroom house. Our landlord is a millionaire doctor who dabbles in properties in his spare time. He has money coming out of his ears, but he's still a tight-fisted stingy old man who's demanded every penny of his deposit in full and up front before letting us step foot in the house.

I'm sharing a double room with Vani this time and Jess is sharing with Ella. Will has his own room and Chris is in with Joe.

Stu quit after first year. He'd done his time and hadn't enjoyed his course so decided to move back home to the island and find a job. I guess uni wasn't for everyone and I wasn't surprised that Stu was the one who'd thrown in the towel. Simon and Maya have moved in together with Teresa and a couple of others.

"Yeah not too bad," I say. "I've just come on my lunch break."

He notices the melancholy tone underlying in my voice. "What's wrong, sweet cheeks, you sound down?"

"I'm ok, it's just these holidays. They're far too long. I was dreading them and now that they're here it's even worse. I miss you loads Chris and I can't even speak to anyone about you."

Now was the time I was wishing more than ever that I had that sisterly bond with Sanya so that I could talk to her about Chris.

"I'm trying to keep myself busy too babe. I wish I could meet up with you. I keep telling you that I'll drive up but you're the one saying you don't want me to."

"Yeah I know you offered, but it's difficult. What do I say to my parents? It'll be hard work. I'll get twenty questions, you know the script."

"Listen, don't get down about it. Try and enjoy your holidays. I'm counting down the weeks too until you get back. Tell your parents you start a week earlier than you actually do."

I grin on the phone "Yeah I'll try."

"Vani's here by the way."

"What? She's moved in so soon, already? How come?"

"You know she doesn't talk much. She's not really said, but I think she's fallen out with her parents so she's decided to stay."

"Oh right. Well I hope she's not nabbed the best side of the bedroom."

"I helped her move some things up into your room. Her bed's on the window side, that's all I know."

"Oh ok. So it's just you two then in the house then?"

"Yeah. But she does her own thing and I do mine. We don't really see much of each other."

"Never mind. Anyway, listen I've got to go babe. A couple of people are on their lunch break with me and I can see them coming up the escalators to join me. I'll text you in a bit and call you later."

"Alright sweet cheeks. See you."

Work is a great sense of relief for me; somewhere where I can unleash myself for a little while. As long as I'm in work, it means

I'm doing something constructive with my time; something that's making my day go faster.

Some days take longer than others to finish, especially when I find myself clock watching whilst day dreaming about Chris.

I'm constantly interrupted in mid thought, by passengers standing in front of my till, waiting impatiently to pay for items that they've forgotten to pack last minute, before jetting off on holiday.

"Fancy forgetting to pack your toothbrush, toothpaste and shampoo?" I said to Dav, as we both stood at the till point ridiculously early one morning on shift. "It's the first thing I think of when I'm packing my stuff to go away."

Dav and I have become good friends since starting our summer job more or less at the same time. He's also a university student, but studying at the opposite end of the country to me and in an extreme opposite course to mine.

Davinder Singh is a first year pharmacy student. His kind nature and annoyingly quick witted humour made me grow fond of him instantly.

"So you're doing a Mickey Mouse course then," he said, when we first met in work. "No wonder you drink. You've got nothing else to do have you?! What, is it about eight hours a week you're studying at uni then or something?!"

"Actually it's a full on course, cheeky! And it's a lot more fun than sitting in boring lectures or mixing potions or whatever you geeky pharmacy students do in labs. I bet, really you're testing all the drugs you're legally allowed to work with, on yourselves, claiming that it's study-related! I know your type. You're dark horses underneath that facade of calling yourselves 'pharmacy students.'"

We both ridiculed each other a little while longer and then laughed together. I knew then that we were going to be good friends for a long time.

To add a little more laughter into our working days, we take it in turns to humour ourselves at the expense of our customers. We discretely examine their purchases as they set their baskets in front of us - forming a picture of their life based on the things they buy. It keeps us highly amused and makes the day pass in a more enjoyable way.

The best times are when we spot young lads from afar walking towards the store. We can pick them out from a mile away and know exactly what they're coming in to buy. One loud mouthed, cocky guy shouted out once, "Go on, just pick em' - whichever, just hurry up man and pay for them. We're gonna miss the flight at this rate." The cocky leader of the pack and his friends starburst from the group, leaving two of them guarding the shelf - to decide which brand and flavour condoms to buy. It tickled Dav and I every time.

As morning turns to night and night back into day, my days are passing into weeks. I've ticked off another week in my diary. That's one more week closer to seeing Chris.

Like clockwork, our phone conversations occur late at night when everyone in the house is asleep, or on my breaks at work. At all other times, I give him a weather update, telling him whether the coast is clear for calls.

Now that I've turned eighteen and recently passed my driving test, I'm allowed to drive the second hand Renault Dad has bought for me. He purchased it about six months earlier in the hope that I'd pass quickly. I thought it was a little premature since I hadn't even taken my theory test at that point, but I imagine that was Dad's way of subtly expressing his expectations of me. Luckily for both him and me I passed first time, which means I've now been given full responsibility of driving Dadi everywhere.

Driving has to be one of the only highlights of my summer - following my job that is. Ironically Chris pointed out to me that even though I have this new found independence with a car, it's a shame I don't have the same control over my own life.

Sad but true.

§

Before I know it it's nearly October. Autumn has settled in and the leaves have begun falling from the trees. The burnt orange and deep red leaves look vibrant in colour against the wet ground, on cold, dark early mornings as I walk to the station to catch the train to the airport.

The days when Dav isn't on shift with me, work becomes boring. I can have a laugh with other people, but not the same sort of banter that I have with Dav. Our Punjabi background is a common denominator, and our love for Punjabi music, another. We've arranged a night out this week, since we're both imminently finishing our summer job.

"Right so this Saturday night, we're having a *glassy* together," he tells me. "Where do you want to go?"

"I don't know. I don't really go out in town to be honest. I don't know where the good places are." He looks at me and laughs.

"Alright leave it to me. I'll figure something out."

We agree to meet outside the old, closed down Odeon cinema

in the city centre, at eight o'clock. I didn't deliberately lie to Chris when he asked me if I had plans for tonight. I just bent the truth a little. I told him I was going out into town with a group from work; it seemed easier. Dav is just a friend, but with Chris hundreds of miles away from me, he'd never understand that. Amongst all the qualities I love about him, his ability to get jealous at the drop of a hat isn't one of them.

"Have fun tonight then sweet cheeks," he tells me.

"Thanks," I reply, guiltily.

Chapter Nine

"Don't forget you're at university to study and get a degree.
I want to see you with that degree one day.
Don't let me down."...Dad

I'm sat in the car looking out of the window - counting down all the stops in my head until I reach Reading; growing increasingly excited that I can hardly contain myself. Another five hours and I'll be seeing Chris.

September felt like moons away back in July, but meeting Dav helped me to enjoy the time in work and also made my days go faster.

Towards the end of the holidays, I even began to enjoy being around my parents more. Sanya wound me up most of the time, and Krish was still an annoying little brother, but on the whole it wasn't too bad.

It's Dadi I'm going to miss the most though. In between shift working, I've spent most of my holidays being her chauffeur, offering to take her places to occupy both her time and my own.

Every Tuesday afternoon Dadi wanted to go to the Temple. Around two dozen ladies congregated in the afternoon for religious prayers and hymns, and Dadi loved to be part of it. It was one of the few social and religious activities she liked to combine into one, because she enjoyed bumping into old friends she hadn't seen in a while.

I on the other hand didn't look forward to those Tuesday's when I wasn't in work. I'd curl up in bed, dreading the moment I heard her call out my name from her bedroom, across the landing. I knew what was coming.

"Anushka, if you're not working today, can you take me to the *Mandir?*" I pretended to be asleep and not hear her; sliding deeper underneath the covers. I hated the fact it was my holidays but I had to spend an entire afternoon at the Temple with a bunch of old women singing religious hymns.

But truth be told, afterwards I felt a great sense of satisfaction when I saw how relaxed, peaceful and content she looked being there. Occasionally I even enjoyed it myself.

Aunties would come up to me and tell me that I was such a good granddaughter for taking the time out, and making the effort to bring my dadi to the Temple. I would feel waves of enormous guilt ride over me at times when I stood facing dozens of statues of Hindu Gods, knowing that I'd built up negative thoughts in my head. I'd quickly ask for forgiveness to all the statues in sight - joining my hands together and bowing my head, in a bid to stop anything bad from happening to me.

Now, Dadi will return to normality - home alone whilst Sanya goes back to college, Krish is at school and my parents are in work. I told her I'd see her in around four or five weeks, and that I'd call and speak to her later tonight. Dadi felt she had to *remind* me that auntie Roma lived in London (like I didn't know already!) and that I could go and spend the weekend with her sometimes if I wasn't coming home. I appreciated her subtle hints and concern for me, but I was secretly amused, because everyone automatically assumed that I'd be bored on my own at weekends when I wasn't in lectures.

It couldn't have been further from the truth.

"So you'll be starting your second year now, huh?" starts Dad, en route to the train station; just when I think I've got away with the big lecture.

"Yep."

"You have to study much harder you know? You won't have time to go out."

"I know Dad." I reply, calmly.

"Make sure you concentrate on your studies and don't spend too much money going out all the time."

"Yeah Dad, don't worry. Chill." I look out of the window, so as not to catch his eye in the rear view mirror.

"You say don't worry, but you know that I do worry. You should know by now that your dad doesn't sleep until he knows that you're safe in bed. You're the one that makes me worry and stress being so far away."

"Nobody tells you to stay up." I laugh out loud. "I'm not going to ring you every time I'm out and tell you what time I'm coming home."

"Oh I know you won't, and I know you don't tell us either. Infact you don't tell us when you're going out, never mind when you're coming home. It's only when we call you that we find out you're out."

The train station is only a five minute drive away but Dad has firmly got into lecture mode. Five minutes suddenly feels like a life time.

"Do you actually stay in your room and study? Whenever I ring you, you seem to be out."

"Of course I do. Why are you giving me a lecture, Dad? I'm not stupid; I do know that I'm at university to study."

"See you always think I'm giving you a lecture. Don't I have a right to say anything to you? I am your father after all. Don't forget you're at university to study and get a degree. I want to see you with that degree one day. Don't let me down."

'Don't let me down!' I mean if that's not pressure, I don't know what is!

"I want that degree too Dad and I will get it."

"Well I hope so. Sometimes I think you're just happy with the freedom you've got being so far away from your parents; freedom to do whatever you want with nobody to stop you. Just don't forget, you're Indian."

This time I deliberately look in the rear view mirror.

"What on earth has being Indian got to do with anything?" I bellow.

"Ok, just stop it both of you," Mum shouts. "She's heard what you've said and she'll listen. Won't you Anushka?"

I stay quiet, feeling confused at Dad's last sentence; repeating it in my head.

"Won't you, Anushka?" she repeats; a tad louder this time.

I reply in an agitated tone of voice. "Yes, Mum."

Every time I feel like I'm turning a page with my parents, in actual fact I'm going back - back to the first page of the chapter, trying to figure out what it is that makes their perception of me so cynical. I fail to understand what sort of person they expect me to return as after three years away; other than their studious daughter with a useless degree, that is.

I wish Mum would stick up for me once in a while, take my side and say to Dad, "Look it's her age to have some fun at university. As long as she's balancing her work and her social life it's fine."

But Mum isn't like that. I've never heard her say anything remotely along those lines. Everything has always been about me working hard, not going out too much, not drinking, and making sure I that I'm in control of my finances. Oh and phoning home everyday to speak to everyone too.

I breathe a quiet sigh of relief when Dad parks the car outside the entrance of the station. He steps out and takes my cases from the boot. Mum gets out and gives me a hug.

"Look after yourself and behave," she warns me. "Make sure you put the food containers into the freezer as soon as you get in, and don't forget that the yellow *daal* and *aloo gobi* is for you to eat tonight, so that is to go in the fridge, understand?"

"Yes Mum, I know. You've told me ten times."

"I know you so well Anu, you'll still forget. That's why I have to keep on reminding you every five minutes."

Dad carries my cases inside the station and waits until I buy my ticket. He walks me to the platform but I tell him to go because there's still fifteen minutes until the train arrives. He takes out a twenty pound note and hands me it cautiously. "Don't spend it on rubbish, ok? And give us a call when you get home." I watch him walk away until he disappears from sight.

A few minutes into my train journey, I purchase a small bottle of wine. I savour my first sip, and try to unwind for my five hour journey ahead.

I ring Chris for the last time, just as I get on to my connecting train from Reading. I've told him I'll be at the station in half an hour.

I can feel the adrenalin rushing through me as I spot him walking towards me on the station platform. It's been nearly two months since I've seen him. He holds me tight for a few seconds, then holds my face and kisses me gently.

"God I've missed you," he says.

"Not as much as I've missed you Chris. Come on let's go."

"Vani and Jess are in. Vani's been cleaning the room for you after the tip she's been living in. Not that you're going to be spending much time in there!" He winks and smiles. I shy away from his look.

It's around five thirty in the evening. I've been home nearly three hours, and have just got round to unpacking and sorting out my things. I phoned home earlier and spoke to Mum, assuring her that the food was in the fridge and the containers which needed to go back in the freezer were in there. She sounded relieved that I'd remembered!

"So when did you get back Jess?" I ask her, as we all settle down onto the sofas to watch TV.

"About two weeks ago."

"And what have you been up to?"

"I've just been working as much as I could over the last couple of weeks in the hotel."

"So you still kept your job in that hotel?" I ask her.

"I did, yeah. I'm glad I did to be honest because they've been really good to me. They've given me all the shifts I've asked for."

"That's great."

I'd given up working at the hotel two months before going home. I couldn't hack all the early breakfast shifts, and it began to impact on my social life too.

"You're a bit quiet hun," I turn to Vani and say. "Are you ok?"

"Yes, I'm fine. Just a little tired."

I sense a hint of frostiness between Jess and Vani. Jess gives Vani a cold stare when I ask her if she's been up to anything exciting over the summer.

It's Saturday evening and the rest of my house mates have now arrived, and there's a unanimous decision between us all that to celebrate our first night together in our new home, we'll go for drinks at our local - and start as we mean to go on!

Saturday is quiz night at the pub. It's more of an old man's boozer, but we don't care. It serves alcohol and that's what we're concerned with. We all have a good laugh; mainly because we decide to play drinking games, taking it in turns to down shots if we can't answer the questions correctly.

In the morning we all drag our sorry little heads out of bed and walk to the local cafe for a greasy fry up. The men who run the place are about six foot tall Italian, gangster looking men, with greasy hair and stern faces. They remind us of criminals belonging to an Italian mafia, so we name our local café, The 'Maff Caff'. But they are the sweetest guys and do a fabulous English fry up.

"You didn't have much to say when we were out last night hun," I say to Vani. "You seemed really quiet, is everything ok? Have I said something to upset you?"

"No don't be daft. You've not done anything. I've just had stuff going on at home that's all. That's why I've not got much to say like everyone else. It's been pretty boring and quiet for me."

"You should have got Chris to drag you out and done stuff."

"Nah, he was busy with his work. And missing you; he was always talking about you."

"Aahh was he? That's sweet. I'm so glad that I'm back Vani. I can only take my family in small doses at times. And this was a really long dose!"

"My parents are the same. Why do you think I came back so early?"

We both smile out of frustration.

Vani is sat on her bed with a book in hand when I return to our room later in the evening.

"What are you reading?" I ask.

"I'm not reading. It's my diary."

"Oh right. I didn't know you kept a diary."

"Yeah I've had it since I moved down here."

"I used to have a lock diary once, when I was around fourteen. My sister found it under my bed, right at the back where I thought I'd hidden it well. I remember thinking that it'd be impossible for anyone to find it unless they were intentionally looking for it. But she did find it, and she broke the lock and read it all. Then she went straight to Mum and showed it her. I got a right bollocking off her that night."

"Why?"

"Because I'd written stuff in there about the boys I fancied in school, and how I wanted to kiss both the Matthews twins. I fancied David and Paul like crazy. They lived around the corner from me and we went to the same school together. I used to go round to their house after school most days to play, but when Mum read my diary, she banned me from going round."

Vani shares my pain. "No way?"

"Yep. I hated my sister even more after that. And since then I never kept a diary. I was too afraid to."

§

I've woken up feeling energized and eager about my first day of second year. I anticipate the workload to increase and become more challenging; but that's what I've been looking forward to.

After an initial welcome back speech, everyone in class is waiting patiently until we're handed our new time table. We all want to know when our days off are. Mine is all day Friday and Wednesday mornings; which is handy because student night is on a Tuesday. That means I have at least half a day to recover from the night before until my class in the afternoon.

Monday afternoon kicks off with my first class, Radio Production with Tony. He starts by telling us all what's happening in seven weeks time.

"The university has got a license to broadcast live radio for three weeks around the campus and within a seven mile radius of the surrounding areas of Guildford.

So this is your chance to take part in an exciting opportunity by using the skills you've learnt over the last year and amalgamating them into your own programme.

All you need to do is think about what you want to bring to the student radio network. And it's not just presenter roles we're talking about. We're talking about a whole host of roles. It's all listed in the brief I'm going to hand to you in a minute.

I want you to think about your idea very carefully. What is it that makes you passionate about working within the field of radio? For those of you who prefer the medium of radio to TV, then it can really be your time to shine. It's not compulsory, but I recommend that if you're serious about working within radio broadcasting, then you should try to play an active role.

If you're interested in taking part, then at this stage all we're asking for are names. But by next week we want you to give either myself or Clara, a brief outline of your three weekly shows and what you intend to include. If your pitch is any good, you'll be given an opportunity to put the package together. Any questions?"

Even though I want to specialise in TV production, I tell Kerry straight after class that I'm thinking of producing and presenting a *Bhangra* music show.

"I think it's a brilliant idea," she says, enthusiastically.

"Are you just saying that to be polite hun? I'm still thinking about it to be honest because I don't know if anyone will listen to it. They certainly won't understand the music I play."

"Who cares, Anu? Music isn't about understanding the lyrics; it's about the sound, the rhythm, and the beats. I've listened to *Bhangra* music in the past. I've got loads of Asian friends back in London. I love it."

"I'm just worried I'll look like an idiot and people won't get it, or listen to it. But you're right; I'm going to educate the students of university and maybe some local listeners."

"If you need any help with anything, you know you only have to ask?" she tells me.

"Thanks hun."

I tell Chris about my idea when I get home, that afternoon. "Go for it Anu," he says. "It's a great idea. And if you need someone to describe to your listeners how to do the light bulb move, then I'm your man! I think I'm an expert now, thanks to that auntie of yours!"

Just as I'm getting ready for bed, Mum rings me on my mobile. We talk for a while before she hands the phone to Dad, who sounds a little moody.

He begins to grill me about my phone bill.

"You opened my phone bill?" I yell.

"What do you think I'm going to do?" asks Dad. "I'm the one paying for it, so I'm entitled to open it and see how much it's come to, aren't I?"

I don't say anything. "Are you stupid that you think I'm not going to open it?" I still don't answer.

"Anyway I want to know something. For the last two months you've been at home. You've been working most days so I want to know, who you have been ringing?"

"I do have friends Dad."

"Yes I know you have friends, but are you telling me that you've been on the phone to them for eight hours of the day? That's what your bill tells me?"

"Don't exaggerate Dad. I can't expect my friends to ring me all the time." I can feel myself getting worked up, and know that I'm not about to win this argument.

"I don't expect to see bills like this again Anushka, you understand?"

"Yes Dad."

"Ok goodnight." His voice mellows down a notch. "Sleep tight."

I lift myself up from the floor, where I'm sat by the window next to Vani's bed. When I tell Chris about my phone bill, he just shrugs and smirks. "Well I won't tell you how much mine came to then, sweet cheeks!"

Chapter Ten

"It serves her right for being blind to
everything that's going on around her."...Ella

The palm of my hands start to sweat uncontrollably and I begin to feel claustrophobic. Panic grabs hold of my entire body, flowing through me like an electric current. I want to get up and run - out of the door and into the fresh air, but instead I sit at the back of the class - still as a statue, unable to physically move.

Thoughts of the ever increasing workload that my life consists of have exploded inside my head. The pressure is on from everywhere. Projects, tutorials, practical and written assignments are coming out of my ears. It's never ending and more demanding.

It's as if a sudden jolt of reality has hit me, and I've only just accepted the fact that my first year is over. I'm no longer a 'fresher,' who can afford to doss about or miss the occasional classes like last year. Maybe Dad is right, I won't have much time to do anything else other than study.

Ged is rambling on about our next assignment, and how it will count towards our degree. I'm looking straight at him, watching words fall out of his mouth, but not taking any of them in. The mobile phone in my pocket starts to vibrate. The little, if any attention I'm paying to Ged quickly gets diverted when I see Chris' name appear on my screen.

I breathe a sigh of relief. It's just the tonic I need to calm myself down.

Just wanted to tell you that I'm thinking about you... Chris x

Somehow I manage to sit through the next half hour of class trying to catch up with what I've missed.

"Have you heard anything back about the radio shows yet?" Kerry asks as we walk out of class half an hour later.

"No nothing," I say, trying to get my breathing to a normal pattern again. "I typed up a proposal and submitted it to Tony two weeks ago. I'm still waiting to hear from him."

"Well Jason's got a spot apparently. The list is on the notice board outside Tony's office. Someone told Darren that your name is on it too."

My face lights up. "Really?"

"I'm pretty sure it is that's what I've heard."

Before I jump the gun and get over excited, I want to see it for myself, so Kerry and I walk to the other side of the media block. I scan the list on the notice board.

Anushka Lamba, Presenter, 'The Asian Groove' Bhangra Show – 3 programmes to be pre-recorded for the grave yard slot.

I can't believe it. Tony and the rest of the lecturers have faith in my idea. I read my name again.

"See I told you," says Kerry.

"Hold on. Why does it say graveyard slot? And pre- recorded? Does that mean that my show is going to be aired around midnight? I'm confused Kerry. What does that mean?"

"I don't know hun, see if Tony's in and ask him. I've got to shoot; I've got Animation class now. See you later. We'll talk then."

I knock on the door to Tony's office. He's inside and tells me to come in.

"Hi Tony."

"Hi Anu, what can I do for you?"

"I've just seen my name on this list outside. It's what I've come to speak to you about actually."

"Oh right, go on. Well done by the way."

"Thanks. I'm happy that my name's on there Tony, but I'm a bit confused because it says I've got the grave yard slot. Is my idea not worthy of better air time?"

"It's not that at all Anu. It was an interesting proposal you put together. The only thing that concerns me with it is that I don't know whether you'll catch a big enough audience during the day time. It's nothing to do with the style of show, it's just we don't know how many people or what the catchment area is that you'll attract. That's no reflection on you Anu, or anything to worry about. I've discussed it with the other lecturers and we feel that if you pre-record it then you could really personalise it and make it your own. Do you understand what I mean?"

I feel a little deflated but decide not to continue with a pointless argument with him in which I know I'm not going to win. Instead I have even more to prove. I have to show Tony and the rest that I can pull in the listeners which they clearly don't think I'll be able to achieve.

"Don't get disheartened Anu. With what you've outlined, it's got the makings of being a cracker of a show."

In the evening I ring Kerry and tell her about my conversation with Tony. She tells me not to be disappointed, and that she'll help me as much as she can.

We also talk about the project Ged was discussing in class earlier today.

"I was thinking about ideas for the World Cinema project" I tell her.. "We've got to depict one genre within World Cinema and do a presentation on it, right? Well how about we do Bollywood?"

"That's a brilliant idea. You already know loads about it so we've already got a head start."

"Exactly."

"Hey can I do some Bollywood dancing in class?" she jokes.

"You can do whatever you like if it will get us extra marks."

Just as one pressure lifts from my shoulders, another one drops right back on. The very next day in Lois' TV broadcast class we get another brief. Working in small groups of four or five, we have to produce a short TV drama, no longer than twenty minutes. Luckily for us all Lois leaves it up to us to decide who we want to work with.

§

Over the next few weeks I work my socks off, researching, gathering material and putting stuff together for various briefs I'm working on, all at the same time.

After spending the last two hours trying to perfect my radio show's audio ident, Will and I are walking home from uni. "I'm so impressed with the slogan and the music," I tell him. "Thanks so much for helping me with that Will."

"Any time Anu. I'm pretty impressed with it too in all honesty! Don't forget a shout out for me on your show!"

"Consider it done. You better listen to it by the way."

"Let me know when you're going to be on and I'll tune in, I promise."

"Cool."

"How did your last recording go, anyway?"

"It was really good fun. Kerry, Martine and Holly were in the studio when I was recording. I got them all on air and we had loads of discussions about the music I was playing. I even got Kerry up out of her seat and showed her how to do the light bulb moves."

He looks confused. "The light bulb moves?"

"I'll show you one day. Next time we're on a dance floor, I'll teach you the moves too!"

"Err, thanks, I think!"

"Hey, can I ask you something?" I ask him.

"Sure."

Have you noticed a change in atmosphere in our house?"

"How do you mean?"

"Well put it this way, if looks could kill then Vani would be the first one to be dead. Seriously you can physically cut the tension in our house with a knife at the moment. I don't know what Ella's problem is, nor Jess'. Haven't you picked up on it?"

I notice a little hesitation in Will's voice before he answers.

"I have a little, yeah, but I don't get involved. Plus because I'm the only one in the house with a room to myself, I don't see half the things you guys probably do."

"Fair enough, I just thought you might know what's going on."

I slot my key into the front door and we walk inside the house. The stench hits me hard.

"Why can no one pick up their dirty fucking dishes and wash them in this house?" I shout out loudly in an attempt to catch anyone's attention. "It's a dump, and it stinks. Seriously is it too much to ask for everyone to wash their own bloody dishes?"

Will bolts straight up the stairs, telling me he's desperate for the toilet.

If Mum could see the state of this place now she'd go ballistic, asking me why my house mates haven't been taught a thing or two about housekeeping.

No one is home other than me and Will. The kitchen sink is stacked high with dirty crockery and I find half empty glasses dumped in various places around the house. I grab a black bin liner from the underneath the kitchen sink and pick up a pair of rubber gloves. I collect all the dirty plates, cutlery and glasses that I can find in every room, carefully placing them in the bin bag, making sure that in my fit of rage I don't break anyone's crockery. I rip an A4 sheet of paper out of my note book and write in large letters with a black marker pen:

I DON'T WANT TO LIVE IN A PIG STY. PLEASE WASH YOUR OWN DISHES FROM THIS BIN BAG OTHERWISE I'M THROWING THE WHOLE LOT IN THE LARGE BINS OUTSIDE. Anu...

I'm sat in Chris' room working on his computer when I hear voices and footsteps coming into the hallway. Jess and Ella are back from uni. My stomach knots as I take a deep breath, envisaging drama to follow within minutes.

"What the fuck?" I hear Ella shout out loud. I'm reasonably confident she's just seen the notice I've stuck on the kitchen door.

"Who the fuck does she think she is putting that up?"

I don't hear a reply; just the odd tutting sound. I walk out of Chris' room, ready to face the music.

"I don't think I'm fucking anything, Ella," I tell her boldly, entering the kitchen.

"Why have you put that up then?" she asks pointing to the kitchen door. "You've got no right to touch our things." Her pale face becomes red. This is the first time I've seen her get this angry.

"Oh right so it's ok for you to use my crockery when you've run out of your own dirty ones, but you can't be bothered to wash them. You're always using my stuff. I never say anything to you because we live under the same roof and I don't mind sharing my things. But that doesn't mean you can take the piss and leave your shit everywhere for me to pick up. All those dishes and stuff are for everyone, they're meant for sharing."

"They're fucking dishes Anu. No big deal. I can't actually believe you!"

She's half laughing and half serious, standing inches away from me pointing in my face, over stepping her boundaries within my personal space.

I assume Will has heard our voices grow louder, because he comes downstairs and attempts to break up the argument. "Come on ladies, why are you all shouting?"

Ella looks at him in astonishment. "Have you seen what she's done Will?" Will hovers by the kitchen door looking slightly bewildered and out of his depth, between three women.

"She's put all the dishes in a bin bag, and is now threatening to dump them in the bins outside if we don't wash up. She thinks we're fucking children."

"Well you're not far off from behaving like it Ella. Even a ten year old child wouldn't make as much mess as you guys."

Jess pipes up. "You just needed to ask us to wash up Anu," she says calmly, trying to diffuse the heated argument. "There was no need for you to do all this, was there?"

"Come on Jess. It's a bit out of order when the place looks like a pig sty all the time. You might be able to live like this, but I can't. It's not the first time I've had to ask you to wash up, but you just ignore me. And anyway, why should *I* be asking you to clean up after yourselves. We're all adults here."

"I'm telling you now Anu, don't touch my things and don't put them in the bin," Ella warns me.

"Well wash your dishes then and then I won't need to." I'm not letting Ella win this one. I storm into Chris' room slamming the door shut behind me. I can feel myself shaking, because this is the first confrontation I've ever had with any of my house mates.

I can hear faint voices coming from inside the kitchen, and expect that both Ella and Jess are bitching about me. I stand with one ear pressed against the closed door, trying to make out what is being said about me.

"It serves her right for being blind to everything that's going on around her," I can hear Ella say.

"Just leave it Ell. Don't get involved," replies Will.

"Everyone's talking about it at uni, she's being made a fool out of right under her nose, and it's been going on for weeks and weeks. I'm the one that's been looking out for her, defending her. Don't know why I bother."

I wonder what they are talking about. It doesn't make sense. *Who* has Ella been looking out for? The conversation becomes hazy and confusing, and I wonder whether they are now talking about someone else. But then I hear Jess mention Vani's name.

"I'm going to speak to Vani and I'm going to say, 'Tell her or else I will.'"

"I'd just stay well out of it if I were you," says Will.

I sit on Chris' bed pondering over what they are talking about and wondering whether I should speak to Vani when she gets back from lectures.

Chris comes home to find me asleep on his bed. He wraps his duvet around me and places a pillow underneath my head. He kisses my head and walks out of the room. I smile in my semi conscious state of sleep, but I'm too exhausted to reach out or talk. I doze off again when he picks up his play station and walks out of the room.

Chapter Eleven

*"Make sure you behave yourself
and show your auntie and uncle respect at all times.
I don't want any complaints about you, from them."...**Mum***

Never in a million years will I make it in on time for my nine am lecture with Godfrey. Especially since I've forgotten to set my alarm clock, and have woken up startled, with Chris' alarm screaming in my ear at eight forty. "Shit, shit, shit," I shout, as I jump out of bed and run up to my own room. Vani is in the bathroom. *Great. She's going to be in there for ages.* I sit on my bed and wait for her to come out. A further ten minutes passes and there's still no sign of her. Accepting the fact that I've already missed the first part of my Animation lecture, I decide to skip it completely and head in after lunch for Lois' TV Broadcast class instead.

I go back down the stairs and into Chris' room again, jumping into his bed. He looks at me in a disapproving way. "You're not going in are you, you naughty girl?!"

"Nope. Vani is hogging the bathroom as usual, and I can't be bothered to wait around for her; plus I'm not in the mood." I snuggle back under the warm duvet.

"Has this got something to do with what happened last night and that notice you stuck up?"

"Might be."

"Will mentioned something about it, and plus you can't exactly miss the great big sign you've stuck up on the kitchen door!"

"You're all filthy beggars, you all do it; including you," I tell

130

him. "There's no favouritism going on, trust me. You all leave your shit lying around, as if the fairy godmother is going to fly around and pick up all your stuff; wash them for you and put them away. I was merely making a point."

"Well you certainly made your point babe. I think the message was heard loud and clear."

"I don't know about that. You should have seen Ella's face. I thought she was going to hit me for a second, she looked so mad."

"Really?"

"Anyway forget it, it's over. I don't want to talk about it anymore. As long as everyone washes up from now on then that's all I'm bothered about. I do think something's going on with Ella, Jess and Vani though," I tell him.

"What do you mean?"

"Well I heard them mention Vani's name and something about Ella looking out for someone. I don't quite know to be honest; I just heard bits and bobs of the conversation. But didn't I tell you the other day that I thought something was up between them all?"

"I'd just leave it Anu. You're already in their bad books. Don't get yourself into more bother. Let them sort whatever it is between themselves."

I arrive in time for Lois' lecture. She wants to talk to each project group to see how we're all getting on with the pre- production stages of our film. After an initial, short spell of blankness from members of our group, we've come up with a script which we show Lois. She skims over it and seems to be pleased with it.

"Ok guys and girls. If this is to be a success, then it's not about the acting ability of your lead roles, it's about projecting the skills you've learnt so far, by putting them into practice in each aspect of production, so we can see your artistic flair through the medium of film. You need to be creative and imaginative with your scenes and shots, and don't forget that post production is just as important. Remember to do a storyboard, because that will become a key focal point when it comes to filming."

"We've already started ours," Fred tells her. He picks up the sheets from the folder and passes them to her.

"Excellent..." She skims through the sheets of paper.

"Listen guys and girls, at first glance this has the potential of becoming an extremely stylish short drama; you need to be sure that you get the balance right between your acting, your cinematography and your script. Don't forget your story needs to come alive through all the elements you've been taught."

We all come out of class feeling positively energized and one hundred percent focused.

§

The next few months fly by. I've immersed myself into my studies that I don't have much time to go out these days.

To top it off, things at home haven't changed. If anything they've got worse. Ella and I brush past each other every day without uttering a single word to one another. Conversations with Jess consist of the odd "hi" now and again, and even Joe is beginning to be distant with me. Although he shares a room with Chris they don't talk much either and he's hardly around in the house.

I don't know exactly when things began to fall apart in the house and I still don't understand why. Everyone has their ups and downs, especially with so many of us living under one roof - we're not all going to agree on everything. Seven different personalities in one confined space - there are bound to be conflicts of interest. But just why it's spiralling out of control remains a mystery to me.

It seems like I'm the only person who wants to sort it out. Everyone else appears to be oblivious, or has no inclination to find out. They seem happy for the environment to remain hostile; and the crockery incident was just tip of the iceberg.

I haven't been home in over seven weeks. Mum and Dad know that I've had so much work going on therefore I don't get the third degree about not coming to visit. Instead I bore them over the phone with a mixture of excitement and pressure about my work commitments, and what I'm doing now that I'm in my second year.

"I'll bring home some rushes of the filming we've been doing for our short film," I tell Dad on the phone. "We auditioned a load of people who wanted to star in our film." I explain the storyline briefly and he genuinely seems interested.

"It sounds like the film you did when you were at college. I remember dropping you off at some house one day where you were all filming. Remember Anu when you went to that house they had a big dog and you couldn't stop sneezing because you were allergic to it? You came home and you couldn't stop sneezing all night."

"Yeah I do remember that, actually. Thankfully though there aren't any dogs that feature in our film."

There's a sinking feeling starting to settle in my stomach. I'm feeling homesick. And that shocks me, because it's not like me at all. In all the time I've been here, this is the first occasion I'm really missing my parents and family, and there's nothing more that I want than to go home and see them, even if it does result in an argument with either Mum or Dad!

My parents sound pleased when I tell them that I'm staying at auntie Roma's this coming weekend.

"Thank God you've finally made time to stay with them," Mum says, in delight. "Make sure you behave yourself and show your auntie and uncle respect at all times. I don't want any complaints about you, from them."

"Complaints? Why would they complain about me, Mum?" I ask confusingly.

"Just, you never know do you? They'll mention the fact you haven't been to visit them ever since you moved there - that's why. Don't get into any arguments with them, that is all I'm saying."

"Yes Mum."

She knows me too well.

A change of scenery is probably what I need. Chris drops me off at the train station and decides to go home himself, to see his parents.

Amber's dad picks me up from High Wycombe train station in the afternoon.

"How long is it since you've been home, Anu?" auntie Roma asks when I arrive at her house.

"It's been nearly seven weeks, auntie. I spoke to Mum and Dad last night, told them that I was staying with you for the night. I'm sure my dad will ring later."

"Yeah I spoke to your dad earlier. I told him you were coming this afternoon. Anyway, it's nice of you to finally come and stay. It's about time isn't it?" she asks with a hint of sarcasm.

I offer her a polite smile, whilst thinking about the conversation I had with Mum last night.

"So how are your studies going?" she asks gingerly.

"Hard," I admit. "There's so much work and lots of deadlines."

"That's what university is about my dear, lots of hard work and dedication. It's the only way you will succeed in life. Education is very important."

Auntie Roma feels compelled to dispense her advice on me, yet I feel like I'm having a conversation with Dad, because they're the exact words I can imagine slipping off his tongue.

"A degree isn't a walk in the park dear; going out with friends once a week should be a novelty rather than a necessity."

I regret opening my mouth, but I agree with her out of respect and so that we can move on from this topic.

"How's Sarika doing?" I ask Amber.

"She's fine, I think. We've not heard from her since yesterday morning.

"She's always too busy with her work as well," auntie Roma adds. "Same as you, she's got lots of assignments on the go and exams coming up."

I wonder if Sarika gets the same treatment as I do whenever I don't ring home; the twenty 'why not' questions and emotional blackmail dropped into the odd conversation or two.

Auntie Roma has served up hot chapatis with *keema*, *aloo gobi* and *raita* for dinner this evening. I don't normally eat more than two chapatis when I'm at home, but the food is so mouth watering that I pick up an extra one.

Amber and I stay up late chatting before going to bed.

"So are you seeing anyone at uni?" she asks, taking me by surprise.

"Me? No. I've not got time for guys. There's too much work going on in my life. I haven't got the time."

"How's your friend doing, the one who came to Arj's wedding?"

"You mean Chris? Yeah he's fine. And so is Jess," I add - making sure I slip her name into the conversation too.

"He seemed like a really nice guy."

"He's a good lad, yeah. They both really enjoyed the wedding."

We continue to talk a little while longer, but I divert the conversation down a different path, so we don't talk about Chris again.

Before I fall asleep I slip to the bathroom to make a rushed call to Chris. He's in the pub with Stu and sounds a little worse for wear.

After tucking into a hearty brunch the next morning, my uncle drops me off at the train station. Auntie Roma hands me some leftover food which she's put into containers, wrapped twice over in small polythene bags.

I travel back home feeling rejuvenated. Chris returns late in the evening, and seems to be feeling the same as me.

"It's amazing what seeing your parents and spending time at home can do to you," he says.

"I totally agree babe. Seeing my relatives has really lifted my spirits. And it beat spending another weekend looking at miserable faces in this house; I can tell you that for nothing."

Vani looks as if she hasn't moved from her bed since I left yesterday afternoon. I enter the room and she's sat in the same position in her bed, with her duvet wrapped around her legs and a book in her hand. The curtains are drawn and her bedside lamp is switched on, even though it's the middle of the day. There's a half empty bowl of cereal lying on the floor beside her bed.

"Hiya," I say cheerily.

"Oh hi," she replies, looking up from her book momentarily to acknowledge me. "Did you have a nice time at your auntie's?"

"Yeah it was great thanks. It was so good to get away from here. What have you been up to?"

"Not much, other than reading and relaxing. I went round to Maya's yesterday and we walked into town for a bit; other than that nothing much."

"How's everything in the house?"

"Nothing's changed. They haven't suddenly started talking to me if that's what you're implying?"

"Nothing at all?" I ask, naively; hoping that over the weekend and in my absence the dynamics would have changed and everything would be back to normal again.

"Nope."

"I don't understand Vani, what's going on?"

"I don't know, and I don't care to be honest."

But I can tell by her face that she cares. I can empathise with her loneliness even if she does hide it. I ask her if she wants to go for a drink in our local pub, but she says no - telling me she's feeling tired and cold and can't be bothered stepping out of the house.

She's engrossed in her book, so I leave the room and head downstairs into Chris' room. Just before kicking back my shoes and settling down to watch a DVD with him, I remember to ring Mum and Dad to tell them I've returned home from auntie Roma's, safe and sound.

Chapter Twelve

"You shouldn't have read my diary Anu."...**Vani**

A turbulent few weeks is on the verge of coming to a welcoming end. I'm in the last stages of finishing off various assignments I have on the go. There's nothing more petrifying than falling behind with my workload and getting into a state of panic, which I'm well aware I can fall into when least expected.

It's just after the May Day bank holiday, and the afternoon sun is sparkling through a large window whilst I'm stood in the media block. But a sudden gust of wind begins to shake the leaves on the trees outside.

As I walk past each classroom I peer inside the glass window. Every room is occupied by students whose faces scream out in panic and stress. Most of them are running around the media block like blue arsed monkeys, diving into editing suites to finish off last minute work to meet their deadlines.

My work is more or less done. Paul and I have taken on the role of Editors for our short film. We've spent hours and hours trawling through rushes, making a post production log and then editing shots with precision; getting our creative juices flowing with each scene. Since I've had sole responsibility of logging and continuity on set I've felt under even more pressure to get the editing - picture perfect.

We've already had to reshoot a couple of scenes because I missed a prop in a shot – something which was vital to the overall scene.

The *Bollywood* themed presentation is in a few days and Kerry and I are putting the finishing touches to our slides and video clips. I've even brought back an Indian outfit from home. We're using anything to our advantage to gain extra points, even if it means bribing Ged, by lending him a selection of *Bollywood* films for his pleasure!

"Indian actresses in *Bollywood* films ooze in sex appeal," said Ged, to Kerry and I last week, as we discussed some of the finer details to our presentation with him in a tutorial. "But I don't get all that dancing around trees stuff. The outfits are beautiful, and the women! Oh they have massive tits!"

He emphasised the word 'tits' with his hands to show us just how big of a handful he was referring to. Kerry and I felt we'd be failing in our duty of care by neglecting Ged's needs, so I grabbed a selection of Bollywood DVD's from home on my last visit.

Just after my Spanish lecture, Kerry tells me to meet her outside the cafe near to the media block.

"Hey you," I say, spotting her sitting alone on a bench outside the café.

"You alright?" she asks, in her broad southern accent. "How was your Spanish lesson?"

"Yeah, it was ok," I say half-heartedly. "I was really good at French when I was at school, but for some reason I just don't find Spanish as easy as I did with French."

"Yeah well I'm glad I didn't opt to study Spanish at all. I can just about speak English!" I take a moment to imagine Kerry talking Spanish in her strong Essex accent, and smile inwardly.

"So what's up?" I ask. "You said you wanted to talk to me about something."

I look closely at her face because I sense something is wrong. Her expression changes almost immediately; her eyes dart to the floor and she begins to fidget with her nails. "What's up hun?" I ask with concern.

"Anu, I need to tell you something, but I'm afraid to tell you."

"Just spit it out," I tell her, feeling anxious and a little confused.

"You're one of my best friends Anu, and what I've got to tell you isn't easy. I feel guilty because I should have told you earlier, as soon as I found out."

My heart begins to sink. I'm scared of what she's about to say.

"The thing is..." she pauses, taking her time to carefully think about how she's going to construct her next sentence.

She takes a deep breath.

"The reason why your house mates have been acting all weird, with Chris, Vani and you isn't because they hate *you* hun...It's because they've been hiding something from you which they didn't have the guts to tell you about, months ago."

I suddenly go numb, paralysed with fear. She's slowly building up to the crescendo, but I just want her to spit it out.

"Anu, Chris has been sleeping with Vani...I'm so sorry hun."

I stare at her blankly for a millisecond before replying.

"What are you on about? Are you messing with my head Kerry?" I ask, almost slipping out a laugh.

"No I'm not messing hun. I'm telling you the truth. I'm really sorry that you have to find out like this, I really am. I didn't want to be the one to tell you, but someone had to Anu. Everyone is talking about it."

My eyes grow large in anger and shock. "Just tell me what you know," I say, abruptly.

Kerry hesitates before answering. "It started over the summer holidays; you remember when you told me that Vani had moved into your house. Well it was Jess who found out when she moved in just after. She confronted Vani apparently, and she admitted it too."

I suddenly get a flash back to the conversation I had with Ella a couple of months ago in the kitchen, when it was just the two of us at home. I came home early after Lois told us that a few of the lecturers had a last minute meeting they had to attend in the afternoon, so we should use this time wisely to study.

Ella asked me a question about something, but I'd ignored her and walked out, heading into the living room. She muttered under her breath, "You need to take your rose tinted glasses off Anu." I turned round and walked back in.

"What are you on about?" I asked her.

"Just that your boyfriend isn't the person you think he is."

"And what's that supposed to mean?"

"He slept with someone, you silly cow."

I remember standing there in a moment of silence, wondering what I'd done that was so bad she'd needed to make up something so cruel; a lie. It was only a few dirty dishes I'd put into a bin liner that day, what was the big deal?

"Oh whatever, Ella. Are you still bitter over the whole crockery incident or is it that you've never liked the fact that me and Chris are together? It's obvious that you're jealous. Even in first year you were always trying to flirt with him. Just admit that you want him?"

Ella expressed amusement at what I was saying, telling me that I had an overactive imagination. "You need to wake up and smell the coffee. When you two got together, he tried it on with me one night."

I wanted to punch her. She was making my blood boil. "You're such a liar Ella."

"Why would I lie to you, Anu?"

What Ella told me in the kitchen stuck in my head that day. I didn't want to believe her. Chris wouldn't do that, not to me. I agonized over the thought in my head but pushed it away into a corner, and refused to think about it again.

I turn my head away from Kerry, in disgust at myself. Chris told me every single day in the holidays that he was missing me, and wanted me to come back quickly. Vani never stopped telling me how much he was pining for me.

He said Vani moved in early because she wasn't getting on with her parents at home. But Jess *was* the first one to arrive back soon after.

I find my voice, but I sound pathetic in my response.

"Kerry, Ella tried to tell me a couple of months ago that something was going on with Chris and someone over the summer, but I didn't believe her."

I want to cry, but no tears surface. Instead my eyes are filled with self pity and rage.

"Why would they do this to me?" I shout. "I've been a complete and utter idiot. I bet everyone's been having a right laugh at me."

"I don't know why Jess didn't tell you straight away. She's supposed to be your friend and you've known her since college."

"But how did Jess find out? How can she say for sure something happened? Or is happening? Oh my God, are they still...?"

"I don't think they are now Anu. Jess found out when Vani said something happened with a guy over the summer. That's the rumour. I don't know the ins and outs. You're going to have to ask her?"

Rumours! I want to die. How can I face anyone knowing that I've been the talk of university over these past months?

Embarrassment begins to eat me inside. I want to run away and hide my face from everyone.

"I bet everyone told you to tell me didn't they, before I looked like an even bigger idiot?"

"You're not an idiot Anu, and you've got nothing to be embarrassed about. It's Chris and Vani that ought to be. They should be ashamed and disgusted with themselves."

Betrayal is overriding my embarrassment. Kerry is right. How could the very people I trusted with so much sincerity stab me in the back?

"I'm here for you Anu."

"I can't breathe the same air as them now, let alone be in the same house as them. Can I stay at yours tonight?"

"Of course you can. Do you want to go now?"

"I'll ring you later. I need to go home first."

"OK, just call me whenever and I'll come and get you."

She offers me a warm embrace, filled with strength and support. I walk away from the university grounds and in the direction of home.

In the space of thirty minutes, my life has turned upside down. I feel the need to vomit. All of a sudden I feel as if the house I've been living in for the past seven months isn't my home anymore. It feels empty, like me. An empty shell to a house made of bricks and mortar. I don't know who any of the people I live with are. My so-called house mates suddenly seem like strangers; one by one they've snatched away my dignity and self-worth.

My head is pounding, as if it's going to explode with every step closer I take towards the house.

The exchange of cold stares between the girls and Vani seem blatantly obvious to me now, in the face of truth. Whenever Chris or Vani entered the living room or kitchen, everyone walked out or made an excuse to leave.

Her diary! She must have something written in there. She writes everything in that diary.

My mind is working on over drive. I have to find that diary before confronting them both.

They can't find out that I know just yet.

My hands tremble in fear as I pull my hand up to place the key into the lock of the front door. I open it slowly, quietly as though I'm sneaking in - half expecting to catch them both in a compromising situation. Chris' car isn't even on the driveway, he's at work. I walk straight up the stairs and into my bedroom. Vani has a towel and some clothes folded in her hands, about to head into the bathroom.

"Oh hi," she says, catching me off guard. "You're back early aren't you? I thought you had lectures this afternoon?"

I'm so angry that I don't want to make small talk with her, but I sound casual in my response. "Yeah they've been cancelled because the lecturer didn't turn up."

"You're lucky. I wish my lecturers didn't turn up for class. That would be a nice change. I'm going for a shower. I'm probably going to be a while because I need to wash my hair; do you want to use the bathroom before I go in?"

"No."

I dump my bag and folder on the bed and sit down for a second looking around the room. My eyes glance at the double sided photo frame sitting on my bedside table. In one frame there's a photo of me and Vani posing with our red, yellow and green traffic lights around our necks.

In the other frame there's a photo of me and Chris, drenched in romance. Jess had taken it of us both at Arj's wedding. Happiness, lust and love pour out of it. It seems obvious now how others at the wedding could see that something may have been going on between us.

Is this really what my relationship has turned into; a big fat lie?

I can feel tears forming in the corners of my eyes, but I don't let them fall. Vani will be at least twenty minutes in the bathroom; I have to find the diary. I look in the most obvious place - under the mattress. It's not there. I search under the bed, behind it, at the side of it; inside the set of drawers that we both bought together for our room. There's no sign of it. I begin to get annoyed. She always has it with her. Her handbag is sitting on the floor by her bed. I open it and feel around in the pockets and zips, until my hand grips a rectangular shaped object. I pull it out of the bag, placing her diary in my hands.

I freeze for a moment, unsure of what to do next. I know I should open it and read it, but I'm scared of what I may uncover. Maybe there are other secrets about them that I'll discover.

I'm just about to open it when her mobile phone starts to ring. I go to pick it up when I stop. To my utter disbelief I see Chris' name flashing on her phone. My heart skips a beat.

Why is Chris ringing Vani? Is something still going on between them?

My head feels fuzzy. I want to answer the phone and tell him that it's me and that I know what's going on between them.

But I don't move. I hold the phone in my hand until the ringing stops. After a few seconds there's a beep. I think he's left a voicemail message. Without any hesitation I immediately press the button that takes me straight to the answer phone message. Right away I can hear the fear in his trembling voice, at being caught out.

"Vani, it's me Chris. Listen Anu's found out about us; about what happened. Just deny it. She can't find out Vani, it would devastate her. I'll be home soon. Don't say anything, please."

I sit on my bed with her phone in one hand and her diary in the other, unable to move. My heart has been shattered into a million tiny pieces. It's impossible to physically feel any worse. Hearing Chris' voice on Vani's phone is the final straw. And I haven't even opened the diary yet. I'm not sure whether I want to. The truth is already staring me in the face, I don't know if I can handle anymore tragedy.

My inner voice is shouting at me to open it and find out just what the hell is going on, for my own self respect. I have to; it's the only way I'm going to know for sure who's lying to me and what's going on. This diary is about the only thing that's going to give me the answers I need.

I have about ten minutes. I know exactly when Vani's finished having a shower because when she goes to draw the shower curtain back, she always yanks it hard so that everyone can hear.

I don't know where to start from, so I just open it at a random page. She's handwritten all the dates. I turn the pages back to July. It was around the end of July when Chris told me that Vani moved into the house. I skim over her entries. It sounds normal; boring. She's talking about being back in the house because her parents are driving her crazy. She needs a job to keep herself busy during the holidays otherwise her parents will be on her case telling her that she's wasting her time. I turn over some more pages, hoping to find what I don't want to read. I come to an entry:

21ˢᵗ July

Been in the house just over a week now and bored out of my brain. Looking to find a job but it's not easy. It's going to be long holidays. There's only me and Chris in the house. He's missing Anu and won't stop telling me. I'm getting sick of hearing it now. They're so mushy, it's sickening. Chris and I are going to the cinema tonight. Not sure what we're going to watch yet, but at least I'll get out of the house.

22ⁿᵈ July

Went into Guildford with Chris to the cinema and watched Jurassic Park III. It was ok, more Chris' kind of film than mine. I sat in his room tonight to watch TV rather than on my own in the living room. He said it didn't make sense us both watching the same programmes in different rooms. It was nice to have a bit of company. I was getting lonely on my own.

We talked; mostly about Anu. He kept telling me again that he was missing her and wanted to see her. He asked me about me, and my life. He said I was really quiet and kept myself to myself. I prefer it that way. He asked if there was anyone in my life that I was seeing, or anyone I fancied from uni. I laughed; told him that I quite fancied Italian Antonio but there was no chance we'd ever get together. He then asked me how old I was when I first lost my virginity. I was a bit taken aback with his question, so I laughed. I was a bit reluctant, or rather embarrassed to tell him that I hadn't yet. But he made me feel so easy about it all, so I told him. He didn't laugh or anything; just said that it was sweet. He asked me if I'd been back to Sri Lanka in recent years and whether my parents were quite traditional like Anu's. I told him that my parents didn't really care what I did. Read a bit more of my sci-fi book and then went to bed.

I can't read all of this, it'll take me ages. I turn over a few more pages until I read a line from an entry which catches my attention and makes me sit bolt upright.

25ᵗʰ July

Sat in Chris' room watching TV and talking. He's really sweet. I wish I had a boyfriend like him. He's not really my type, but he's not bad looking. He's cheeky and funny, so my evenings pass quicker.

It happened for the first time ever tonight, when I was least expecting it!

He was telling me about his first time, and how he fancied the girl so much. He said it didn't hurt her either, but I told him I was still scared. He took my hand in his and stroked it. Then he leaned forward and put his face close to mine. I was trembling. He touched my lips and then put his lips to mine. We kissed for a while. I felt really guilty. I told him we shouldn't, but he told me it'd be ok. He slowly placed his hand on the top of my thigh and then slowly travelled downwards and inwards. It made me tingle. He was gentle. He undressed me and started to touch me everywhere.

We had sex, and it hurt quite a bit.

I felt really awful afterwards. I felt bad on her.

I start to shake uncontrollably; struggling to comprehend what has gone on within the last hour. My day started off so well.

Chris mentioned that his mum had invited us both to the island in a couple of weeks to celebrate his dad's fiftieth surprise birthday bash at a country club. Sally specifically told Chris to bring me along. I was looking forward to it and thinking about what I should wear.

But I wasn't even mildly aware that within a matter of minutes, my world was going to collapse around me; forever etched in my memory to be one of the bleakest, blackest and worst days of my life.

Chris has ripped my heart out and trampled all over it. And Vani has gone beyond all the boundaries of the meaning of friendship.

Even though she hasn't mentioned Chris' name as the guy she's had sex with, it doesn't matter. I have enough evidence which indicates that it's him.

I don't want to read anymore. I've had enough; enough of all the lies and betrayal. I refuse to take anymore heartache, so I shut the diary and sit on my bed in silence.

I hear the yanking sound of the curtain go back on the shower rail, yet I don't do anything. I don't put her phone back beside her bed, or the diary back inside her bag. Instead I place it on the bed next to me and wait for her to enter the room.

I wipe away the tears that have pooled in my eyes, with no idea of what I'm going to say or do.

She walks in humming to herself. Her back is towards me and she continues getting ready. "Hey, what are you up to? I thought you might be with Chris. Isn't he back from work yet?"

"No he's not back. But I guess you'd know all about his timings wouldn't you?" I say, my voice rising in fury.

Vani turns her body round to face me. "What do you mean by that?" She glances at her phone and diary lying next to me on the bed and her face loses its showered glow.

"What's going on?" she asks.

I laugh at her question. "Don't you think I should be the one asking you that? After all, you're the one that's been sleeping with my boyfriend."

Her face drops. "What the hell are you talking about Anu?"

"How can you stand there and blatantly lie to me Vani? I thought you were my friend. Kerry's told me about you both. In fact everyone knows about it, so you can stop acting all innocent."

"They're lying Anu."

I stand up in anger. "I've read your diary for God's sake. You're the one lying to me Vani. Why are you denying it?"

She remains quiet, refusing to look at me. I'm standing inches away from her face, unable to control my emotions. "In fact I've just listened to a voicemail on *your* phone from *my* boyfriend, telling you to deny everything, because I've found out about you both. So tell me the fucking story. I mean it sounds like my relationship is common knowledge if it's already got back to him."

"You shouldn't have read my diary Anu," she says, with guilt written all over her face.

"And you shouldn't have slept with my boyfriend, Vani!"

"I can explain Anu."

"You bet you're going to explain. You've made me a laughing stock of uni and of my friends."

"I made a mistake, I'm sorry."

She can't even look at me in the eye.

"Sorry! Is that it, sorry? It's such a meaningless word. What exactly are you sorry for? Are you sorry for me finding out, or that you and Chris haven't had the chance to corroborate your stories with each other. Or that you have to explain to me before Chris? ... Or are you actually sorry for what you've done; what you're doing?"

"There's nothing going on between us," she says, looking more worried.

"You seriously expect me to believe that?"

"There's not. Whatever happened it happened over the summer. Not when you came back."

"Oh really, so it happened all over summer then?"

"No, it didn't. I don't mean it like that."

"I don't believe you."

"It's true Anu. If you've read the diary then you'll know what happened. Nothing has ever happened since you've been back. In fact it was over before you even got here."

I don't know what to believe now. I didn't read any further than 25th July, because I couldn't face knowing anymore.

"How many times?" I need to know.

"Why?"

"Just answer the damn question Vani, you owe me that much."

"Three times," she says quietly, bowing her head down in shame.

I want to be sick. I can't bear to think of them both together. I want to smack her across the face. Let out all my anger on her; but Chris is the one I want to vent most of my anger on. He's the one who's betrayed me the most and caused me the deepest pain.

"You're supposed to be my roommate; my friend," I yell at her in disgust. "What a joke. You're not a friend of mine."

"I'm so sorry Anu."

"Too late. I don't want to hear any more lies. I'm done with you. I'm just sorry that I didn't believe Ella when she tried to tell me. I spent hours helping you with that stupid music video that you were filming. I offered you my help. I laughed and joked with you; gave you the time of day when no one else would. And this is how you repay me. All this time you were keeping this from me. You're a fucking bitch, Vani."

With that I walk over to the cupboard and take out a small holdall; the one I usually take when I go home for the weekend. I grab a few of my clothes in a hurry and pack them. I walk out of the room, without looking or saying anything more to her. I want to get to get out of there so that she can't see the tears that are streaming down my face.

Vani shouts after me, "Where are you going?"

I ignore her. I run down the stairs, hiding my face from her. I grab my phone and ring Kerry. "Are you at home or still at uni? Can you come and get me, or I can walk to yours if that's easier?"

She tells me she's on her way to collect me.

I sit on the sofa in the living room in complete silence, until Kerry arrives and knocks on the door. I open it and walk out with my belongings."

On the drive to Kerry's house I tell her in detail exactly what has happened at home. She's as horrified as I am.

An hour later, after everything is beginning to sink in, Chris rings me. I ignore his calls. My state of mind won't allow me to handle any more lies right now.

Kerry opens a bottle of wine, which she picked up on our way back to hers. I want to drink the whole bottle and drown my sorrows; block everything out and feel sorry for myself. Kerry doesn't know what to say or do, apart from tell me that she's here for me. She can only share my shock and anger; not the depth of pain which sits heavy in my heart.

It's early evening and I decide to call home just in case I'm not in a fit state later on - both physically and mentally to be speaking to my parents. The last thing I need is trivial questions after the day I've had.

My phone hasn't stop ringing. The sound of it is giving me an earache and driving me crazy, so I switch it off. Minutes later Kerry's mobile phone rings. She answers it on her way into the kitchen. Through the closed living room door, I hear Kerry's raging voice. "Haven't you got the bloody message, she doesn't want to speak to you."

There's a pause for a couple of seconds before she speaks again. "No I'm not going to give her the phone. If she wanted to speak to you, she would have answered her own phone, wouldn't she?"

Kerry walks back in to the room having cut Chris off. "For fucks sake, he doesn't get the hint does he?" I lean back on the sofa with my feet curled up beside me; a cup of wine in my hand.

About fifteen minutes later the doorbell rings, followed by vigorous knocking. It can only be Chris. Kerry and I look up at each other. "Do you want me to open it?" she asks.

"I'll get it. I've got to face him sooner or later, haven't I?"

"Yeah but you don't have to do it right now if you're not up to it."

"I know, but I just want to get it over and done with." I place the cup on the coffee table and drag myself up from the sofa. I can make out the shape of Chris' body through the frosted glass.

He's standing on the doorstep looking sheepish with his tail between his legs.

Chapter Thirteen

*"I didn't think I'd fall in love with you Anu."...**Chris***

A long, awkward and frosty silence stands between us. Neither one of us know what to say and how to start a conversation. For hours my head has been buzzing with questions that demand answers, but I'm stood here unable to string one sentence together.

In front of me stands the guy I dote on; idolise and love with every broken piece of my heart. But when I look at him, venom runs through my veins, pumping through every muscle in my body. I want to cry and shout, *"Why me?"*

The only image I can picture when I force myself to look at him is of Vani and him together. The passion within me - which up until now ignited with his every look - is slowly burning inside me.

"Anu, we need to talk," he says.

"What do you want to talk about? What pack of lies are you going to feed me with this time?"

"I'm not I swear. I'll be honest about everything. Please can we just talk?"

"You're not coming inside," I warn him. "And I'm not coming back to the house either."

"Ok, ok. Well come and sit in my car then, it's out here."

There isn't an alternative, so I agree. I pick up my jacket from the banister and put on my shoes that are lying in the hallway. I pop my face around the living room door and tell Kerry that I'm sitting outside in Chris' car. She asks me if I'm ok. "We'll see," I reply.

He's already sitting in the car when I walk down the driveway, so I open the passenger side to get in.

Silence finds its way between us again.

I spot a stain on my jacket pocket, and stare at it, waiting for him to start the conversation.

"I'm sorry Anu, about everything."

He tries to hold my hand as he apologises, but I pull away. I don't want to be touched by him.

"What are you sorry for exactly, Chris? I mean a few hours ago you left a voicemail message on Vani's phone telling her to deny everything; that I couldn't find out about what had happened, so I don't understand what it is you're sorry about."

"There was a reason I didn't want you to find out Anu. It's not about not telling you, it's..."

"Of course it's about not telling me," I cut him off sharply. "What else can it be? It started in summer. I'm almost coming to the end of my second year. It's not like it happened last week."

"It was over before you came back. And we weren't having a relationship."

"No, you were just having sex with her, weren't you?" I answer for him.

"We had sex yes a couple of times, but that was it. Anu I don't know why it happened. I don't want to be with her. I felt sorry for her."

I laugh out loud. "Ha, that's the most pathetic excuse I've ever heard Chris. Come on if you're going to lie at least make it a good one. You've had plenty of practice lying through your teeth."

"I did feel sorry for her Anu, it's not an excuse. It's the truth. She'd never done it before, and... it just happened."

I'm struggling to comprehend his reasoning.

"Why would anyone have sex with another person because they felt sorry for them?

You know something, all those times you made comments about me jokingly; saying that I was 'gullible', 'innocent' and 'naive', well you weren't wrong were you? Those three words pretty much sum me up at this moment in time."

His face drops. "I'm sorry, I really am."

"It's a bit too late though," I say, with a heavy heart. "You've broken me completely, to the point where there's nothing left to break."

I look out of the window and stare into thin air.

"I've got nothing to say to you. There's nothing left anymore. You cheated on me simple as that. I trusted you wholeheartedly, but you did the worst possible thing a guy can ever do."

"We can work it out, I know we can. Don't say that. I made a huge fucking mistake; yes I agree but please don't let it ruin what we've got."

"Don't you tell me not to ruin it! You're the one that's ruined it already. How dare you?!" The anger in my voice is evident within the confined space.

"I don't mean it like that, Anu. I just mean let's not throw what we've got away. I'll make it up to you, I promise."

"I don't think you can make this one up to me Chris. It's well beyond repair."

"I love you Anu."

"And I love you too, but..."

"Then let's work through this," he says in a pathetic plea, picking up my hand and placing it in his.

"I can't stop thinking about you and Vani together. You made a fool out of me for months. You hid it, and you were still going to hide it today, even when I found out."

"I didn't want you to find out like this."

"You weren't going to tell me at all," I remind him.

"I was. It's just difficult to explain."

"Well you better try hard and tell me now Chris, because I'm not going to sit here all night in the car. Just be truthful for once. Did you ever love me?"

I cling onto a little hope from all the lies facing me. I'm already hurting; if he tells me he didn't, that'll be like another stab in my heart.

"Of course I did. I do."

I don't know if I'm relieved or not.

"Then why?"

"I was stupid and had stupid thoughts over summer about us."

"Like what?" I ask, moving my hand out of his.

"I've never been out with an Indian girl before. I just felt a little uncomfortable at what was going on between us."

"Uncomfortable? About what? I don't understand."

"I'm not making much sense, I'm sorry. I mean you met my parents and I met yours. But we've still not... you know...you've not given yourself to me completely."

"So is this what it all boils down to; sex? I should have known. You weren't getting it from me, so you went to her?"

"It's not like that Anu," he says mincing his words...

"Or do you just have this thing for Asian women?"

"No, I just never got to see you. Everything was a secret between us from day one. I didn't know how I felt for a moment. I was confused with the whole set up."

"So instead of speaking to me about it you decide to sleep with Vani to get your answers?" I say sarcastically.

He doesn't have an answer.

"I'm going to go Chris because there's no point sticking around. I've heard enough."

"No don't go," he says hurriedly.

I turn to open the door, but he stops me. "What do you want Chris?"

"Please let's sort this out."

"I'm so confused with what you're telling me. You say you were uncomfortable with what was going on between us. And what, now you're suddenly comfortable with us. What's changed your mind? And at what point did you decide that everything was ok and that you were comfortable again?"

He presses his lips together; I can see sweat gather in the corners of his mouth.

"I didn't think I'd fall in love with you Anu. I admit at the beginning I was confused. We weren't even intimate and things were moving so quickly, with me coming up to your cousin's wedding and everything."

"But you wanted to come. I didn't force you or anything. If you didn't want to come, you only had to say."

"I did want to come, of course I did. Look I just got scared, and did the stupid bloke thing. We were both a little lonely and it just happened."

"I was lonely. Beyond belief Chris, but I didn't go find attention from someone else. Did you just conveniently forget that you were my boyfriend or something?"

So far I've resisted from showing him my tears, promising myself that I won't let them drop for him. But I've finally defeated. Tears start to stream down my cheeks, in tiny rain drops.

Every word I utter is filled with cries of heartache. "We spoke virtually every day over the holidays. Did I not mean anything to you?"

"You mean the world to me babe."

"Well obviously I don't because you wouldn't have treated me like this; done this to me."

I move my hand towards the handle of the door.

"I need to go."

"Please Anu, don't give up on us."

I open the car door and before I know it I bolt out, running up the drive way and into the house.

I stand with my back against the front door for a few seconds, in a moment of complete stillness.

Kerry is sat in her bedroom watching TV when I enter. "Stupid question, but are you ok?"

"Sort of," I manage, wiping away the tears.

"I've made your bed on the sofa, is that alright? Do you want to talk?"

"No, it's ok. Listen thanks for this. I owe you one."

"No you don't silly. I hope you get some sleep."

"I doubt it," I reply. "Night."

I lie in bed awake, but my eyes remain shut. I can't sleep. My phone is buzzing with messages from Chris. They all say, "I'm sorry", "I love you" and "I'm not going to give up on us." I don't respond to any of them.

The writing in Vani's diary whirls around in my head. I can picture the pages when I shut my eyes; it's all there in black and white.

Chris' voicemail message goes round and round, like a song

stuck on repeat. It's impossible not to doubt all the feelings he says he's had for me and all the sweet things he's ever said. How do I decipher what the truth is, in all this mess?

The way he told Vani to deny everything so easily is unbelievably hard to accept; as if I meant nothing to him. I go over and over the conversation we've just had in the car; Chris telling me that things were moving too fast. That he was scared and didn't know how he felt about me. Ultimately though that I hadn't given myself wholly to him.

I thought we were on the same page; that his feelings mirrored mine. How could I have got it so wrong?

My head is spinning like a whirlwind. My brain eventually decides to switch off and I slip into some form of sleep; but it accompanies an aching heart filled with sadness from a betrayal I never imagined.

When I awake, I wonder if yesterday really existed, or whether it was a fragment of my imagination. But it takes me all of ten seconds to realise that I hadn't dreamt the last twenty four hours. It really did happen.

The love of my life really has crushed me to my core, and my roommate is a lying, poisonous bitch who doesn't have any morals or value for friendship.

I despise them both with every bone in my body.

PART TWO

Chapter Fourteen

"Normal! Things can never be normal again."...Anu

They say that you never really know someone until you move in with them. I wish it hadn't taken me so long to learn what the truth behind that *really* meant to me.

I lived with six, so-called 'friends' and it took me almost ten months to discover that every single one of them was cheating on me in some form or another.

I can never forget the look in Vani's eyes when she lost the trust and friendship of some of her closest friends, including me. There was no pleasant or lasting memory she could take back with her when she finished uni for good. No laughter and banter of her final days. She looked melancholy and there was sorrow, almost regret in her eyes.

After her final exam finished I never saw her again. She slipped away - vanished into thin air and no one heard from her; because the day my life turned upside down, it was the day Vani's and Chris' did too.

It felt like only yesterday when I arrived on campus. I waved my parents goodbye after they helped me to settle in to my new home.

There were no tears of sadness in my eyes, like there was in Mum's, when she and Dad, Sanya and Krish rode away in the taxi.

Instead an enormous wave of relief overcame me. I settled into a new way of life almost instantly, without any hesitation.

Five months have now passed of my final year.

I wait patiently in a queue outside the equipment room, waiting to pick up a camera. It's my second attempt at filming an interview which I'd messed up the first time round as a result of a technical glitch.

I'd returned from central London on a high after filming an interview which had gone exceptionally well. But when I checked the rushes, I realised that there was no sound to go with any of the footage. I cursed myself for not having checked it all whilst I was still there.

Luckily the interviewee is more than accommodating with me returning for a reshoot.

This dissertation is my last attempt at boosting my chances of securing a half decent grade which is not only going to determine my future, but also, either make my parents immensely proud of me, or utterly ashamed of me. Either way there's pressure.

From scripting, to filming, directing and editing, the twenty minute video documentary has to blow their socks off!

"Good afternoon again," says Reece, director of the online dating service I'm here to interview.

"Hi," I reply, all embarrassed. "I am so sorry about this Reece. I should have checked to see if the sound had recorded last time."

"Oh don't worry about it. I'd offer you lunch again, but I'm not sure whether you will have time?"

"No I'm just going to get this done and get out of your hair, but thanks for the offer."

The first time I came to interview Reece he picked me up from Waterloo train station and insisted on taking me for lunch first. I was overwhelmed at his generosity; but more so because this successful businessman was offering to buy me lunch - a mere university student. And it wasn't any lunch either; it was a fancy restaurant where they served poncy food that I couldn't pronounce. Luckily I'd worn something half decent and hadn't opted for the stereotypical student look, in jeans, trainers and a scruffy looking top.

"I'll let you set up and whenever you're ready just shout," he says, leaving me to get on with it.

"That's great. I won't be long." I set up the tripod and camera; insert the digital video into the camera, take out the mini microphone for Reece, and put on a set of headphones to make sure I can hear the sound.

"I'm ready Reece," I call out.

An hour later I'm sat on the train again, heading back to university, with rushes of yet another interview in hand. I hope to God that I won't need to return for the third time.

I watch a plane in the distance, which looks as though it's getting ready to land at Gatwick. I think about the summer holidays and my second stint working at the airport. I was over the moon that Dav came back to work there with me.

Dav always knew about my relationship with Chris. I remember his initial reaction. He seemed surprised when I told him I was seeing a White guy, as if he wasn't expecting that from me - the girl who loves Indian clothes, Indian music and the Punjabi banter. He didn't thrust any opinions he might have had on me though; strangely he told me that he envied me.

"Why on earth do you envy me, Dav?" I asked him curiously.

"Just the way you are. You're a strong minded girl. I haven't met anyone quite like you. You know what you want and you don't let anyone stand in the way of that; even your family. I wish I could be more like you."

"Being Indian doesn't mean that you can't have your own thoughts and your own mind, Dav. Anyway I'm probably more stupid than anything else. I shoot my mouth off all the time without thinking, and I'm always getting into trouble with my parents."

He frowned. "Yeah but that's because you stand up for what you believe in."

I poked him on the shoulder. "Or that I just don't know when to shut up. Anyway, you need to stop getting all weird on me."

"Nah Anu what I'm trying to say is that… yeah I'm having my fun at uni and doing my own thing; don't get me wrong I love it. But I know that as soon as I get home I'll probably have to settle down with someone of my parents choice."

"Who says?" I asked, scrunching up my face.

"I just know that's all. It's like this pharmacy course for example. I don't have that much interest in it and I probably wouldn't have chosen it myself, but I'm doing it for their sake. They want me to do it."

"But why?"

"Because it's what makes them happy."

"What makes *you* happy? Are you going to fulfil all of their dreams and none of your own?" I asked crossly. But I knew the script, even before I asked him the question. I knew about the hassles, the responsibilities, and the expectations that are tagged with being Indian. But for a guy, I was surprised at Dav's unusual talk.

I never mentioned to him about what happened between me and Chris. Not because he might have given me the third degree or anything, but because I was embarrassed and ashamed to tell him that Chris made me feel like the biggest joke; that he destroyed my trust in him, and he slept with my friend - that girl who was my friend first and became my roommate later. But the biggest reason I didn't tell him about what happened with us was because I did something which would have gone beyond most people's comprehension.

I'd forgiven Chris. And after all that he did to me, I even took him back.

Kerry and others told me I was stupid and naive; that leopards never change their spots. I knew that already though.

But love doesn't warn you when it hits. It's like a drug. You're on an awesome high; but when you try to wean yourself off, knowing that in the long run you'll be better off without it, you start to get withdrawal symptoms. So you go back for more, hoping that it'll make you feel the same way it did when you first experienced it.

Christian was my drug; he was my addiction.

§

The flat is empty when I return home which means I have peace and quiet for at least a couple of hours before the others get back. I hook up the camera to the computer and watch rushes of the interview I've just filmed. Everything is still fresh in my mind and so I start to make a scene log of the shots I want to use.

By the time Chris walks through the door, I'm at the end of watching the rushes. "Hey, how did the interview go?" he asks.

"It went alright, I think. The only frustrating thing is that when I filmed this interview the first time round it felt more natural, because the questions were off the cuff. This time he already knew what I was going to ask him so he'd rehearsed his answers. It just didn't flow the way I expected it to. Do you know what I mean?"

"Yeah I think so. But you'll just have to use the best bits I guess. Suppose you're going to have to accept that now babe. You're the one that messed up."

I look up and roll my eyes at him. "Thanks, like I didn't know that already!"

He smirks. "Have you made sure you've got the sound though? You know the most important thing?!"

"Ha ha," I say, sarcastically. "You can stop with the little digs. Yes I did. I've just been going through it all now." He bends down to kiss me.

"Do you want to do anything tonight?" he asks. "Go to the cinema or something?"

"Kerry asked me earlier if I wanted to go to Basement Jaxx. There's an 80's theme night going on tonight. Some of her house mates are going, but I said no. I'm shattered after traipsing around London carrying all that camera kit. I just want to stay in tonight. Do you mind?"

"I forget you're only a tiny person. How on earth did you manage to carry all that stuff?"

"I managed, you cheeky git."

"I'll get a few beers in and get a take-away then."

"Is Jenny around this weekend?" I ask.

"No, she said she was going to stay with some friends in Milton Keynes."

"Cool."

§

The end of my final year is fast approaching. My exams are done; the documentary is complete and the tenancy agreement for the flat is coming to an end.

Every time I think about going back home, my heart sinks. It's an even deeper sinking feeling than before, because I know that this time I won't be returning; ever. This is it. My three years are finally up. I'm getting ready to say goodbye to my independence and the real me - slowly preparing myself with having to justify my existence all over again, and not knowing where the love in my heart for Chris is going to take me. The grim reality slowly starts to seep into every pore of my body and terrify me.

In the end I'd surrendered to my heart and returned to getting my fix each day from Chris. He vowed a clean start, with no lies, no cheating, only honesty. He realised - however late it was - just how much I meant to him; when he came so close to losing me forever.

The truth was that I couldn't live without him either. He'd become entrenched in me, like the biggest piece of a jigsaw puzzle in my life which completed me, and I found it physically impossible to let go of him. Deep inside him I knew there was a kind, loving heart which ached for me. An ocean of regret filled the tears in his eyes for all that he'd done and put me through.

I came home to pack the rest of my things a couple of days after that unforgettable day. I told him I was going to stay at Kerry's place until uni finished. I knew it was going to be difficult but I didn't have a choice. I was even willing to return to halls of residence until the end of term, but there weren't any rooms available.

Chris' appearance looked dishevelled when I stepped inside the house. He looked as if he hadn't got out of bed for days. His hair wasn't in its usual, immaculate state - gelled and spiked up. It was shabby and he hadn't shaved in three or four days.

I hadn't seen him since our conversation in the car, and didn't answer any of his phone calls. I couldn't even bring myself to read his text messages.

When I walked through the door, he literally jumped up to greet me. "Anu, are you ok, sweetheart?"

"I'm fine," I said coldly.

I started to walk up the stairs but he grabbed my hand to stop me.

"I'm so sorry Anu. Please I beg you, don't do this to me. Talk to me. Let's sort this out."

I yanked my hand away from his. "I'm moving into Kerry's house."

"Don't. You don't need to. Look I'll go if that's what you want, but please don't leave the house."

"I can't be under the same roof as the both of you Chris. It's just not going to happen." I pulled out cash notes from my back pocket. "Here's the money I owe for the bills and the council tax. Take it."

"Leave it Anu. Stop this," he pleaded.

"I'm not having you pay for me Chris. Just take it." He refused to take the money from my hand, so I left it on a ledge in the hallway. "Where is *she* anyway?" I asked, my voice suddenly sounding bitter.

"I don't know. She's not around. She's not been here since that day."

The house was empty, it didn't sound like anyone was home other than us. "I don't want us to fight or argue anymore," I said.

"I don't want that either. I just want us to get back to normal."

"Normal! Things can never be normal again," I laughed out harshly.

"It can if you let it babe. I love you Anu and I'm an idiot for doing what I did to you." I looked up to see tears fall from his eyes.

I didn't know what to do. I'd never seen a grown man cry before, and even after all that he'd put me through, it hurt me to see him like this.

"Don't Chris," I said. "It's done. Whatever's happened has happened and you can't change it."

He started wiping away the tears with the palms of his hands. "I want you back Anu. I swear I will never do anything to hurt you ever again."

"You say that Chris, but you've done a really good job of that already. How can I trust you? You obviously wanted to be intimate with someone in the way you couldn't be with me and I guess Vani was your ideal bait. You reeled her in, what more can I say?"

"It's not like that."

"It is. No matter how much you try and dress it up, it really is. And if that's what you want, you're welcome to her, or whoever else you want to do it with. I'm not the girl for you. You know my thoughts and where I stand on all that. You can either accept it or leave it. But I'm not letting you trample all over my emotions again."

He vowed that he'd never hurt me again or let himself get that weak. He told me that nothing was more important to him than being with me.

I let my heart over-rule my head because it was impossible to walk away from the person I'd given my entire heart to.

Chapter Fifteen

*"I'm on the mainland, driving up to see you
and to tell your parents about us."...Chris*

Two slices of a twelve inch ham and pineapple pizza sits on a plate, firmly resting on the armrest of the sofa, while Chris and I lie comfortably in each other's arms, full to the brim and unable to move. We've worked our way through a bottle of Blossom Hill white wine whilst watching crap on TV.

I've been preoccupied for days thinking about the imminent future. And the wine isn't helping my mood to forget either. If anything, its making me think about it more, but I dread bringing it up in conversation with Chris.

But the wine has given him the Dutch courage needed to bring up the subject that I can't bring to my lips.

"Anu, in four days time you finish uni for good," he says, with sadness on his face.

"I know." I say, turning my face to the floor, with the same look.

"I don't want you to go."

"I don't want to go back."

"I know you don't have a choice sweetheart, I'm just saying. When you go back home, I don't want to stay here, not if you're not going to be here with me. So I've decided to go back to the island."

§

"I love you Anu," Chris tells me, as he watches me buy a one way train ticket. "We'll make it work, sort something out I promise."

He stands watching the train depart from the platform, waving me goodbye and leaving us miles apart with an unknown future ahead of us. I look out of the window one last time to see him; then I sob my heart out as he disappears from sight. I begin my journey home all alone, not knowing if I will ever see Chris again.

Everything at home has changed and I find it difficult to adjust. Life as I knew it hasn't changed though. Everyone is on top of me making me feel claustrophobic. I desperately want my own space; the space I'm so used to having only weeks ago, without any questions or obligations. I want Chris, and the happiness I felt being with him. I long for his hug, his touch and his smile.

Four weeks have passed between us, and our only contact has been on the phone.

It's the August bank holiday weekend and I'm in the middle of a spring clean of my bedroom when Chris calls.

"I need to speak to you about something," he says, with an excited tone in his voice which I haven't heard for a while.

"Go on then."

"Can you talk for a few minutes?"

"Hold on," I say, walking over to the radio to turn up the volume a notch, so I won't be overheard by anyone. "Go on, I can now."

"You know I love you don't you Anu?"

"I love you too," I reply in a whisper, covering my mouth as I speak.

"I love you and I want to be with you always. I need to know how you feel."

His words send a sudden rush of warmth inside me, instantly making my face glow like a spark.

The last few weeks have been extremely hard to deal with. Mum and Dad have picked up on my change in mood. One minute I'm happy, because I've spoken to Chris, and the next I'm down because I miss him. "You're like an alien since you've come back home," Dad said to me a couple of weeks ago. "What's wrong with you?"

"Nothing," I said. "I just miss uni and my friends."

"Listen Anu, you can't keep thinking about university. You're home now, it's over. You have to move on in your life. We'll be going back when you go to collect your degree. You can see your friends then."

I wanted to scream at him and shout out,

"How can I move on when my boyfriend is hundreds of miles away from me? I can't tell you about him because you'll never let me see him again. I wish you could just be like my friend's parents – understanding and happy in my happiness."

But I knew I couldn't say it. There was nothing that I could say to make either of my parent's understand that the reason I was so withdrawn and unhappy was because I was trying to do the right thing. I was trying to distance myself from a forbidden love.

It was at that moment that I fully understood the depth of Dav's emotional turmoil that day, when he explained to me that he'd probably have to live his life pleasing his parents.

I feel as though I'm on that road now.

"I want to be with you as well more than anything Chris," I say with conviction.

"Then let's tell your parents about us."

"You what?!"

"Let's tell your parents?"

"Are you being serious, Chris? Do you know what you're saying?"

"I do, yeah. My life feels incomplete without you in it. I want us to be out in the open and I want to be able to see you and spend time with you like a normal couple." As he delivers each word I hear the certainty and passion in his voice. I yearned for him to say those words when he dropped me off at the train station.

But I feel more than a little anxious. Our relationship can never be normal, not in the sense he wants it to be anyway. "Let's talk about it later, properly and figure out what to do," I tell him.

"I need to know now Anu, not later."

"What's the rush Chris? We've been together for three years and not spoken about this, what's a few more hours going to do?" I'm puzzled by his urgency.

"Because I'm on the mainland, driving up to see you and to tell your parents about us."

"What?! Are you kidding me? You're on your way here? Now? To my house?"

He starts laughing. "Yes, I'm on my way. We have to do it someday don't we, if we want to be together?"

"Yeah of course, I just didn't think it'd be today or this soon."

"There's never going to be a right time to confront your parents about us, is there? We may as well do it now, together."

My heart is telling me to say, 'Fuck it and let's tell them.' But my head is saying something else.

Do you know what you're doing Anu? Do you have any idea of what the consequences will be telling Mum and Dad? What happens if they throw you out of the house, forbid you from ever speaking to Chris again? What if something happens to them? What if Dadi collapses in shock?

I don't know what to do. I know that I love Chris and that my feelings for him are real, they're not about to change. And he's right, there's never going to be a good time to tell them.

But am I brave or am I a coward? Do I risk it and suffer the consequences in the hope of being happy with Chris, or do I remain unhappy within, in a secret relationship, not knowing where it's going to take me?

"Let me call you back Chris, in about ten minutes."

"Ok, but be quick, because I'm not lying Anu, I am on my way. I'm about an hour away from Birmingham already."

"I'll call you back soon, don't worry." I end the call.

I don't know what the right thing to do is. All I know is that I'm frightened.

I walk down the stairs, biting the skin off around my nails in fear of the unknown. I want to see what everyone is up to, to get a feel of what the general mood is like. Dad is in the back garden mowing the lawn. Mum is in the kitchen. Dadi is lying on the sofa in the living room. Sanya is in the shower and Krish is watching TV.

"Have you got any plans for today Mum?" I ask casually.

"No, nothing yet. Your dad's still in the garden. I was going to make *choley bhature* for lunch. Why, have you got something planned that you're telling me about at the last minute?" she asks, sarcastically.

"No, it's just, you remember Christian from uni?" I wait for a second for her to remember, but she doesn't. "Christian, Chris," I remind her. "Well he's coming up north, near here for a conference or something with work, and he thought he'd come by and see me on his way. I was wondering if he could come home for lunch."

I haven't planned what I'm going to say or do. I want to test the water, gage their reaction first.

"He's coming today? Where is he going?"

"I don't know Mum, he just rang me. I didn't ask him lots of questions." The last thing I need is twenty questions right now. I'm just making this up as I go along. I don't need to think about answers to even more trivial questions.

"I don't know. I don't mind, but ask your dad if it's ok. I don't know if he has anything planned."

I put on a pair of trainers that are lying in the pantry and walk out of the house into the front garden. Dad looks worn out having already cut the grass in the back garden, and now on a third of his way round the front. "Do you want a hand Dad?" I ask.

"You're asking me now when I've done the back and nearly the front," he says.

Great, this is not getting off to a good start. He's already annoyed at me that I haven't volunteered to help him.

"I was cleaning my room, I'll do the rest for you if you like?" I offer.

"Tell you what, pick up the brush over there and sweep up the grass that has fallen on the pavement."

"Alright," I say, picking up the brush; my heart dancing a thousand beats.

"Dad, you remember Christian? Chris who came to Arjun's wedding; you know my friend from uni?"

"Hmmm yeah, why?"

"He's coming up here today for a conference with work and he asked if I was free to see him while he's up."

A bemused frown appears on his face. "He's coming up here? Why?"

"I don't know Dad. He's just coming with work."

"Where does he want you to meet him?" He asks, sounding a little uneasy at the prospect of me meeting up with a White man alone. I wonder if it has slipped his mind that over the past two years I've been living in the same house with him.

"Actually I thought he could come over and have lunch with us."

Dad flicks the switch back on the lawn mower and carries on cutting the grass.

Is that a yes or a no? He looks as though I've asked him a difficult question which requires a huge amount of thought before answering.

"Well?" I say loudly, over the noise of the Flymo.

"Well I don't know. Have you asked your mum?"

"Yeah I've asked her. She said to ask you."

We're playing that game of table tennis again where I'm the ball in between the two of them. I should have known better than to ask Mum first. Mum never makes decisions about anything without consulting Dad. When I want to go out anywhere; if I ask Mum first, her response is always, *"I don't know. Ask your dad."* I end up wasting time getting permission about the most insignificant of things.

I begin to feel frustrated, but this is definitely not the time to be showing it. He turns the Flymo off. "If your mum says it's ok, then I guess it's ok with me."

"She said its fine."

"What time is he coming?"

"It'll be about two o' clock."

"Ok, fine."

"Dad says that it's fine," I shout out to Mum, hurrying through the kitchen and up the stairs.

"He'll be here around two o' clock."

"Ok," she replies.

"So?" he asks when I ring him back. "What are you saying?"

"I've told them that you're coming up for a conference with work and that you're popping over to see me, ok?"

"Right, ok." He sounds confused. "And what's going to happen when they find out that there's no conference?"

"I don't know Chris. I haven't thought that far ahead. I just said what came into my head. I couldn't exactly tell them that you're coming over so that we can both tell you we've been seeing each other for three years, and we thought that today would be the best time to tell you all the truth."

"You know best hun."

"You reckon you'll be here for about two ish?"

"Yeah I should be."

"Well I asked if you could stay for lunch."

"Oh right, OK." He doesn't say anything for a few seconds. All I hear is the noise of passing traffic on the motorway.

"I don't know how this is going to work Anu. I'm nervous too you know, but I'm ready to face whatever I need to, as long as you're by my side."

I want to jump down the phone and kiss him. I've committed myself to this huge decision, and I'm frightened to death of the consequences. I need to hear some reassuring words from him, to help me get through, what I *know* is going to be a tough afternoon.

"Chris. What would you have done if I said No?" I ask curiously; "that I don't think you should come over to the house today; that I want to be with you but just not ready to take such a big step yet."

"I'd just accept it Anu. I'm coming up anyway. I've already booked a hotel for the night, so I'd just stay and head back tomorrow."

"Is that it?" I say, a little disappointed.

"Well I'd be upset but I wouldn't have any choice really would I? I couldn't come over unless I got your say so?"

"OK, listen I've got to go babe. I'm helping Dad with the gardening. I may as well get in his good books. It might be the only chance I get. I'll see you when you get here."

"I love you, no matter what babe," he says.

"I love you too."

After three years of being with him; dreaming of how it would be and how I would feel telling my parents about us if we lasted the distance, it's finally about to come true. I'm filled with dread, nerves, fear and relief at the realisation that everything is going to be out in the open. But my mind is still in a conflicting state. I can't help but feel a pang of worry; guilt and selfishness too, that I am about to drop a huge bombshell on my family without any warning.

Can I really do this to them?

Thoughts and fears engulf me to the point where I start to shake. I have to tell someone in the family before Chris arrives. It will be too much for everyone to hear our news without any prior warning.

I don't want to ring him and tell him that I'm in two minds. He sounds pleased and relieved that we're about to do this together. But something doesn't feel right. I know my parents inside out; I can pre-empt them about virtually anything. I've had so much practice.

I hear Mum's footsteps coming up the stairs. I take a deep breath and walk into her bedroom, closing the door behind me. "Mum," I say gently. "Yes?" She replies, worryingly, noticing that I have shut the bedroom door fully.

I can feel my heart beginning to thud erratically in my chest, as I stare her in the face.

"I need to tell you something," I utter, with an unmistakable shudder in my voice.

She gives me a worried look. "Are you ok? What's wrong?"

"I'm fine. It's...it's about Chris coming over later."

"What about it?"

I can't believe I'm about to do this.

"There's another reason why he's coming over to see me," I say. Mum's face looks confused, almost frightened. She gives me the same expression she normally does when she knows I'm about to drop something unexpected on her toes. She has no idea that this is by far the biggest bombshell I'm about to drop.

"What?" she asks, looking at me closely. Her eyes dart to my lips anxiously as she waits in anticipation to hear what I'm about to tell her.

My mouth feels dry. I inhale a large amount of oxygen, filled with nerves before answering.

"He's coming over so that we can tell you and Dad that we're together."

There, I've said it. Those words which I'd only dreamt of saying in my head and in my dreams, I've finally blurted them out to Mum.

Her facial expression changes immediately. "What, what?" she repeats, sounding baffled.

I continue to speak but without making any further eye contact with her. "Chris and I are seeing each other Mum, and he's coming over so that we can tell you and Dad."

I look at her, half expecting her to scrunch her face up and smack me across the face. But she just stands still, not moving or speaking.

"Mum, do you understand what I'm saying?"

Looking completely taken aback at what I've just said to her, she sits down on the bed.

"Have you told Dad?" she asks with a worried look on her face.

"No I haven't said anything. I wanted to tell you, so you didn't get a shock when Chris blurted it out."

She's silent, and doesn't say anything for a few seconds.

"Tell him not to say anything to your dad when he gets here."

"What? Why?"

"Just tell him not to say anything, I said. You can't just tell your dad something like this - just like that."

"That's the whole point though Mum."

I'm trying to figure out her unusual reaction, but fail to. I have no idea what is going through her mind, and I'm scared of asking.

"Please Anushka, tell him not to mention anything to Dad, I will tell him."

Without questioning her further, I go back to my room and shut the door. I pick up my phone and go to the call log menu, to dial the last number stored at the top of the list.

"Hey," Chris says.

"Chris, I've told Mum."

"What have you told her?" he asks intriguingly.

"I've told her the reason you're coming here?"

"What, the truth? I thought we were going to do it together."

"I couldn't risk dropping it on them both Chris without any warning. I know my parents, and I know how they take things. I just had to say something to Mum."

"What did she say? How was she?"

"I don't really know," I say, confusingly. "She hasn't said

anything, but she has told me to tell you not to tell Dad when you get here."

"But why not?"

"I don't know. She said she would tell him, but said make sure you don't."

"What's the point of me coming over then? I mean obviously I'm coming to see you but..."

"Well you're having lunch anyway, so just keep it as that. I'll have to speak to her later on."

"Alright, if you say so." He sounds disappointed.

"I better go. How far away are you now?"

"About an hour and a half away babe."

"Ok, I'll see you later."

I sit down on my bed for a moment, to stop the overwhelming shakes that are running through my body. I don't know if I'm feeling relieved or worried because I was half expecting Mum to yell and shout at me, or show some sort of emotion that I would half expect of her; like a complete mental breakdown or an attack on my morals and values as an Indian girl, accompanied with a stream of tears. But there was none of that. Instead she appeared calm at my revelation, and more concerned about exposing the truth to Dad.

What have I done?

A few seconds later Sanya enters the room and asks what's going on. "What were you speaking to Mum about when you shut the door?"

I wonder whether I should tell her or not. She's going to find out sooner or later so I tell her.

The unsurprising expression on her face rapidly turns to shock. "Why are you going to tell Dad about him? Are you mad?

"Wow, that's brave of you. I'm surprised Mum didn't go mental." She pauses for a second. "I wonder how Dad's going to react."

Suddenly I feel a jolt of angst. I've told Mum without any real difficulty, but that doesn't mean to say that there isn't any trouble waiting for me later. I convince myself that everything will be ok. After all I've done the hardest thing by breaking the news to one of my parent's. I just want to get everything over and done with right now; face the music once and for all.

It doesn't quite feel like a weight has been lifted off my shoulders yet. I'm not even half way there. The biggest hurdle is Dad; and I haven't even begun to think too deeply about Dadi and how this is going to affect her. How will she handle the shock of knowing that her granddaughter doesn't *just* have a boyfriend, but a White boyfriend?

After grabbing a shower I head downstairs and into the kitchen where Mum is preparing food for lunch; stirring something in a pan, looking undeniably preoccupied.

She looks up at me in apprehension. "Have you told him?" she asks, in a voice just louder than a whisper.

"Yes, I've told him."

"He won't say anything, right?"

"No he won't."

"Good, because I don't want your dad finding out."

I wonder for a second whether she means today, or she means ever. But I don't want to clarify that point with her.

I check the time, its approaching two o'clock.

Nerves start to kick in again.

Sanya is sat in the living room with Krish. He flashes me a worried and disapproving look. Sanya has obviously told him something.

I'm on tenterhooks. At two twenty sharp the doorbell rings. I open the front door to Chris standing in the porch, ready to greet me with a warm smile. He leans in to me to give me a kiss on the cheek and says, "Hi." I push him away quickly, in case Mum sees us.

"Don't look so worried Anu," he says in a low voice. "It'll be fine."

"It's not that," I quiver. "I don't want Mum to see you kissing me in case she gets funny about it."

I quickly change my demeanour so as not to arouse any suspicion. "Come in, come in," I say cheerily, acting normal as I possibly can.

Chris walks in asking if he should take his shoes off. I tell him he doesn't need to. I follow him through the hallway leading into the kitchen. It's Mum who greets him first. I keep my eyes on her face, weighing up her mood towards him. She walks towards us with a rolling pin in her hands. She's been rolling out dough ready to make *naans* to eat with the *choley* for lunch. But my overactive imagination and paranoia kicks in, because in my mind's eye all I can see is Mum's angry face. Her eyes are full of venom and she's armed with her rolling pin heading towards us, unafraid of using it. Hitting it round Chris' head and then taking it to mine! I get so worked up that I feel my cheeks burning up.

"Hi Sita." Chris says, cutting my paranoid state of mind by engaging in conversation. He wears an unusually big smile on his face. I wonder if he's trying too hard with her, under the circumstances.

"Hello Chris."

It feels odd hearing Chris call Mum by her name. For a second the memory of meeting Chris' parents for the first time spring to mind. And how it felt odd calling his dad, Rick. I had wanted to call him uncle.

Mum signals with her hand and points to the living room. "Come inside."

I hover behind them both as we walk in, afraid of leaving both their sides in case something leaks out of their mouths accidentally. Dadi is sat cross legged on the sofa. Chris brings his hands up, presses them together and says, "Namaste Dadi."

I want to smile but I don't let so much of a crease pass my lips.

I look to Mum through the corner of my eye, but there is no emotion or change in her expression; which only continues to make me feel uneasy. Dadi smiles to acknowledge him and returns his gesture with a "Hello," in English.

He shakes hands with Krish and pecks Sanya on the cheek. I glance over to Mum. Once again, she's expressionless.

"Hello again Vinnay," Chris says, pulling out his hand to shake Dad's.

"Hi Chris. Good to see you again. So what brings you up here? It's a bit of a long way from the Isle of Wight, isn't it?"

Chris lets out a laugh and replies, "Err just a bit, yeah. It was sort of last minute with work."

Dad gestures for him to sit down. I observe the pair of them from a short distance whilst Chris is stood up in the living room. I hadn't noticed at any of the wedding functions, but looking at him closely in the house Chris looks like a giant in comparison to every member of my family.

Whilst Dad and Chris make small talk, I follow Mum into the kitchen. I'm still clueless as to any of the thoughts swirling around in her head. She's doing a pretty good job at not expressing or showing any emotion to anyone.

"Do you want a beer Chris?" Dad asks. He nods to say no. "I better not, I'm driving later. If I have one, I'll want another."

"Yes you're right, you shouldn't in that case." While Dad gets a beer for himself, I grab some soft drinks for everyone else.

I could murder a glass of wine right now.

The glasses clink against the tray in my hands as I nervously walk in and hand out the drinks. So far mum seems to be taking this all too well.

Maybe this isn't such a big deal after all. I could be making a mountain out of a mole hill.

But I'm not convinced. The cauldron is bubbling, and I know she's going to unexpectedly throw something into it causing it to explode violently.

Throughout lunch there are pockets of silence around the dinner table, where nobody utters a word. Generally though, Chris and Dad seem to be nattering between themselves.

Chris tears a piece of *bhatura naan* using both his hands, and dips it into the spicy chickpea dish. I glance at him sneakily as I raise a glass of juice to my lips. I can't help but wonder if the food is too spicy for him.

At uni, Chris loved to eat the food I brought from home, particularly *aloo keema* - the spicy minced lamb and potatoes dish. It was amusing to watch him wolf down curries which I'd bring back because it was guaranteed that within seconds, sweat would be pouring down his forehead uncontrollably and his cheeks would blush like a girl's.

He takes another mouthful.

Sunshine sweeps through a window behind him catching one side of his face. I can see his forehead glitter in the sunlight. I want to reach over and wipe the sweat with a tissue and tease him, but I daren't do either.

"So what are you doing at the moment?" asks Dad. "Are you living with your parents?"

"Yeah I'm living at home with the folks, they absolutely love it, and so do I if I'm being honest. Mum likes to make a fuss over me and it's nice to be pampered again. I'm working in I.T software on the island. It's not been that long since I started the job so I'm just finding my feet at the moment."

"That sounds interesting. I.T is where the money is, that's for sure."

Dad continues with the questioning. "And who's in your family? Do you have brothers and sisters?"

"There's my Mum and Dad and my younger brother Graham. That's it."

"You came to my nephew's wedding," Dad says. "You enjoyed it, right?"

"Yeah I loved it. I don't usually like going to weddings, but I must admit I won't forget that one in a hurry. It was a crazy and colourful wedding. What was that stuff we put on your cousin's face Anu?" He turns to ask me.

"Oh, err it was turmeric paste."

"I remember putting it on him. He didn't like that stuff, I remember him saying."

"Yes but its traditional," Dad tells him. "Every Punjabi person who gets married will have that put on them. It's a sign of good luck in your married life."

"Yeah I remember Sita saying." Chris turns to look at Mum, but she doesn't respond; instead she gives him an awkward smile.

After dinner we all settle down on the sofas. Dadi insists on watching her Indian soap on the Asian channel. The volume is turned up and the cringe worthy music to the opening credits of the soaps kicks in. Dad grabs the remote from Dadi's hand and decreases the volume. "It's too loud Mum," he insists.

Chris makes curious faces as he tries to make sense of what is going on in the soap. I watch his eyes follow the subtitles along the bottom of the screen.

An hour later, I decide to text him from my bedroom, when he's sat downstairs with the family.

Maybe it's time you were starting to make a move hun? I know Mum's giving you smiles, but I don't know what she's really thinking inside. We'll see what happens later and I'll text you. Love you xx

I head back down a few minutes later and casually walk into the living room where they're all still sitting. I notice Chris' mobile phone in his hand.

A few minutes later he announces that he's leaving, and Dad asks him where he's staying.

"It's a hotel in the city centre. I don't think it's too far from here."

As Chris gets up to leave, nervous tension comes flooding back, making me feel more anxious and frightened. We'd promised to tell my parents together, and I'd felt safe and protected knowing that Chris would be by my side when we did. But he's leaving; knowing full well that Mum knows about us but Dad doesn't. I feel sick at the thought of what faces me once he's gone. What seemed like the right thing to do a few hours ago, now feels like the scariest thing in the world.

I stand in the porch to see him off. "Call me later," he tells me softly. "Let me know how everything goes. And if you need me, just say. I'm only up the road from you."

I force a smile.

"Do you want me to come back in and we can tell him together, now?" he asks, noticing the fear and vulnerability prominent on my face.

"No no you better not. I told you what Mum said to me. She's probably going to tell him herself, when I'm not around I imagine."

"Ok, but if you need me..."

"Yeah I know babe, thanks."

I watch as he sits in his car and drives off out of the estate, waving me goodbye. When he's no longer in view I step back into the house, gently closing the door; praying in my head:

Please God, help me get through this. Please be with me.

Chapter Sixteen

*"I sent you away to university for an education,
to get a degree, not to mess around and get boyfriends."...Dad*

When night falls, so do all my hopes. I draw the curtains, switch off the lights and lock my bedroom door. I lie in bed in total darkness; my body shaped in the foetal position under the duvet. I shut the world out and sob quietly and uncontrollably.

I've never felt so vulnerable and lonely as I do right now. The last few hours are a blur, but the harsh words spoken to me are far from a distant memory.

The tears in Mum's eyes haunt me; the shock and anger in Dad's voice, and the confusion on Dadi's face.

In the space of an afternoon I've gone from being an opinionated but lovable daughter, to a deceitful, dishonest, disrespectful and devious one. The trust, faith and confidence I once held in high esteem, in the eyes of my parents - those values which they worked so hard to instil within me since childhood - I have completely destroyed within minutes. In their eyes I've become one of them; a *gori,* a White girl.

Dad raced up and down the house, not quite knowing how to handle the situation. I was sat on the sofa when Mum broke the news to him in a shocking fashion. Chris mustn't have even arrived at his hotel, and unbeknown to him my living room had become a set; a stage where an explosive and powerful drama was about to unfold. There was no warning; no opening credits and no introduction.

Dadi sat cross legged on the floor with her back to the radiator.

Sanya and Krish were floating between rooms - lurking behind doors, waiting for the fuel to ignite, the fire to explode.

It took Dad a few minutes to register and digest what Mum told him. But what hurt and confused me the most was the manner in which she told him. In my mind I'd convinced myself - based on the sober and unexpected reaction I encountered this morning - that she would break it to him gently and with compassion; not only for Dad, but for me also.

I didn't expect what happened.

"Do you want to tell him, or should I?" Mum shouted out unexpectedly in anger, as we all sat watching TV. I looked at her in disbelief at the startling and sudden transformation in her behaviour. She appeared cold.

"What's going on?" Dad replied, switching his momentary look from Mum to me and then back to Mum again, demanding answers. "Tell me, what's going on Sita?"

I couldn't bring myself to open my mouth.

"Anushka has been keeping a very big secret from us, which she was going to tell you today without even thinking about how it would affect any of us."

How could she say such a thing? I'd spent three years thinking about this day and how it would affect them. I lay awake at night trying to figure out what words I'd use to help ease the blow. I never expected them to take it lightly, but I had hoped that they would try to understand.

"Tell me what? What's going on Sita? What was she going to tell me?" Dad asked, looking increasingly worried and eager for answers.

Mum's face became stern. "She and *that* boy, Chris have been seeing each other at university, behind our backs and today they were going to tell us. They were going to give us a heart attack! That's the real reason he came to the house today."

I couldn't believe my ears. Thirty minutes ago she was making polite conversation with Chris.

Dad's eyes grew large; his eyeballs nearly popped out at the revelation. He stood up, put one hand on his head and then brought it down to cover his mouth. I could see the muscles in his throat expand and contract slowly as he swallowed hard in a state of shock.

I didn't know what to do. He looked at me with a mixture of anger, disappointment and shame.

"Is this true Anushka? That boy has been in my house, he sat at my dinner table and he had the cheek to lie to my face. All this time he had a hidden agenda. You both did."

All eyes were on me. Mum, Dad, Dadi, Sanya and Krish. I sensed that Sanya and Krish wanted to say something in my defence, but they didn't speak up, in fear of what reply they may get in return. Poor Dadi kept speaking in Punjabi. She looked baffled, asking why voices were being raised and why the sudden hostility towards me in the room. *"Ki hoya, ki hoya,"* she repeated. "What's happened, what's happened?" No one said anything to her.

Instead Dad continued to point out more of my failings and assume the worst in me.

"That means when he came to the wedding, you were seeing him then? Now it makes sense, why you wanted him to be there. Have you been lying to us since then?" Before letting me speak he carried on shouting at me.

"I'm absolutely disgusted with you Anushka. I never expected this from you. I had faith in you and trusted you. I sent you away to university for an education, to get a degree, not to mess around and get..." He paused, wondering how to say it; "boyfriends," he uttered with disgust, as if it was a shameful and dirty word.

When I looked up at him I saw him holding his hand to his chest, taking deep breaths.

The last thing I wanted was the burden of causing pain and misery to any of my family, but looking at him and seeing how distressed the news was making him made me feel sick to the stomach.

I wondered whether I'd made a huge mistake.

Could Chris and I even last the distance? If not then all this heartache will have been for nothing.

But we made a conscious and mutual decision because we love each other. I was tired of all the lies and secrets. I hated the loneliness I felt when he wasn't with me, and I wanted them to know that we were serious about each other.

I couldn't breathe. I felt suffocated. Questions came pouring in one after the other from both of them. Tears fell from Mum's eyes; every drop filled with disappointment and failure as she looked and spoke.

I could feel my windpipe tighten; my face burning up. I was having trouble swallowing my own spit and I urgently needed my inhaler.

I stood up to go upstairs when Dad asked, "Where are you going; upstairs to ring *him?* He should be ashamed of himself."

"No," I shouted back. "I need my inhaler."

I raced to my bedroom and grabbed it from the bedside table. I inhaled two sprays and sat on my bed. A few seconds later, I could feel my lungs expand and I started to breathe normally again. I heard footsteps creeping up the stairs. It sounded like two sets of feet. They were slow and quiet. Dad walked in to my bedroom first, Mum followed behind.

"Are you ok," Dad asked, noticing the inhaler in my hand. There was a shade of concern on his face, but an air of anger still evident in his voice.

"I'm fine," I replied.

It took only a few seconds for that concern to turn into disappointment and disgust again.

"I want to know everything," he demanded.

"What do you want to know," I said. "What's your problem with Chris?"

"I don't have a problem with him Anu. I have a problem with this whole situation. We thought he was your friend, not anything else. You brought him to Arjun's wedding as your friend, you deceived us. And now you're telling us there's more. What do you want me to think? You've been lying to us for goodness knows how long. Telling us one thing and doing another."

Surely I'm not the only daughter in the world to have kept a secret like this? At least I'm brave enough to finally be telling you. That has to count for something doesn't it?

"He's *gora*. White. I just don't know how..." Dad was struggling to comprehend what I'd done.

"He's not even Indian. If he was Indian then maybe we could have discussed this. But this is totally unacceptable."

Mum eventually piped up, as if she'd suddenly found her long lost voice since this morning. "Didn't you know it was wrong Anushka? You knew didn't you that your parents wouldn't accept this, so why did you even think about it?"

I heard more footsteps coming up the stairs. They were a lot slower this time and a little heavier. It was Dadi. I could hear the thud, thud, thud sound of her walking stick from the landing, coming towards my room.

"Tell me, what's going on?" Dadi demanded, entering my room, struggling to prop up and sit on the bed. Both Mum and Dad proceeded to take it in turns to tell her a piece of my sordid affair with the *gora*!

"She's totally shamed us. Imagine what people will say?" Dad said to Dadi, with an unmistakable worry on his face. "How will we face anyone in the community if they find out?"

That's what this all came down to; what other people's perception of me and my family would be once they found out! I was waiting patiently to hear that line, and here it was bang on cue.

What took me almost years to pluck up the courage to reveal the most private part of my life I'd kept hidden for such a long time, and all they could think about was their reputation in the Indian community.

It clearly didn't matter to them how *I* was feeling, what *I* wanted and what made *me* happy. Everything was about what *other* people would think and how *they* would react.

"I can't believe we let you live in the same house as him," said Dad. "No wonder you never wanted to come home at weekends. It's because of him. Slowly it's all making sense now." I sensed another kind of disgust in his eyes towards me; like I'd let my Indian values extinguish.

My head hurt. More and more accusations were being thrown at me.

"You have no respect for your parents. What haven't we done for you our whole lives, huh? And this is how you repay us! We didn't bring you up to throw this in our face," said Mum.

I wanted to know what I'd done which was so bad. I mean, the way they were talking, anyone would think I'd stabbed someone and left them to die. Any of my close friends listening to this would laugh at all the melodrama.

But this was one thing they just wouldn't understand. Even though I felt that I was very much like them in a lot of respects, there were still some aspects of my life that required parental approval no matter what my age.

To make matters worse Dad decided to call uncle Ashok and auntie Renu over to discuss the "situation." The shock to their system was clearly too much for them to handle alone and amongst the four walls of our own house.

The thought of my parents discussing my business with them infuriated me. This was the last thing I wanted, but naturally I didn't have a say in the matter.

"Why are you calling them round? What's it got to do with them? You're my parents and I'd rather discuss this with the both of you sensibly. What's the point of getting everyone else involved?"

Mum looked surprised at my outburst. "You expect us to sit here quietly and accept what you've just told us, and not discuss it with anyone?"

"What do you need to discuss and what is there to think about?"

Dad looked at me bewildered. "What do you mean what do I need to discuss? I never imagined that I would see this day, where my daughter tells me that she has a *gora* boyfriend. You've been lying to us and I can't trust anything you say or do anymore."

"This is exactly the reason I didn't tell you before. Look how you're reacting. If I'd have told you when I was still at university, you would never have let me stay there."

Mum turned to Dad, pointing her finger at him. "This is your fault," she said. "You agreed to let her study away and this is the end result."

All I wanted was the ground to open up and swallow me. I needed Chris by my side. I wasn't brave enough to do it on my own. He'd know the right words to use. All I was doing was arguing back and it wasn't getting us anywhere. If he was here, he'd tell them face to face how serious he was about me and how much I meant to him. On my own my words were meaningless. Nothing I said or did was making the slightest bit of difference in convincing them otherwise, and it was futile trying.

§

Within half an hour, I was sat on the sofa under a cloud of suspicion, with five sets of eyes fixed on me, all listening to me intently as I tried to express into words, mine and Chris' unprecedented, emotional and psychological attachment. Krish and Sanya were ordered to go upstairs. When I tried to speak, I was repeatedly interrupted by Mum and Dad wanting to know the *whys, where's, and when's* to everything I was saying. Auntie Renu had to stop them from intervening a few times.

Uncle Ashok and auntie Renu remained quiet throughout; but their unspoken words spoke volumes. I knew exactly what they were thinking. I felt like I had lowered their opinion of me, especially when I was always regarded in such high esteem with them.

Chris tried to call me on my mobile. I could hear the constant attempts. My phone was vibrating in my pocket, but there wasn't a second where I felt I could take it out and answer it. I knew he'd be going frantic with worry.

I wanted to tell him that I couldn't do this without him and that I needed him here with me. But I stuck like glue to the sofa, physically unable to move or shift the glares I was receiving from everyone. I was being scrutinized from head to toe. I'd brought shame on the family and now I was being looked at in a different light.

"You associate with White people at work," I said to Dad. "You're friends with them. They're you're business acquaintances, so why are you so against me wanting to be with one?" I asked.

I was expecting to hear a remark that would expose his ignorance, but it was auntie Renu who responded to my question.

"Anushka, listen to me. We're not here to curse you or shout at you or anything else. We just want to listen to what you have to say, and then ask you some questions."

I didn't say anything. "We associate with English people all the time, yes of course we do. But this isn't just about being colleagues or friends with them. What you are saying is more than that. You're talking about a relationship with a White person; someone who has no idea about our culture, religion and traditions. They don't have any barriers or limits."

I kept my face down, rubbing a stain on my jean, getting more and more wound up at the things being said. Chris was the one person who knew more about me than my own parents.

Mum interrupted, "*Gore* people don't know the value of marriage like we do. One minute they're in one relationship, the next minute they're in another. They live together for years, and then have babies, and only then do they decide to get married. Is this the kind of lifestyle you want to be part of?"

"Did I say that Mum? Is that what you think of me? That just because I want to be with Chris, I'm going to forget my roots? What do you take me for?"

It was Dad's turn. "We've been in this country over thirty years Anushka; we know how English people live."

I wanted to scream at them.

"Not every White person is like that Dad. And what about Indian people, do you think they are perfect? I don't think so. Unless you fit their stereotypical criteria, Indian people don't even want to know you. The only thing they're interested in is their reputation in society and their bank balance. They're so two faced it's unreal."

"Now you're being stupid," Dad said. "You're just saying that because you've been brainwashed into thinking like that."

I wanted to laugh at their stupidity. The way they thought they knew everything.

"You just assume everything don't you? Nobody has brainwashed me into anything. I am my own person with my own thoughts. Nobody said that I don't like being Indian. This isn't even about that. It's about me wanting to be with Chris, and he wanting to be with me, that's all."

Admittedly, the memory of Chris and Vani crossed my mind at that point, but I wasn't about to disclose that to them.

"You don't even know Chris. Why can't you just get to know him?"

Dad turned his face in disgust at the mere suggestion.

"At the age of eighteen *gore* people tell their kids to find their own place, you know?" Dad continued, completely dismissing what I was saying. "Some don't even keep in touch with their parents;

out of sight, out of mind. Have you ever seen them looking after their grandparents the way we do?" he asked. "They leave them in a home and never see them again."

Chris' parents had put his grandmother in a home because they couldn't look after her. I wasn't about to tell them that either!

"I think you're generalising Dad, and completely over exagg-erating. Not everyone is like that."

Auntie Renu came to my defence. "Come on, you can't say that Vinnay. That's not fair."

"But it's true; I'm only saying the facts."

Facts! The fact is that you're so narrow-minded. You live in this bubble world where you believe everything should be in accordance with your thinking. And God forbid anyone to go against that thinking.

I was glad in a way that Chris wasn't around to listen to any of it. He'd be pulling his hair out. Rather than trying to convince them about us, Chris would give Mum and Dad more ammunition, and another excuse to tell me why I shouldn't be with him.

After remaining quiet for a long time, watching us all talk loudly in English, Dadi spoke up. "If you get married, and it doesn't last, you know that he'll just divorce you. That's what they do; they think divorce is the answer to everything. It's such a simple word to them."

"Who said anything about getting married?" I said, "let alone divorce?"

"What do you mean? You think we're just going to allow you to have a boyfriend that you can see freely?" Dad proclaimed.

"I'm not ready to get married," I said.

"So you just want our permission so you can carry on seeing him then?" I was scared of saying, *"yes, that's exactly what I want."*

So I didn't reply; instead I let them draw their own conclusions from my silence. After all they were good at making assumptions.

"Well I'm sorry but that isn't going to happen. There is no way that we are going to give you permission. You can get that idea right out of your head."

With that, he got up and walked out with a stern look on his face. "I'm your father and whilst you're still living under my roof, I make all the decisions around here."

I rapidly managed to find the power in my legs to run out of the room and up the stairs, bumping into Sanya and Krish who shot up from the top step.

"Are you ok?" asked Krish. I couldn't speak. Tears streamed down my face instead and answered his question.

§

Under the duvet I dial Chris' number. The bright light of the phone in the confined space I'm lying in hurts my eyes. He answers before I hear the first bell ring.

"I've been so worried about you Anu. Is everything ok? I've sent you so many texts and tried ringing you for ages."

I want to tell him everything. Mum's impromptu change in character; the heartless manner in which she took Dad's side and turned against me. I want to tell him that I got accused of being brainwashed by him, and that I'm a wicked daughter who has no respect for her parents and their happiness. I want to laugh and tell him that my parents have no idea of how to handle their daughter's happiness that they have to hold a family discussion first.

All I do is cry.

"Anu, Anu please don't cry. What's happened sweet cheeks?"

I fight through the tears and whisper, "Dad knows. Mum told him as soon as you left, and he's gone up the wall."

"Oh babe, do you want me to come round, because you know I will if you say so?"

"No, no don't. It's late. They need time to absorb everything. They don't want to see you."

"Do *you* want me Anu? Forget your parents for a minute, do you want me there?"

"There's nothing more that I want than you here with me Chris, but I can't. Please. I'll call you tomorrow as soon as I get up. I'm in bed now and I'm tired; I just want to sleep. I promise I'll call you when I get up."

"Alright babe, I love you."

"Me too."

I've reached a new level of exhaustion and my body cries out. Sleep engulfs me within seconds.

Chapter Seventeen

"These children, they're not going to rest until
they have completely destroyed our peace of mind."...Mum

The sun peeps its head through the curtains as I stir, leaving me with a warm feeling on my cheeks, before hiding its face and disappearing out of sight.

My body feels numb, as if I've woken up after suffering a massive trauma. I lie still, listening to the sound of birds chattering outside my window, thinking about the events of yesterday. In spite of everything that was said - mostly by my parents - I wake up clinging on to a glimmer of hope; that maybe now everything is out in the open, there's a slight chance that mine and Chris' relationship will be accepted. Granted, it's going to take time, but at least they know that I'm serious about him and that's why I've taken such a big step in telling them.

I'm not sure if I'm being naive, over confident or just optimistic.

I slip out of bed and stand at the window sill looking out onto the back garden. A small flock of pigeons are picking at bread crumbs, which is scattered across a small patch of grass. Its seven thirty on bank holiday Monday and Mum is already awake. The bread on the grass is a big giveaway.

Every morning her routine is the same. She gets up, goes downstairs, tears up slices of bread into tiny little bites and scatters them onto the grass. As soon as she turns her back, pigeons fly over her head so fast, and huddle in a circle with their beaks to the ground.

Mum religiously carries out her routine and the birds too wait for her in anticipation - sitting in the same spot until the exact moment she opens the back door holding their feast.

"Birds get hungry as well you know," she says. "Not just us. They have hearts and stomachs, and they need food to survive. You know, they're always waiting for me, my birds. If I'm a few minutes late they get anxious and start chirping louder. As soon as I open the back door, they all gather round, ready to pounce on the bread."

She hides the loaf of bread from Dad that she uses to feed the birds. She doesn't use the two thick slices you get at either end of a loaf either. She buys a whole loaf especially for them. Dad always complains. "Why do you buy separate bread for them, Sita? Just give them the leftovers. You waste your money every week." Mum doesn't argue, but she still keeps her cheaper, smaller loaf of bread out of Dad's sight to keep the peace.

In the kitchen she'll make two cups of tea, one for her and one for Dad and bring them up to bed. At eight thirty, she'll come back down stairs and make another cup; this time for Dadi, and she gives it to her in bed.

I pull down the lock on my bedroom door slowly, trying ever so carefully not to make a noise. Once I hear the sound of clicking, the door pushes slightly ajar. I creep out, walking quietly across the landing towards the bathroom. On my way, I have to pass my parents room. I tiptoe gently avoiding the creaking spots.

I hear voices coming from inside. I stop to listen.

Mum's voice is quiet and melancholy. "I told you it wasn't a good idea sending her away to university. There was nothing wrong with her staying at home and going to a local one. At least she would have lived at home, where we could have kept an eye on her. But it was you who said, *'It's ok, if that's where she says the best course is then she should go there.'* Have you seen the consequences now!

"I didn't expect her to do this Sita. I don't know what is going on in her head. The girl doesn't think about anything or anyone but herself. She has no idea of the implications of her actions. She's always been a problem, ever since she went to college, and now she's landed us with another one. We don't know anything about him, only what we saw when we met him at the wedding."

"Ever since she told me I've just been mentally distressed," Mum says. "I can't think about anything else."

"When did she tell you," Dad asks in almost a whisper.

"She just came into the bedroom yesterday morning and said she wanted to tell me something. I knew there was something wrong when she closed the door behind her. You know what I'm like; I got nervous. You don't know what's going to come out of her mouth."

I stand still as a statue, listening with a heavy heart.

Is there any hope out there for me? They're never going to accept Chris. I've always been a problem child, they've said as much. I spring things on to them and then expect them to accept it and deal with it. But why can't they just accept that I want to live my life, my way? Why does there always have to be barriers?

"I asked her what she wanted to tell me," says Mum. "When she did tell me I thought my heart was going to stop."

Oh come on, stop being so melodramatic.

"I didn't know what to do, I was speechless; shocked. There was no warning or anything. To be honest I was more worried about you. I was thinking that if he comes here and blurts it out like that, what it's going to do to you."

"Give me a bloody heart attack probably," Dad cut in sharply.

"I couldn't let them tell you the way they planned. So I told her not to say anything to you and that I would tell you in my own time. I was so angry. I wanted to shout at her so much. But what could I do? She put me in an impossible situation."

The TV is on in their room. I can hear an annoying advert on one of the Asian channels for Rubicon mango drink.

"I couldn't sleep all night."

"And you think I could?" says Dad. "She's completely disturbed my mind. I don't know what to do. I'm worried about Mum and what she's thinking. I know she's a strong woman but this... it's another headache and stress which she doesn't need at her age."

"These children, they're not going to rest until they have completely destroyed our peace of mind," Mum cries out.

I creep past their room and into the bathroom, quietly shutting the door behind me. I've heard more than enough.

The glimmer of hope I've woken up with gets flushed away instantaneously. I wash my hands and splash cold water onto my face. It aches with all the tears I've cried. I slip back into my bed and pick up my phone. I have one text message waiting to be read.

Morning sweet cheeks. I couldn't sleep, been thinking about you all night. How are you? I want to see you. Is there any chance? Chris xx

I ring him.

"Morning hunny," he says cheerily. If only he knew of the conversations which took place last night.

"Hey," I manage to say, in a colourless tone.

"How are you feeling?"

"I'm ok."

"No you're not, I can tell in your voice."

"I'm just scared Chris. I don't know what's going to happen. I don't know if they're ever going to let me see you."

"They will babe, don't worry. Once they see the Jamo charm they'll never be able to resist me."

A hint of a smile passes my lips, if only for a fleeting moment.

"I don't know if that's going to work this time. You don't know how mad they are."

"Can you get out of the house and see me?"

"I don't know if I'm ever going to be able to see you Chris. Seriously, I don't know what's going on in their mind."

"They can't stop us from seeing each other," he laughs.

"You want to bet?"

I hear their bedroom door open and I jump up.

"I'll call you back," I say to him. "I can hear footsteps."

"Call me back soon as you can babe. Let me know if we can meet. I want to see you and speak to your parents."

"I'll call you back," I say in a hurry. "Bye."

I throw the covers back over my head and pretend to be asleep, when someone pokes their head round the door.

As soon as I hear the door shut again I lift the duvet off my face.

Sanya walks in twenty minutes later and I'm still lying in bed feeling sorry for myself. After the conversation I heard between my parents earlier I'm a little apprehensive that they're hatching another plan involving more aunties and uncles.

"Are you going to come down?" Sanya asks.

"Yeah in a bit. Is everyone up?"

"Mum and Dad are downstairs, Krish is asleep and Dadi is still in bed."

"Oh yeah it's bank holiday Monday," I remember. "Wish it was

Tuesday. At least they'd be going to work then," I say snuggling deeper into the covers.

My phone vibrates. I pick it up and read the message. It's from Dav:

Kidha? How you doing? What's it like being back home? I want to be back at uni so bad man! Everything's so different at home. If you're free sometime soon, let's catch up?

He's right. Everything is completely different at home, especially for me. I leave the phone next to my bed with the intention of replying back to him a little later.

Dragging myself out of bed, I put on a dressing gown over my bed clothes before making an appearance downstairs. The atmosphere is filled with tension before I even get half way down the staircase. When I enter the living room, my parents look like they're sitting in mourning.

My stomach growls but I can't eat. I decide to make a cup of *masala chai* instead. I walk into the kitchen and switch the kettle on. Whilst waiting for it to boil I drop a tea bag into the stainless steel tea pot and add a cardamom seed, a pinch of fennel seeds, and a spoon of brown sugar. I pick up a newspaper lying on the breakfast table and pretend to read it, twitching nervously; my fingers trembling as I turn each page wondering what they have discussed for my future and the problem that I've landed them with. I want Chris here with me so badly.

I pour water into the teapot and let it simmer for a few minutes on the hob and then add a generous amount of milk to it.

I used to laugh at storylines in soaps where the characters would drink tea in the kitchen, in a bid that they'd miraculously find a solution to their dilemmas. That somehow they'd find all the answers to their troubles as they sipped a cup of tea. But right now a hot cup of Indian *chai* is about the only thing that is close to making me feel less on edge, albeit for a few minutes.

I walk back into the living room with my mug and take a seat on the single sofa facing the TV. But it isn't switched on. They continue to sit in mourning. Although I know the reasoning in my own head, bizarrely I still have this urge to ask them why they aren't watching an episode of one of their dreary Indian soaps. I bite my tongue because I know that this isn't the most appropriate time to be cracking a joke with them. I can just imagine their response:

"Are you being smart? There's a bigger drama going on in our own house, why do we need to watch it on the TV?"

Sitting on my own in the same room as them makes me feel uncomfortable. I want Krish to come running down the stairs and be his annoying little self; but it's a holiday and the chances of him getting up before midday and gracing us with his presence is less than likely. I wait impatiently for the sound of Dadi's walking stick to knock against the banister as she makes her way down the stairs. But I can't even hear that. I desperately want her to be sitting here with the TV on and the volume turned up to the highest decibel. I wouldn't complain.

It's unnervingly quiet.

Mum and Dad are not in any hurry to make small talk with me. It feels like torture. If they could just get to know Chris the way I do, then I know they'll fall in love with him, I'm sure of it.

"Have you spoken to him?" asks Mum, with anger still evident in her voice.

"If you're talking about Chris then yes I have," I reply stiffly.

"Is he still here or has he gone back?" Dad asks, nervously twitching his brow.

"He's still here. He's not going back till later."

"What is he going to do?"

I'm unsure of what he means by that question. "I don't understand. What do you mean, what's he going to do?"

"Well is he going to go back home?"

"Well yeah he's going to go later." I pause for a few seconds before plucking up the courage to say what I really want to.

"He wants to see me...and you?"

I wait patiently for a response. I know this is a big deal and no matter how I feel I have to see this from their point of view. I don't push it with them. Instead I wait for them to say something; anything.

Finally Dad speaks. "Where does he want to meet?"

"I don't know. He didn't say and I didn't ask."

"If he wants to meet us then tell him to come to the Thistle Leisure Club and Hotel," says Dad. "We'll meet him there."

This is a turn up for the books. This time it's me wearing a shocked expression on my face. I wasn't expecting him to agree so quickly. I was preparing myself for another round of heated arguments.

"What time because he's got to drive back home, so it can't be too late."

"Well what time then? About two o'clock?" he asks.

"Yeah that should be ok. I'll ask him."

Nobody says anything more. The conversation has run dry and so I continue to drink my tea in silence. A few seconds later Dad gets up and walks out without so much of a look in my direction. He can't even bear to be in the same room as me.

I call Chris and tell him of the plan. "That's fine with me," he says. "Just give me the directions and I'll find it."

I explain as best I can, but he knows that I'm no good at giving directions. He calls me, "a typical girl!"

"Just call me if you get lost," I tell him, "and I'll try and guide you from wherever you are." He doesn't sound reassured.

§

I sit anxiously at the table playing nervously with my hair; twirling strands of it around my fingers in anticipation. A waiter comes over and asks if we want to order any drinks. I ask for a pineapple juice.

Dad orders a beer. I assume he needs to calm his nerves before talking to Chris and I sense apprehension in his demeanour; the trepidation in his voice about the imminent conversation. That makes two of us. I have no idea what he's going to ask or say to him.

I could do with an alcoholic drink myself, but I know if I ask for one, they'll be horrified.

"You're asking for a vodka and coke at two o' clock in the afternoon? Is this what you've been doing in all your time at university? Drinking yourself into shameful state and messing around with boys I imagine."

As much as I really want it I don't ask for one, in fear of adding more fuel to the fire, which is already burning in my direction.

Mum doesn't order anything. She sits on her chair with a grave expression on her face, looking extremely uncomfortable.

The emotions running through me are ten times worse than last night, when I was being scrutinized and interrogated by everyone after Chris left. I'm nervous beyond belief, because this time, when they see us together - they'll both know the real story - well most of it. Everything about them is bound to doubt every inch of us, our words and our intentions.

Just as I finish praying that he arrives on time so I don't feel this awkwardness, I spot him walking towards us. There's a sense of relief. I want to jump up and run into his arms.

I still manage to notice how good he looks. His hair is spiked up, and his sun glasses are resting on top of his head. He's wearing jeans and a round neck white t-shirt, which shows off his broad shoulders and big chest.

Dad gets up as Chris approaches our table. He has cleverly picked a spot at the back, and in a corner; hiding us so that we're not in view of many people. It means no one can eavesdrop into our conversations either.

"Hi Vinnay," says Chris, holding out his hand to shake Dad's invisible hand. Dad has no choice but to extend his hand out and shake Chris'.

He takes the empty seat next to me. My parents are facing us; I feel as if I'm about to be interrogated by the police.

There is an air of uneasiness between us all and I wonder who is going to start off the conversation.

Dad breaks the ice. "Do you want a drink Chris?"

"I'll have a diet coke, thanks." Dad signals for the waiter to come back and he orders another drink.

"Well Chris," starts Dad. "I think we all know why we're holding this meeting."

Meeting! Why is everything a meeting with him? Why can't it be a chat, or an informal discussion? We're not having a business meeting to discuss statistics and strategies. 'Meeting' makes it sound so official and formal.

"I want to know..." he begins. "...We want to know," he says, pointing to Mum too, "when and how this started? I mean, when you came to my nephew's wedding, you and Anu were just friends? In fact I distinctively remember you saying that you had a girlfriend, so how come you suddenly realised you had feelings for my daughter?"

"All I can tell you Vinnay is that Anu and I felt that once we'd come to the end of our time at university, we wanted to be together. We had a very tight friendship over the three years and we both wanted to develop it into something more."

Something more! Oh no Chris what are you saying? The first bit was really good. You remembered the sequence of events, but you've made a fundamental error. Telling my parents that we wanted to develop our relationship into something more sounds like you wanted to sleep with me.

I turn my head around to face him, hoping that he'll look round and realise what he's said. But he doesn't and it's proving difficult to make any eye contact with him.

"What do you mean you wanted to develop it into something more?" Dad asks.

He shifts around in his seat, looking uneasy with Chris' answer.

It shouldn't have been Dad making that comment this morning about having a heart attack. It should have been me. Over the last forty eight hours, my emotions have taken me to another level. High one minute, low the next; up through the roof and then the next minute crashing down on all fours. I've been sat on a rollercoaster taking the ride of my life, but with no idea of the duration and destination it's taking me to.

"Well, we've always liked each other, and been fond of one another, we just didn't know how deep those feeling were until a few months ago, when Anu came home to visit you and I went back to my parents. It made us both realise that there was more to our friendship, and we wanted to make a go of things."

There's no way that they will ever be able to handle the real truth; that we've been together since first year and not since only a few months ago. Dad remains quiet, a little taken aback with Chris' reply.

"Hmm, I hear what you're saying," he says, "but don't you think that this is wrong? I mean two different religions can't mix together like this."

I knew it was too good to be true.

Chris looks shocked. "Two religions can't mix? Are you serious?"

Dad looks slightly embarrassed at the way his sentence has been perceived.

"I don't even have a religion."

Mum and Dad look at each other and then turn to Chris.

"What do you mean you don't have a religion?" Dad asks, now looking confused at this new revelation.

"Like I said, I don't have a religion. Neither do my parents; I'm an Atheist. I don't believe in God."

We've already gone beyond the boundaries of taboo subjects over the last twenty four hours; throwing religion into the mix doesn't seem like a good idea. "You must have a religion," Mum says. "You have to believe in something. It's strange that your parents named you Christian when they don't believe in God!"

I hadn't thought of that. That was a surprisingly quick observation from Mum.

In a matter of two days, this has got to be the worst possible news to fall on her ears. Firstly she finds out that her eldest daughter wants to be with a White man and then being a devout practicing Hindu, she learns that the White man her daughter wants to be with doesn't believe in God. It must be the icing on the cake.

I wish Chris hadn't mentioned it. I knew he didn't believe in God, but I had no idea it would become a further obstacle in our relationship. "I think they just liked the name. They never associated the religious meaning with it. They never have done. But yeah..." he chuckles, "I see where you're coming from."

Silent takes over again.

"Look Mr and Mrs Lamba, I have never disrespected anyone's religion or way of life, don't get me wrong. I love to learn about other people's faith, but I just don't believe in God myself. I believe there's something out there that controls the universe, just not God."

This is going from bad to worse.

"What do your parents do?" Dad asks, swiftly changing the subject.

"My dad's a mechanic at a garage, and my mum's a social worker." I scan their body language and facial expressions, to see whether Chris' parent's occupation meet my parents approval. I know what's racing through their minds; that if his parents have a decent, respectable job and a nice home, if they aren't divorced or separated, then maybe there's a slight possibility they could think about this.

"Is it his own garage, like a family run garage?" asks Dad. I can see where he's going with this. "Like ours. We have a family run business."

"No, no it's not his own. He works there. He's been in the mechanics trade for most of his life though."

"You told me you had a brother, yesterday?"

"I do yeah, Graham. He's two years younger than me."

"And what does he do?"

"Graham's a nurse."

Dad's face perks up a little. "A nurse? That's good. Where? In a surgery?"

"No in a hospital."

"That's good, that's good," Dad repeats.

"And you're working in I.T?"

"For my sins, I am. I actually studied Sports Science at uni in my first year, but I wasn't enjoying it in the end, so I dropped it. I've always been quite good with computers, so I managed to get work within I.T when I quit, and they even funded an I.T course alongside me working with them. I've been lucky enough to find the same sort of work back on the island, like I told you yesterday."

"So you've not been a student since finishing your first year?" Dad asks suspiciously. I know he's wondering why Chris didn't just move back to the island when he quit, but he's figured out that I'm the reason behind that – and he looks disappointed in me once again.

I want to know how many questions he has in store for Chris. "This is a lot for me to take in and I'm not very comfortable with all this," admits Dad. "I don't know what you expect us to say or do," he declares.

Chris looks at me. He picks up my left hand and places it inside his.

My heart starts to beat erratically.

"We just want you to know that we're serious about each other Vinnay. My parents have met Anu and they really like her."

Dad's posture suddenly alters. "When did your parents meet my daughter?"

Oh shit! He's landed us in it again.

I take my hand out of his and quickly step in before things spiral out of control. "I met his parents when they came to visit him at the house a couple of times."

"I'm not happy with this situation," Dad states, as if we didn't already know. "And I'm being honest with you. I need to go away and think about it. I can't give you an answer just like that."

We're not expecting an answer but Dad is making it sound like we're asking for his permission to be together, when in actual fact we just want them to know about us and to accept it. In my eyes, it's gone beyond the permission stage. I've already made the decision, but I can't help sounding annoyed with his reply.

"An answer about what?"

"Well you've told us to get our permission haven't you?"

"We're not asking for your permission, Dad. We're letting you know how we feel about each other."

His face looks horrified, as does Mum's. "Then why have you brought us here to talk," says Mum. "You're either asking us, or telling us."

I can tell Chris is feeling harassed at the way this is going. The politeness in his voice is starting to turn into a slight irritation instead.

"We don't want to argue with you Vinnay, and Sita. That wasn't the idea. My concern is Anu that's all. I care very much for her."

"Are you saying we don't care about her?" Dad asks defensively. "You don't think that this has been a huge shock to us; it's something that we never expected from her. We want the best for our daughter, nothing less. We are her parents and we've always wanted the best for her."

"Then you should be happy in her happiness," says Chris.

"It's easy for you to say that. We are the ones that have to face all the questions."

"And you're worried about a few questions?"

Chris is pushing it a little far with Dad, but I don't know how to stop him.

"You don't understand..." starts Dad.

"Look it's getting late," I interrupt, sharply. "You need to be getting back don't you Chris? You're going to get traffic as it is because of bank holiday. Maybe you should be thinking about leaving."

I want all the questions to stop now. I've had enough. I know this is all new to Chris, and he wasn't quite expecting such a cold and unwelcoming response from my parents, but he's not naive or stupid.

"I'm willing to do whatever it takes to be with Anu, Mr Lamba; even if it means moving up here to be with her."

With that, he gets up.

Does Chris really mean that? Would he really move up here to be near me?

"I'll see you soon," he tells them.

He turns around to face me and plants a kiss on my forehead.

"I'll speak to you later Anu, I better be off."

"I'll call you later," I say softly.

On the journey home, I sit quietly in the back of the car, thinking about Chris' departing sentence.

He's willing to do whatever it takes to be with me; even if that means moving up here.

A tiny smile crosses my lips. When we arrive home I head straight to my bedroom. I'm still unsure of how I'm feeling, other than lonely. Chris is on his way back to the other side of the country, and I'm still no clearer about my present or what my future is going to hold.

Chapter Eighteen

"We're still going to have to meet in secret even though it's out in the open. We've got a long way to go."...Anu

The way I see it is there's only two possible conclusions from being in a long distance relationship.

If your love is true and sturdy enough then it'll withstand anything.

Or on the other hand, the more time you spend apart from one another, then the easier it becomes for the thread to break – that bond to weaken.

Chris' messages and phone calls are the only things that keep me going on days where I feel immense emptiness in my life. Every day brings a personal hope that we'll be accepted by everyone wholeheartedly. It's painful to think that my family will never accept us, so I avoid the thought and push it to the back of my mind.

I don't know if that day will ever arrive but I hold onto hope, because it's all I have.

The relationship between my parents and I was always tense, but it's now turning rapidly fraught.

Chris has travelled up to see me a couple of times since the afternoon he left - telling my parents that he was willing to move so he could be closer to me. I never told them he'd been up to visit me since then. I think they thought, or rather hoped that the long distance between us would prove difficult for us both, and that whatever feelings we might have had would disappear into thin air, like a silly teenage crush.

Logistically we both feel the pressure of not being able to see one another as often as we want.

I've managed to sneak out on a few occasions to spend time with him.

"Nothing's really been resolved. They're not accepting this. They won't even talk about it, as if you don't exist, and they're not talking to me properly either. I don't know what we're going to do."

"Tell them, I'm moving up there."

"What?"

"You heard. I'll move up there, find a job and show them that I'm serious."

"Are you serious?"

"Deadly. I said as much that day when I met up with them. You heard me, right?"

"Of course I did. I heard it loud and clear. But I don't want you to do anything you're not comfortable with babe. You do realise that they might never accept you at all?"

"Do you want to be with me Anu?" he asks, cautiously.

"Of course I do, you know that."

"Then this is the only option we have."

I wanted to cry, with joy this time. If this was the only way then who was I to stop him? Wasn't this what people did when they were in love? Make sacrifices for one another?

Chris understood that I didn't have the luxury of just getting up and leaving, like he could and never once pressured me into anything I was uncomfortable with.

I decided not to be hasty, and tell my parents immediately about Chris' decision to move, just in case it took longer than expected.

Four weeks later and Chris found a place to live, about six miles away from me. I was ecstatic.

I received a message from Dav asking me if everything was ok because I hadn't replied to his last text all those weeks ago. With the entire goings on at the time, I'd completely forgotten to text him so I rang him and got him up to speed.

"Anu, you're so brave. I can't imagine what you've been going through these last few weeks. Why didn't you tell me *yaar?* I thought we were friends?"

"We are friends. It's just been a very difficult time and it's not been easy to talk about it. I've been trying to get my own head round it. They've not taken it well; they keep having these late night discussions at home with my dadi and my auntie and uncle. They don't involve me. I mean I'm the one that's at the centre of all this, but it's like they're trying to decide what's best for me and then when they've decided they'll inform me. It's shit Dav."

"That sounds unfair hun. Have you spoken to them about how you feel?"

"What's the point? I don't get anywhere with them. They know that Chris and I speak on the phone. I don't hide the fact that we do, although sometimes I still get a little jittery when they're around and I'm on the phone to him."

"Man, I can't believe you've actually done it. I'm in shock." Dav sounded completely dumfounded at my news.

"I'm in shock too, I think. I can't quite believe that after all this time I decided to finally tell them about us. Do you think I'm mad?"

"Yeah I do! You've got guts, that's for sure. But you've always been a strong willed person ever since I've known you, so I'm not surprised one little bit...well maybe a tiny bit!"

"Ha ha."

"What's happening now then?"

I told Dav about Chris finding a place to live and moving up.

"So it's serious then?" he asked.

"The way I see it, is that I've taken a massive step telling them about us. We have to show them that we're committed to each other. We've not got any other choice."

"Good on you then. I mean it Anu; I really hope it all works out. And if you want to just get out and meet up, chat, go for some lunch then call me."

"I will thanks."

I felt a little lighter unloading my problems onto him. Kerry was the only other person I told after Dav. She wasn't too pleased that I'd got back with Chris at first, but she knew that it was what I wanted and that I'd thought long and hard about it before taking him back, so she was happy in my happiness. She was almost screaming with shock and excitement over the phone, when I announced it to her.

"About bloody time," she exclaimed. "You've both been through a lot together and you've obviously thought about it seriously to get to this stage, so fuck it and deal with the consequences, it'll be fine. Feed him lots of curry and tell him to sit on a sun bed every day, he'll fit in in no time!"

§

It's been two weeks since my state of affairs has been off the radar in the Lamba household. There's been no interrogation and no mention of Chris' name. I'm unsure if it's a good or bad thing.

I'm sat in the living room with Dadi, when out of the blue she decides to ask me whether I'm still talking to 'him.' I wonder why she thinks I wouldn't be. When I tell her that I am, she tries to pile on her best *I-know-what's-best-for-you* grandma speech; trying to make me see things from a different angle - a totally one sided one. It's the same stuff I've heard before, and although it gets me wound up hearing it again and again, I suppress my annoyance and listen to her out of respect. But I can't control my sharp tongue anymore, and words spit out of my mouth like a leaky tap unable to turn off.

"Why does nobody understand what I'm telling them?" I say angrily. "It doesn't matter to me that he's White, or that he's not Indian. There are plenty of people out there that are in mixed race relationships. They do work. Not all White people are bad Dadi. If they were I'm pretty sure you wouldn't be living in this country, would you?"

The questions and answers go backwards and forwards like a game of tennis. The force of my racquet becomes harder with every game served. Mum and Dad walk into the room, and suddenly we're no longer playing a game of tennis anymore. It's become fiercer, more like a game of rugby, where I'm being tackled and held down at every point so that I can't reach my opponents in-goal area. It feels grossly unfair - three on one. I want Sanya to speak up and take my side to show some support, but she stays quiet.

"Chris is moving up here soon," I shout.

"What do you mean he's moving here? What for?!" asks Dad.

"What for?" I exclaim. "He did tell you that he was willing to do anything to prove he's serious about me, and that's exactly what he's doing."

"When is he coming?" asks Mum, a little apprehensively.

"In a few weeks."

Another look of disappointment creeps over their faces. Without waiting around for a further barrage of questions to follow, I leave the scene, to let them stew over another grim reality.

The day finally arrives when Chris moves into his new place. We conveniently forget to tell my parents the exact date of his arrival and instead decide to enjoy our freedom for a little while longer, before the restrictions kick in. Chris is a little puzzled when I tell him that there will still be barriers to face and obstacles to overcome even though we're out in the open.

"Why can't I see you when they know about us?" he asks, looking confused.

"It's not that easy Chris, you don't understand. Just because we've told them doesn't mean that they're going to accept it so quickly and let us see each other whenever and wherever we like. It's going to take time for this to sink in. It's a massive deal to them babe. No one in my family has ever done this before.

I'm going to get frowned upon from everyone when they find out and it's going to begin with my own relatives. And you've seen how big my family is, haven't you?

We're still going to have to meet in secret even though it's out in the open. We've got a long way to go."

Chris looks bewildered at the new complications which have arisen out of nowhere.

Ironically, neither the secret nor the freedom lasted long enough, because that very night I got an ear bashing from my parents. My car was spotted by them on their way home from work; parked outside Chris' new place, and I was subjected to more accusations after getting rumbled.

"How was work?" asked Dad.

"Yeah it was fine."

"What time did you finish?"

"About seven o'clock."

"So when did you say Chris is moving up?"

"Next week sometime."

"So he's not here yet then?"

"No he's still on the island."

He was quiet for a split second before exploding like a firework.

"Can you tell me then please..." he started, with a detective's style of questioning, "...if you were at work and he is on the Isle of Wight then why have I just seen your car and Chris' car on Millbrook Road, outside a block of flats?"

I could feel the walls closing in on me. I'd been caught out once again. I felt like a naughty thirteen year old once again, getting a telling off after Mum was handed a love letter from Sanya - who'd gone rifling through my personal belongings, even though I tried so hard to hide it in a safe place.

Mum confronted me with the letter, in which I had declared my undying love for a family friend's son.

The situation now was by far grander and more serious than my adolescent crush, but the emotions weren't far off from feeling the same.

I could feel my cheeks turning crimson; sweat forming at the corners of my mouth. I was unable to think of the right words to get me out of this situation unscathed.

"It was supposed to be a surprise that's why. I was going to tell you that he managed to move up quicker than he thought. I was helping him to move his things in."

They didn't fall for it though. Instead I get accused of lying again and Dad said he could no longer trust a word that came out of my mouth.

Chris doesn't understand what all the fuss is about.

"What difference does it make whether I come up now or in two weeks?"

"It's not about you being here, it's about me lying about being in work, when I was really at your flat with you. He's annoyed that I lied about it all. But I don't know what he expected, because he'd never have agreed to me coming over to your flat if I'd have told him."

"He needs to stop making something out of nothing," Chris says, in an annoyed tone of voice. "He gets himself in such a state when there's no need to."

"You think he'd be comfortable knowing that his daughter was alone in her boyfriend's flat? Come on Chris, you know he wouldn't."

"Yeah I know. It just frustrates me, that's all."

"I know it does babe. It frustrates me too, but I have to deal with it. And you're going to have to as well for the time being."

I remain in the bad books with Mum and Dad, and ponder over whether Chris is having doubts that he's made the right decision.

§

My parents eventually let us see one another alone and in public, on the proviso that we meet their conditions. I pull a face when Dad explains.

"You can't meet him whenever you want to, it's only if we

agree and we're comfortable with it. I don't want you to meet at his flat because there's no need to go there. You don't need to take both cars when you go out somewhere, just go in his. Leave your car parked up somewhere nearby. Make sure it's locked and parked in a safe place where it won't get damaged. And I don't want you to wonder anywhere in town or in the local area in case you're spotted by someone we know. And I want you home at a reasonable time; we must know when you're coming back home before you've left."

I feel physically drained after listening to what sounds like his Commandments:

Thou shall not meet up without seeking prior permission and approval from mother and father.

Thou shall not be seen in public where one can be recognised by nosey aunties and uncles who have nothing better to do than spread rumours and gossip about persons who have no direct influence on them.

Thou shall return home at a time which is reasonable and acceptable by parents.

Being with Chris and spending time with him the way we used to at university has become virtually impossible and a distant memory from the world I once knew. When we're out together I feel like Cinderella; out with my prince charming but clock watching until the alarm bells start to ring and I have to race home.

We cope as best we can though - taking it on the chin and in our stride. We don't have much choice.

§

On a few occasions, Dad allows Chris to come to the house for dinner or for Sunday lunch. But even when he invites him, he's always worried that someone might pop round unexpectedly and find him sitting cosily around the table with the family.

Chris has become the entertainment this Sunday afternoon at home, after Dad challenges him to eat a whole green chilli at lunch. He always rises to a challenge no matter who it's with, and my dad is his biggest challenge so far. There is no way Chris is going to back down. He confidently accepts his dare and Dad deliberately eggs him on.

"Indian people love eating chillies," says Dad. "The hotter the better; it's a sign of a strong man when you can eat a whole green chilli, you know."

Well that's it. Chris will never let Dad question his manliness, so he picks up the greenest and biggest whole chili he can find off the plate and throws it into his mouth.

Seconds later, Chris' face changes colour, becoming red as a beetroot. Sweat trickles down his face from every angle. Everyone is laughing at the tops of their voices while he gasps for air and shouts out for water. Krish fetches a glass of water from the kitchen whilst Dadi and Mum express concern over his flustered state, telling Krish to hurry up.

Chris gulps water down and says to Krish, "I'm going to need more than a glass bud. I need a jug. I'm dying here." Mum rushes up to go to the kitchen, bringing back a jug of water filled to the brim. He knocks back the entire jug until the flames that are burning in his mouth are under control.

Dad relishes in his victory and Chris gracefully takes it on the chin. I'm feeling more relaxed today and quietly confident that we're finally making some headway.

After the laughter dies down and Chris' mouth is no longer on fire, Dad asks him how his parents are doing. Chris slips into conversation that his parents are looking at selling their house. "Oh right. Where do they want to move to?" Dad asks with interest.

"Well, that's the interesting thing," he starts. "They want to sell their house and buy a mobile home."

Dad scrunches up his face. "You mean a caravan?" he says, in a shocked tone of voice.

Mum and Dad exchange confused and worried glances with each other. I can see them contemplating the possibility of telling people that their potential son-in-laws parents are gypsies and live in a caravan.

"It's not a caravan. It's bigger and much more luxurious than a caravan. It has everything in it; all the mod cons."

Chris talks about his parents new adventure of buying a mobile home with enthusiasm, but all I can focus on is the uneasiness and embarrassment on Mum and Dad's faces.

The doorbell rings.

Krish gets up to answer the door while the rest of us look round at each other, holding an uncomfortable look in silence; wondering who has turned up uninvited.

Jaya and her family walk in to find us all sat around the dinner table. She seems more shocked than anyone else to find Chris tucked in at the dinner table amongst us all, and sitting comfortably between Mum and Dadi.

Although Mum, Dad or Dadi don't tell any of them why Chris is here, I can see their brains ticking; they're dying to know why he is having lunch with us. They don't stay long and don't have much to say either, so make small talk and then leave quickly.

But they return later in the evening once Chris has gone to quench their thirst for information.

I want to shout, "What bloody business is it of yours?" But Mum and Dad feel obliged to tell them what is going on.

"He's Anu's university friend," Dad says. "You remember he came to Arjun's wedding." He begins to tell them a much shorter and edited version of the truth, omitting some minor details which he feels doesn't need disclosing.

"You kept that quiet," Jaya's Mum says, disapprovingly.

"Well we weren't going to go round broadcasting it to everyone on loud speaker," Dad replies, sounding annoyed at auntie Lalita's snooty comment.

"No but you should have at least told us. And you're happy about this?" asks uncle Arun, as if I'm invisible in the room.

"We're not entirely happy with it, no" admits Dad. "But what can we do, if she says she wants to be with him?"

Auntie Lalita and uncle Arun begin to throw more and more questions at Mum and Dad, and demand answers. I want to scream with anger because it's none of their business.

"Vinnay, you had so many things to say about my family in the past," says Jaya's mum. "You were so quick to judge them, and now when your own daughter is doing things behind your back, you don't have a bad word to say."

A war of words continues between auntie Lalita and Dad as everyone watches on quietly. For the first time ever since the day I exposed my secret to my parents, Dad is fighting my corner and sticking up for me. He tells auntie that she shouldn't compare me to her daughter because the manner in which they found out about me and Chris is much more dignified compared to the lies that their daughter has subjected them to.

"It's completely different," says Dad. "She at least had the decency to tell us what was going on rather than us finding out through more unsavoury ways."

I want to hug Dad and thank him for supporting me, albeit it's in a fit of rage. I can see with the intensity in his eyes that he means every word. I feel special for a tiny second.

The conversation ends sourly and they all leave with a bitter taste in their mouths.

Days later Jaya's brother, Neel comes round to get a slice of the story, and to throw his two pence worth in as well. I happen to be in my bedroom at the time when I hear him tell Sanya what he thinks of it all. "So she's bringing shame on the family eh? After what she's done she's dead as far as I'm concerned. I don't want anything to do with her."

My blood boils.

What right does he have to make judgment over me when he has no idea about my intentions?

I'm annoyed and disgusted that Neel, who is only four years older to me, has become this prejudiced man with unjustifiable views. At Arj's party he was the perfect companion and host to Chris, welcoming him and embracing him into the celebrations and traditions with such enthusiasm and vigour.

But when it really comes down to it, he has the same outlook as everyone else. Indirectly he's saying to me, you can have White friends but you shouldn't cross the line of that friendship into a relationship.

I wonder if he knows that he sounds like a racist.

I decide from that moment on that I don't want anything to do with him anymore.

But I can't get his comment out of my head. I should leave it, let it go and ignore it, but I can't. Instead I send him a text message telling him what I think:

I can't believe you're saying and thinking such disgusting things about me. We live in a society where we should embrace all cultures and communities; integrate not segregate ourselves. You're obviously blinkered by your tunnel vision. I suggest you get out more into the real world. I'm embarrassed to call you my cousin, so as far as I'm concerned you're dead for me too.

Chapter Nineteen

"I don't care whether you're twenty two or thirty two;
whilst you're living under our roof
*we make all the decisions in this house."...**Dad***

It's been almost four months since Chris moved up north to be closer to me, but he's still struggling to find a suitable job that matches both his expansive skill set and desired salary. Luckily he has the luxury of not having to worry about money for a while because his grandmother left him and his brother a significant amount of money in her Will.

He leisurely spends his days filling out application forms for a number of different jobs that interest him. He's even been offered a couple of them, but he's turned them down because he doesn't see any career progression or longevity in them. But rather than thinking that it's a good thing that he's not accepting any old job, Dad says he is being far too fussy, and asks whether he knows that jobs are hard to come by these days. He also thinks that he is wasting his money.

"I don't understand why he's spending so much renting a flat; it's dead money. He should be out looking for a house to buy."

"It's not that easy," I say with frustration. "He only moved up a few months ago. It takes time to settle down and find your feet."

"Yes but it's been four months now; he should be investing that money and buying a property; a house. How are we going to take anything further and tell people about you two if he hasn't even got a job or his own place?"

Chris mentioned to Dad in passing a while back that he wanted to go travelling before settling down. Dad feels obliged to bring it up at this moment. "Does he still have that silly idea to get up and go round the world?"

"Yeah he still wants to do it. It's his dream."

"Time is getting on you know. He's been here for a long time now; he should be thinking about his future and taking things forward, not planning to go on a big holiday."

By taking things forward, Mum and Dad mean that once he's found a house, and got a full time, credible job; one they can tell people about, then he and Mum can get the ball rolling by telling people about us. Ultimately they want us to at least get engaged as soon as.

It is something that Chris and I have spoken about on a few occasions, but I don't want to bring it up too often or push it in case I scare him off. I don't know how I feel about it all myself at the moment and the last time we spoke about it, we ended up in a heated argument.

"I've proved enough to your dad that I'm serious about you Anu, that's why I'm here. But I'll be damned if he starts to put pressure on me to start finding a house quickly just so he can announce to the world that we're a couple. He should have done that months ago himself regardless of me having a job or a house."

"I know Chris. But that's him, you know that. He means well. They just want us to move forward."

"I'm twenty-two, Anu, and you're twenty-one. We're so young. I haven't even got a job yet."

"I know, and I know that you're trying to find one, and so does he."

"But it's not good enough for him is it. He wants everything now. He'd probably be happy if I put a ring on your finger this minute."

"I don't know about that," I joked. "Like you say, you haven't even got a job or a house yet."

We've spoken on many occasions about his dream of going around the world. It was in our first year at university when he first mentioned it, but over time his determination has only intensified. He often asks me to go with him.

There's nothing more that I want than to be able to share this once in a life time opportunity with him - to go on an amazing adventure around the world and for us to create some fabulous memories together. I imagine us sitting on beautiful beaches watching the sunset together. But I know that it's just a beautiful dream; it could never be a reality. That's why, as quickly as I let the thought enter my head, I let it exit just as fast.

"Indian girls don't go on holidays with their boyfriend's Chris," I told him, when he first asked me to go with him. "Once they get married, then it's acceptable for them to do anything they want with their husbands, but before marriage it's out of the question."

My parents don't even like me going to Chris' flat to see him; they would never in a million years let me go travelling with him.

"Me and Graham have bought the tickets now sweet cheeks," Chris tells me.

"Have you? That's fantastic," I say with half hearted enthusiasm. I am happy for him, but I also feel a pang of uneasiness and a hint of envy. We've just started to make real progress with my parents, and I desperately want to hold on to that acceptance. Chris going away now means that Mum and Dad will only doubt our commitment.

I have no right to stop him from going. It's *his* dream, and I'm not about to shatter it for him.

So when he tells me he's booked it and is going in two weeks time, I tell him that I'm extremely jealous.

"I just wish that it was you coming with me," he says.

"Me too babe. You don't know how badly I want to... How long are you away for?"

"I'm away for seven months, and my first stop is India. It's all sorted."

"Good I'm glad. Mum will be pleased that you're going to India."

"Yeah I know. I'll have to ask her if she wants me to give anything to her family."

"Yeah," I say in almost a whisper. I'm confident that Mum will not want our relationship being made public, especially to her family in India.

A few days later I decide to inform my parents that Chris has booked his round the world ticket and he's off in less than a fortnight, for seven months.

"What for? Can he afford it?" is the first two questions out of Dad's mouth.

"He must be able to," I tell him. "His grandma left him and his brother quite a lot of money between them when she died."

"What about his job?"

"Well he hasn't got one yet, which is why he's decided that now will be the best time to go, since he doesn't have any commitments."

Dad looks at me with bemusement on his face.

"You should be his commitment right now."

"I am, Dad. He just wants to fulfil this dream of his. He's not going to get the chance again, not like this. So let him do it."

"Well I can't stop him, can I?"

"This is what *gore* people do," starts Mum. "They just get up and leave without a thought for anyone. What happens if later on in the future he does the same?"

I'm not in the mood for another round of meaningless arguments. No matter which way I put it, they're not going to fathom why this trip is so important to Chris, and why he wants to do it. I'm already feeling deflated after telling them the news, the last thing I want is more confrontation.

"Well he's going soon, and that's it," I say. "I thought you'd be happy that he wouldn't be around for a long time."

Mum doesn't respond.

I'm confused. Even though I want, more than anything for Chris to be rightfully accepted by them, I half-expect, even wish that they will be happy about him going. But for some reason they aren't and I don't understand why.

The day of his departure arrives too fast and I've begun to worry about how I'll cope without him for all those months. But he's promised that he'll stay in touch and email me as often as he can. He tries to make me feel better about the situation, but he knows that I'm anxious.

"When I get back we'll look for a house together, I promise."

"I'd like that."

He heads down south to stay with his brother for a couple of days before they fly out together from Gatwick airport.

The day he leaves I'm an emotional wreck. And for days after he's gone, I barely eat or speak to anyone in the house. I'm feeling this new hole in my life that is filled with emptiness and sadness. The more I think about him being away for all those months, the more it breaks my heart. And although I know that it's a big adventure for him, I pray that his feelings for me will remain the same after all that time apart.

§

Work is the only thing keeping me going. This time the feeling is different though. I don't count down the days until I get to see him, like I did at uni. Instead I wait to hear from him on his travels. That way I can cross off all those places I know he's visiting until he's back at home with me.

Some weeks I don't hear from him at all, but I don't worry. I don't expect to hear from him every day, and when I least expect it that's when he phones me up out of the blue, or sends me an unexpected email. This is when he unknowingly brightens up my days.

In my last email I told him all about my graduation ceremony. How I looked like an idiot dressed in my cap and gown because it was three sizes too big for me and I couldn't walk properly in it. I told him that even with whatever had gone on over the last few months my parents still looked proud to watch me collect my degree on stage; cheering me on when they heard my name - recording the precious moments on their camera.

I left the best bit till last because I knew he'd laugh his socks off when I told him that I walked off stage in the wrong direction to everyone else after receiving my degree.

I wish Chris could have been there to watch me receive it. He'd have been so proud of me.

§

I'm working as ground staff for an airline, and lucky to be working with a close knit bunch of colleagues, whom I endeavour to socialise with when out of work too. My work colleagues have undoubtedly become my confidantes; people I can talk to about my complicated love life. Some of the girls try to understand my situation but are surprised that it is the way it is.

"You're the most westernised person I've met in this place," Danielle said to me last week. "Some of the Asian people working here have got a right chip on their shoulder, but you don't. You're not like them and you don't come across as having strict parents either."

"It's hard that I can't talk to my parents about Chris, because I miss him loads. But we don't have that kind of relationship. At least I can talk to you guys though, right?"

"Of course you can."

Six weeks have raced by and I've spoken to Chris as much as possible. When I miss him I send him a text, and when I just want to hear his voice, I pick up my phone and dial his number. Our conversations aren't very long but I know that he's missing me just as much as I am.

"Hey I received that photo you sent me of you with the snake around your neck in Rajasthan," I tell him.

"Excellent, I'm glad you got that. What an awesome experience that was, Anu. It was a four foot python – almost as big as you babe, and it was placed around my neck. I was shitting myself, but oh my God what an incredible experience."

I hear the excitement and energy in his voice. He's living his dream. I'm happy for him and secretly thrilled that he's finally getting this out of his system.

The next month I receive my mobile phone bill. My eyes almost water when I open up the bulky envelope which contains an itemised bill. I can't quite believe it myself how I've managed to run up a bill for £438.96 in just one month! If my parents get hold of it they'll hit the roof. Thankfully I've started to pay for my own phone bills now.

After university finished and I found full time work, Dad said it was about time I paid my own phone bills. I was fine with that, since I was living rent free at home anyway.

That was another thing that my friends at work found strange; that I wasn't paying my keep.

"Asian families don't really take money from their kids," I said to Tammy one afternoon, when we had two hours down time before setting up to check-in a Malaysian Airlines flight.

"So you don't contribute to bills or food or anything?"

"No, not really," I replied.

"If I take my grandma out shopping and stuff, I pay for any food we might pick up, but that's about it."

"Wow you're so lucky to be living at home rent-free. I have to pay a hundred quid each month, and contribute to the shopping bill."

I didn't think that was that bad, and if my parents did ask me to help out with bills and stuff then I would have happily done so. But Mum and Dad never asked me, and I never offered.

I guess there were advantages to living with Indian parents!

Two days later I'm summoned into my parents' room late at night, just as I'm coming up to bed.

Whenever I'm asked to come into their room late at night, I know I'm going to be in there for a while. It all started after I exposed my relationship with Chris. I'd end up spending a lengthy amount of time in their room in discussions, as they wanted an update every so often as to what was happening between Chris and I. Ever since then I hated it when they shouted my name from the other side of the landing, asking me to come into their room. I knew I'd walk out of there not having the will to live; feeling absolutely drained with all the grilling.

This time they've caught me off guard. I'm geared up to tell them where Chris is up to on his travels; which country he's presently in and what he's up to. But they don't want to know about Chris' adventure. They want to know why I've run up a mobile phone bill of nearly five hundred pounds.

My heart begins to pound from my chest when Dad pulls out the broken down bill in front of me, which details page after page exactly when and for how long I've made and received international calls.

My first reaction is one of madness - that they've gone snooping through my things.

"Why have you gone through my drawers and taken out my stuff behind my back?" I shout at them. "Can't you let me have my own privacy ever? Why do you always open my post? Your name isn't Anu, so why do you open mail that clearly has my name on it?"

My voice grows in pitch and tone as I remember that this isn't the first time they've gone rifling through my personal belongings; they've done it before.

"Because I am your father, and I have every right to know what you are doing, and what you are spending your money on. And anyway we didn't go snooping through your drawers, ok."

"So how did you find it then?" I ask, suspiciously. "It can't have mysteriously walked out of my drawers, could it?"

"I was looking for the hair dryer," shouts Mum, "and I opened up your drawer to see if it was in there. That's when I saw the envelope was open."

"That doesn't mean to say you had to pick it up and read the contents. I don't go reading your letters."

"Listen what's done is done now. We have it and that's all that matters," Dad says, matter-of-factly.

Their reply gets me fuming even more. I'm twenty one years old, and being treated like a disobedient, adolescent teenager who's out of control.

There's no trust from their side. I know I've not given them opportunity to gain that from me in recent weeks, but still, they don't have the right to barge into my private space and invade it; then tear it into pieces whenever they feel like it.

A war of words continues between us. Mum as usual takes Dad's side in everything. When I tell them that I'm nearly twenty two and I don't require keeping an eye on in everything I do in my life, Dad's response is predictable.

"You don't need to remind us how old you are. I don't care whether you're twenty two or thirty two; whilst you're living under our roof we make all the decisions in this house."

I storm out of their room and slam the door shut. I walk into my bedroom and slam the door harder this time to release more of my anger.

I've decided there are definitely no advantages of living at home.

§

There's still an hour and twenty minutes to go before check-in closes for the PIA flight bound for Islamabad, and we still have another two hundred and thirty passengers waiting to be checked in.

The red coloured barriers are set in place, cordoning off a bank of nearly twenty desks; nearly a quarter of the airport terminal space in landside.

A family of five, including three small children arrive at my desk, and the male passenger who I assume to be the head of the family hands me six passports. I begin the check-in process by comparing each passport to its holder, but whilst doing so I notice that there's either a missing passenger or an extra passport belonging to someone else in my hand.

"Where's the elderly lady in this passport?" I ask the group, holding up a Pakistani passport.

"That's my mother, she's sat at the back in her wheelchair," replies the gentleman in his thick Asian accent.

"I need to see her so that I can check her in. Can you bring her to my desk please?"

"It's very difficult for her to come here, actually." He points to the back of the terminal. "She's over there; see right over there in the wheelchair with some family members?"

"Sir I need to physically see the lady here at my desk. If she's travelling with you, I can't print out her boarding cards or send the luggage through without verifying her passport and asking her some security questions."

"But it's difficult for her to come here. Look you can see over there, she's sat in her chair. I can tell you anything you need to know."

I look up to a sea of passengers standing in front of me. Waheed and some of the other airport security staff are arguing with relatives and friends of passengers who have come to drop them off. They're trying to restrict the number of people joining the queue, to only those who are travelling and have a ticket.

"With all due respect sir," I begin. "There's about fifteen elderly ladies over there sitting in wheelchairs, I don't know which one you're referring to. And anyhow she does need to be here at my desk."

He pleads with me to check her in without seeing her, but I'm growing increasingly annoyed at his attitude. "I'm not going to ask you again sir. I need to see the lady otherwise I'll have to ask you to move away from my desk. There's a long queue behind you. I haven't got time to be arguing or justifying the role and duties of my job with you."

He reluctantly wanders off to bring his mother to my desk. In the meantime I start to weigh all the bags to check that they aren't over the combined weight limit.

When the man returns, I tell him that he's over on his weight allowance.

"Sir you have twenty kilos of excess baggage, so you need to either pay for it or take it out."

"Come on love, it's only twenty kilos. There are six of us travelling. You can at least let one bag go for free."

"They're not my rules, sir. It's the airlines policy. If I did that for everyone then I'd get into trouble. If you want to take it you need to pay for it."

Failing on his last attempt to try and sway my decision, he starts to get out the keys for the locks on his suitcases. But at that moment, I give in a little too. I charge him for ten kilos rather than twenty, because there's a long queue of passengers and I haven't got the energy or the time to waste watching a family of six unpack their belongings in front of me.

Danni is sat next to me dealing with a family of five. None of them can speak very good English or so they claim, and when she tries to tell them they have fifteen kilos of extra luggage between them, they make a non-verbal communication gesture by shaking their head, to signify they don't understand.

"No English," states a middle aged man.

Danni proceeds to speak a little slower, using her hands and facial expressions to explain that they have too much luggage.

I could help her out and translate for her but I'm having too much fun watching her play a game of charades with them. Danni starts to look a little agitated with the passengers so I decide that now's the time to step in.

Just as I'm about to, I hear a woman in the group mutter, 'White bitch' in Punjabi, under her breath.

"We should have gone to the Asian girl next door; she would have let our luggage through. This white bitch was never going to let it go."

I don't know if I'm more het up because I'm already in a foul mood after last night's argument with my parents, or whether I'm feeling sensitive because my boyfriend is White. Either way it's got me mad. I turn my back to the desk, pretending to weigh some bags.

"Danni," I whisper. She looks around to acknowledge me.

"Those people in front of you, they just swore at you under their breath." I tell her exactly what they've said.

Danni's cheeks turn red, making her golden blonde long hair stand out against her pale skin tone even more.

"Right," she shouts at the top of her lungs, getting up out of her chair. "No one is going to swear at me, even if it is in a different language, and expect me to take it. I'm refusing to check you in. Can you all get your stuff and move away from my desk?"

I carry on dealing with the next group of passengers at my own desk, refusing to look at the family in front Danni's because I know they'll realise soon enough that I was the one who told her what they said.

But the lady clocks me and shouts out loudly that because I'm Indian that's the reason I told the White girl what they said.

I spot the badge on my blazer pocket displaying the Indian flag, and take a deep breath. I ignore her completely before I say something that I regret and risk losing my job in the process. Instead I call my supervisor over who politely explains to the group that she will not tolerate any racist or abusive behaviour towards her staff; and that they can wait till the end of the flight to be checked in.

Diwali, Christmas and New Year slip by quietly. When an unexpected Diwali card from Chris turns up on my doorstep, I'm overjoyed to see that it's addressed to not only me, but to the whole family.

This year it felt weird that Chris wasn't in the same country as me to celebrate Christmas. Even though every year I've been at home with my family and Chris has been with his, I know that he's only been a couple of hundred miles up the road and across the sea. We could speak as much as we wanted to and wish each other a Merry Christmas.

But he's thousands of miles away somewhere in Australia enjoying the sun, sea and endless barbeques no doubt. I feel a little envious and extremely frustrated that I'm not in a position to pack a bag and fly off to see him. From time to time, I struggle to stop myself thinking about the possibility of him finding someone else.

Chris has always been a free spirit and it's been difficult to pin him down to one place. When he told me he was going to move to be closer to me, at first I thought he was joking and that he wouldn't really move across the country to be with me. But when he proved it, my dream came true and I was overjoyed that that there was something special he found in me which made him lay down his roots.

Chapter Twenty

"Just be happy and true to yourself, that's all I ask.
*I can never forget you."...**Anu***

By the middle of March, a storm of emotions are running frantically inside me. Something has changed, and I can't quite put my finger on it.

I miss Chris, but my heart doesn't ache for him the way it did when he left. I put it down to the fact that he's been gone a while and I've got used to it.

Work is keeping me entertained and I don't know where the time goes. It's not even the best paid job, or even as glamorous as it sounds. Waking up at three in the morning to get into work for four thirty can never sound appealing, but once I'm in work I love it.

Mum finds my job highly exciting, as I often come home from work with stories.

"Passengers leave their brains at home Mum, when they go on holiday. I can prove it." I then go on to tell her some amusing stories that occur in work.

Dad is a little more cautious with displaying his enthusiasm towards my job. He wants to know how long I'm going to be working at the airport checking in passengers on flights and what happened to my dream of getting into the "Media".

I tried my best to find work within the media field after finishing university. I filled out application forms in the dozens. But everything was so hard and so competitive; and after a few short stints of work experience with the BBC and a few unsuccessful interviews I stopped looking at trying to get into the media.

After feeling deflated and hungry to start making money, I applied for work in a different field where I could still use my communication and people skills.

§

Chris has just returned off his trip. I'm excited to see him, but a little apprehensive too. I wonder how I'm going to feel when I see him after so many months apart. The thoughts whirl around in my head as I sit on the train and head to London to see him.

He's staying with Graham for a couple of days before returning up north. But I need to see him straight away. All I've been thinking about over the last few weeks is how I'm going to feel when I see him and what I'm going to do or say.

When he comes to collect me from the train station, he lifts me high in the air and twirls me round. He's ecstatic, telling me how much he's missed me.

"I've missed you too babe, lots," I tell him, convincingly.

"You look great, you've not changed one little bit," he says.

I smile. He has no idea that behind my smile, I'm hiding a multitude of emotions. Everything has changed. I'm no longer the same Anu he left behind seven months ago.

"How's the family?"

"They're ok," I reply. "You've got a tan, and you look like you've lost some weight."

"Yeah I have lost some weight actually and I think Delhi belly played a part in that if I'm honest."

We talk for a while about his adventures around the world and he tells me about the people he met along the way. His life has changed so much in the months he's been gone but he's still so excited and happy to see me.

What he doesn't know is that my life has also changed. Even though I didn't go away anywhere, in my head I feel a world away from him. The feelings I held for him, which were so strong and unbreakable, are slowly fading.

I could have waited for him to return home in a couple of days, but I needed to see him; to see if that feeling, that excitement, that passion and adrenalin was still there for him. I wanted to feel butterflies in my stomach the moment our eyes met. All of those emotions should have been there in abundance.

But they weren't.

I know that I've come to a cross road in my life but I don't know which way to turn. I've spent four years with Chris; sacrificed my parent's happiness and put them through so much, to reach the point where I am at today - where they not only approve of Chris but have happily accepted him into the family and begun to love him. I never imagined in my wildest dreams that I would ever see this day.

He could have walked away from me months ago. Who would have blamed him? He could have easily swopped his life and chosen an uncomplicated path to walk down. But he didn't. He chose me, and he chose to walk back into my life and prove his love for me.

I don't know if I have the courage to throw all that we've achieved together, away in a flash. It's hard not to feel indebted to him but by the same token feel obligated to my family too. I've come so far in my relationship with Chris, and in the relationship with my parents that I don't know if I'm strong enough to express to either of them that my feelings have slowly burned from within me.

No matter what, I have to stay committed to him and see this through, because the consequences will be far greater to deal with.

Two days later Chris is home and settling back into normal life. My family are happy to see him and Dad is even keen to hear all the stories he has to tell.

Week on week the relationship between my family and Chris grows stronger. Chris tells Dad he's looking at finding a place to buy for us both, and that he's going to take on a good job. They seem pleased and it looks as if the time away has done him and my parents the world of good.

Looking at him and my family interact makes me feel artificially happy on the outside but on the inside guilt is eating away.

We've spent hours viewing houses and Dad has even given us his advice on the best locations to look in.

Chris came so close to buying a house, but at the last minute it fell through. It was selfish and mean but secretly I was glad it had fallen through.

If we buy a house it more or less cements the commitment between us and I don't think I'm ready for that anymore. Everything is moving too fast. The next step is unquestionably going to be a marriage proposal.

I should be over the moon that things are moving forward in the direction I've longed for. But that's not what each bone in my body is shouting. I'm petrified and battling with my emotional turmoil.

Chris has noticed. He senses my melancholy mood and asks if everything is ok between us.

"Everything's great," I lie.

"Are you sure, sweet cheeks because you seem a little on edge and quiet these days?"

"It's only work babe," I tell him. "It's all this shift work, my body clocks all over the place. I'm tired that's all."

He leaves it at that and doesn't pursue it anymore.

But it's more than just the distance and time apart that have made my feelings sway.

I've enjoyed my freedom away from Chris in a way I never thought I would. I've found a big wide world out there filled with lots of interesting people. I'm questioning myself whether I'm giving myself a chance to find someone better than Chris; perhaps someone who might even be Indian too. I've begun to question my every intention for being with him.

I don't even know if it was or is infatuation with Chris; or is it love? Do I want to be with him because he's White and it's the thrill of defying everyone that I'm attracted to rather than actually him?

And if those thoughts are going through my mind, then who's to stop them going through Chris' too? I could just as well be a huge challenge in his life because of my background.

On par with those disturbing thoughts are the ones of the few girls' names he has dropped into conversation with me on more than one occasion recently. At first it didn't bother me, because I was excited to hear his stories. But after a while I noticed that there was one name, one girl in every photo he sent to me who kept popping up. How could I be sure that after everything that went on between us he hadn't met someone whilst he was away, and wasn't up to his old tricks again?

I couldn't help but feel uneasy, so I questioned him.

"Anu, why are you being so paranoid? She's just a girl, like lots of people I met when I was away. Nothing's going on, I swear."

But how could I know for sure? I could only take his word for it, just like I did when he swore to me that nothing went on between him and Vani.

I left it and didn't say anything more.

Then a couple of weeks down the line I sensed a change in his behaviour. Whenever we met up, he'd hide his phone from me. When he got up to go to the toilet, he'd pick it up and take it with him.

Whenever I'm around him his phone is on vibrate or silent and he'll answer his calls in another room, away from me. That never happened in the past.

We plan to spend the afternoon looking through a handful of brochures from the estate agents. Chris decides to grab a take-away for us both and insists on picking it up, so I stay in the flat and wait for him.

As soon as he leaves my inner conscious stirs unexpectedly and I find myself rifling through his things.

Starting with his paperwork inside a box file stored at the side of the TV, I start rooting. I know it's wrong of me to do it, but I don't have any other option. Chris has so easily lied to me in the past, that deep down I don't think I've ever let myself regain that trust in him. Doubts are never too far away from my mind, and a huge part of me cannot believe that he went away for so many months and didn't meet someone else.

I come across mobile phone bills. His latest bill is in its envelope. It's already been opened, so I pull it out and scan it. I feel a moment of guilt as I remember the way I exploded with my parents when they confronted me about my phone bill.

My number appears on the bill repeatedly, but then so does

one other. It creeps up time after time as I examine his bill in more detail.

He's spoken to this mystery person at various times of the day and night and sent frequent text messages. It isn't Graham's or his mum or dad because I have their numbers stored in my phone.

I dial the number from my mobile, with-holding my own number. A female voice answers after three rings. I put it down straight away; she doesn't sound English.

In a state of panic I walk into his bedroom and rummage through his shelf and drawers to find more clues. Under a pile of papers and books on his shelf I come across a photograph which is turned over – picture side down. My hands tremble as I go to pick it up. I'm afraid of who and what I might uncover. In my mind I picture myself at uni; in my second year and in the room I shared with Vani - sitting on my bed about to open her diary, petrified of what I was going to unearth.

It's her. The girl I've seen in many of the photographs with Chris. Although it isn't a compromising photo, I can see that there's an intimacy that only the two of them share in the picture.

I feel numb.

But I'm not sure if I'm entirely disappointed or even bothered at the discovery.

The predicament I'm in is that no matter how hard I've tried to forget the past, it hasn't ever really left my thoughts. It's always been there lurking in the corners, waiting for the right moment to stir and awaken with life - to remind me of the heartache.

Chris and Vani are there, like an open wound that I can't get rid of. No matter how hard I treat it the scar is always going to remain; visible and exposing me to unforgettable hurt and pain.

Chris returns a short while later. I'm sat on the sofa with the TV on and sound turned off. He asks me why the sound is off. "I'm not in the mood to watch TV," I say. He sees his mobile phone bill in my hand.

Panic instantly sweeps across his face.

"What are you doing?"

"It's funny that, because I was going to ask you the same thing. You've been acting weird for weeks Chris, ever since you came back,"

"What do you mean acting weird? I thought you'd be happy that I'm looking for a house to buy for us and that I've now got a job. Your parents will be happy."

"Just forget about my parents for one minute. What is it that you want?"

"I don't understand Anu. What is all this about?"

I pick up the phone bill in my hand lifting it in the air, pointing to the mystery number with my finger.

"I want to know whose number that is."

"What number?"

"Please don't act all innocent with me Chris, like you don't know what I'm on about. Something's been bothering me for weeks; like the way you pick up your mobile when you're just going to the bathroom. You cling on to it with dear life as if I'm going to go through it if you leave it lying around for even a minute. And it's always on silent these days."

"You're being silly Anu."

"I'm being silly. That sounds familiar. You've said that before Chris, when you swore blind to me that there was nothing going on between you and Vani?"

"I wondered how long it would take you to bring her into the conversation."

"I have every right to. Who is this person Chris, because looking through the bill, I can see that you've called this number about twenty times in the space of a week, and sent about fifty text messages."

He fumbles around with words. "...It's no one, just a friend that I met when I was away."

"Who is it you met? Which friend?"

"I met lots of people Anu."

"I'm not asking about everyone, I'm asking about this particular person." I pull out the photo from my bag and lift it in front of him. "Is that number, this person?" I ask, pointing at the girl next to him in the photo.

The colour drains from his face instantly. He has nowhere to go and hide.

"Where did you find that?"

"Does it matter where I found it? I just want to know who she is."

There's a long pause before he answers.

"Her name's Isla," he finally admits.

"And is she the one that you've been talking to. Is it her number on your phone bill?"

Chris puts his hands in his pockets and stands facing me; a look of guilt pouring out of him. "Just say it," I snap.

"It's not what you think Anu, seriously."

"Care to tell me what it is then?"

"Isla was having a bit of trouble with her boyfriend while she was away. He was out there with her travelling with us all. They just had a few problems going on."

"And don't tell me, she came to you for help?" I say sarcastically.

"She just wanted someone to talk to. We still talk. She's still going through a hard time."

"Clearly! Why has she come to you though? Has she not got any female friends or closer friends than you?"

But before I give him a chance to answer, I tell him that I don't believe him. "Chris, lying is like breathing to you. You can't help it. It comes to you so naturally. I mean why would you have a photograph sitting on your shelf of the both of you with a load of books and paper stacked on top of it? It doesn't make sense. It looks to me like you keep this photo close to you, and since you knew I was coming to see you, you hid it so I wouldn't see it or question you."

"You're wrong."

"I'm not wrong Chris. I'm right. Whatever you say, I don't believe you."

"This is about Vani isn't it?"

"It's always been about Vani. I've never got her out of my head. I thought I could get over it but I just can't."

"So why didn't you talk to me about it?"

"Because I thought I could deal with it."

I don't want him to see my tears, but it's too late. They start to roll down my cheeks.

Chris comes close to hold me, but I push him away.

"I don't want you to hug me. I just want the truth."

"I am telling you the truth, Anu."

"You're not. And to be honest with you, I've not been either."

Chris looks confused. "What do you mean?"

Wiping away my tears I attempt at explaining to him what's

going on inside my head. "I don't feel the same about you as I did, Chris."

"How do you mean Anu? I don't understand. We've kept in touch all the time I've been away," he says. "I've emailed you, sent you photos. I've told you all the time that I miss you and love you. I don't understand."

"I know you did. But I can't help the way I feel. I can't explain it properly."

"Try to because I need to know what's going on in your head."

Suddenly it's me in the spotlight. I'm the one being interrogated instead of him.

"I just think we've grown apart. The distance and time has been too long."

"It's been the same distance and time for me Anu and my feelings haven't changed."

"Maybe not, but you're still hiding things from me."

"I'm not."

"I've been thinking about this since before you got back, but I needed to know how I felt about you when I saw you. That's why I came to see you straight away, as soon as you got back."

"And what did you feel?"

I hold his look with sadness; my voice becomes quieter, softer. "Not the same as I desperately wanted. I can't help it. We've both had time apart and met different people; I'm not sure whether it's you that I want to be with."

His shoulders drop and his face falls to the floor.

"I'm sorry Chris."

He looks up. "Have you met someone else?"

"No."

At nearly twenty two I thought I knew what love was. I was adamant that I knew my heart well enough to make tough and big decisions. But the truth is that I'm not. In reality there is so much more in life that I want to do and experience. There are so many other people that are going to enter my life and I want to let them. I want to find my inner self and explore it.

Part of me has grown used to being without Chris and I'm starting to enjoy this new found freedom.

I know that I'm not ready to commit to him. Not because I don't love him; because I do. I'm just not in love with him anymore. And I don't think I'll ever be able to find my inner strength to forgive him for what he did to me.

"I'm not seeing anyone Chris."

"So why are you doing this?"

"You're not telling me the truth babe. I know you're lying about that girl. But it doesn't matter, because it's probably for the best."

I go to pick up my bag.

"So you're just leaving it like this," he asks.

"I don't know what else to do. It's done my head in for weeks and weeks. I've put you and my family through so much. Even with all my doubts I still tried to give it my best shot, because it's what I wanted. I couldn't let my parents down. They really like you."

"So you've stayed with me because you've felt sorry for me and you didn't want to upset your parents again?"

"No of course not."

"That's what it sounds like." He gets angry with me.

"Maybe if they'd have been a bit more open and chilled out with us from the start; given us the freedom to spend time with each other more often, then maybe you wouldn't have gone travelling, or we'd be a lot closer right now and things would be very different. But I feel a million miles away from where you're at. I'm not seeing anyone else, but I feel like I want to Chris and maybe I need to, so that I know what it is that I want. Can you understand?"

His eyes look glazed as tears pool inside them.

"You've put me through a lot of heartache and I don't want to keep rubbing it in your face, honestly I don't. I know it's in the past, but it's the not knowing of things in your present too that I can't deal with. You went away for all these months and I think you met someone else. I'm not entirely convinced that you want to lay down your roots with me. I think that deep down you're trying really hard to make a go of this, like me - because of what we've both been through and with everything we've had to face along the way."

I suddenly feel this strong power of self control wash over me. There are no more tears.

"You're not ready for marriage Chris and neither am I. We're both very young and we need to find our self; figure out what it is we want in life...you know I'm right. You've been pushed into buying a house and moving up here, and I feel so guilty about it. But it's not what I want. Be honest with me, is it truly what you want?"

He lifts his head to make eye contact with me, but he maintains a strong, silent expression. His unspoken words speak volumes.

An overwhelming wave of relief showers over me, lifting a thick fog from above my head. The misty clouds begin to feel as if they're washing away to make room for a sparkle of sunshine.

I start to make my way to the door, but Chris tries to stop me. "Please, don't stop me Chris."

We walk down the spiral staircase in silence. He opens the

door and stands at the top of the steps to the entrance of his flat.

He asks if he can give me a hug. I let him. He holds me in his arms so tight before I inch away from him.

"I could never break up with you Anu, even if I tried to; never in a million years."

I realise then that he knows we're making the right decision.

"Just be happy and true to yourself, that's all I ask. I can never forget you," I tell him.

He kisses my forehead, holding his lips tightly. I tear myself away from him and run down the steps to my car. I drive away almost instantly, refusing to look back at him. If I do, I may not have the courage to leave. I may change my mind, in fear of the unknown waiting for me at home instead.

I don't know how I'm going to break this to my parents, but it seems irrelevant right at this moment in time.

I don't care. Nothing matters anymore but this welcoming courage pouring out from me.

I can do this. I can walk away and be happy knowing I've done the right thing, I know I can.

§

Six months later

As I make a final call for the last remaining passengers to board the Thomas Cook flight to Rhodes, a young couple sitting to the side of me, catches my eye.

The girl appears to be of Indian appearance and looks slightly older than me. She's sitting hand in hand with her White boyfriend, I'm assuming - a glow radiating from both their faces.

He turns to look at her and wipes away something from her cheek; then tucks whispers of hair behind her ear, before kissing her on the forehead.

A dull ache creeps into my heart as I evoke thoughts of Chris for a moment. All those dreams, hopes and promises we'd made to each other seem like another life time ago; as do the dark days and nights I'd spent fighting a battle with my parents just to win them over.

Different forms of guilt consumed me for weeks after Chris and I parted, which coincided with relief. It started with a sad, confusing feeling.

How could all those emotions I once had for him disappear so easily? Should I have given us more time to adjust after he returned? Perhaps those feelings would have come flooding back. Was it still worth fighting for after we'd come this far? Could I really face a life without him in it? And if so, what would it be like?

There was the guilt I faced every time I looked into my parents eyes; a constant reminder of all those hours I'd spent convincing them that Chris was the one I wanted to be with, and could see my future with. Them coming to terms with the disgrace I bestowed upon them and then having the courage to accept it and tell everyone in the family. How would they face everyone again? What would they tell them?

But I quickly came to the conclusion that it didn't matter what anyone thought. It was about what I thought and what I felt in my heart. And in my heart of hearts I knew that I'd taken the right course of action.

Chris has unquestionably shaped the person I am today; that of a feistier, more confident, and strong willed individual, who doesn't shy away from life's constant and unexpected twists.

I will never forget and never regret.

EPILOGUE

"I will never crave for acceptance from anyone,
but my heart."...Anu

I wait until uncle Arun has finished singing, 'For she's a jolly good fellow' before I cut my birthday cake. Nobody's birthday is ever complete until uncle Arun belts out the words at the top of his lungs. Everyone claps their hands once he's finished singing. Mum and Dad are stood at either side of me.

There are about fifty people circling me, all watching me as I'm being fed cake one after the other by my relatives.

"Smile," shouts Arj, as I stand with my mouth half open and Dad feeding me a generous slice of chocolate cake.

"Do you have to take a photo of me being fed Arj? It's such a typical Indian thing to do... I know let's take photos of your mouth half open and a spoon shoved in it!..Can you take another one, without my mouth wide open and on show, please?"

"Why? You can put it on Facebook, Anu!" He lets out a cackling laugh. "Make it your profile picture, your mum and dad feeding you cake in front of all your friends on your thirtieth birthday!"

"Ha ha very funny."

"Right can we have a speech now please Anu?" auntie Renu says.

"Come on, we know you're never short of words," shouts Ritu.

Dadi is sat on a chair by the side of me. Everyone gathers round to hear what I'm about to say.

I clear my throat in jest. "Well you all know that I'm not shy when it comes to public speaking. So firstly I want to thank my mum and dad, and my auntie Renu and uncle Ashok who have made this party possible. Without them it wouldn't have come together and have been as special as it is."

I turn to look at my parents. "I'm well aware that I've not always been the easiest of people to see eye to eye with, and god knows how much I drive you mad; but you are the best parents in the world and I love you both very much. So thank you Mum and Dad for everything you've done for me over the last thirty years. I'm very lucky to have you as my parents."

A bout of clapping erupts from around the room.

"I also want to say thank you to everyone who made it tonight. This year has got to be the first time ever I've seen so much snow and that too on my birthday. I just wish it didn't snow quite so much because there's some family and friends that haven't been able to make it tonight, which I'm totally gutted about.

"It can't be helped though, and those of you who have managed to dig yourselves out of your homes and be here tonight to share my special day, I'm really glad you could make it. It's been fantastic to see each and every one of you."

"It's been a brilliant party," auntie Renu shouts.

"Can I say something now?" says Krish.

I wonder what he wants to say.

Krish picks up Dadi's walking stick, which is hung on the back of her chair, and he holds it up in the air.

He turns to her and starts speaking in Punjabi, in front of all my friends and family.

"Dadi, what Anu has just told Mum and Dad, in front of everyone, is that she's extremely sorry that she's not yet married yet."

"Hang on, hang on," I say. "When, did I say that you cheeky monkey?"

He ignores me, continuing to talk to Dadi in Punjabi in front of all my guests.

"She knows that you're all waiting for her to get married and leave the house, so you can make some home improvements; so she's promised that within the year, she'll try her hardest to find a nice man and settle down. She also says that she's very sorry that she's such a fussy person, but she'll make more of an effort now that she's thirty."

Laughter fills the room, and Ritu translates what Krish has just said to my non-Punjabi speaking guests.

I thank Krish for his wonderful speech and tell him that just because he's twenty it doesn't mean that he's not old enough to start looking for a wife. He looks at me with a horrified expression.

"Forget that, I'm happy on my own, thanks. It's you that we need to get rid of!"

"Don't worry little bro, I'll help you find a bride when it's your turn, but remember she'll have to be vetted by Dadi first."

§

Two notifications ping up in my emails one after the other. A Hindu Gujrati guy has expressed his interest in me, and the site tells me that I should respond back immediately to keep my ratings high. I was almost certain that I'd filtered my preferences, but I'm still receiving matches from a whole spectrum of Indian guys around my age; Hindu Gujrati, Hindu Punjabi, Hindu Bengali, Hindu Spiritualist.

At first I found the Indian dating site a little daunting. I'm a big fan of modern technology and social networking, just like anyone else, but this new age virtual dating platform sits a little uneasy with me. I feel like I'm selling myself over the internet, exposing my world and my heart to millions of complete strangers in the hope of finding that one perfect, potential partner.

It's taken a lot of persuasion from people close to me to even log onto the website, let alone sign up to it. But nearly twelve months have passed and I'm still dipping my toes in the pond searching for that special frog.

I read the opening line of his profile:

My friends would describe me as fun loving, caring, romantic, funny, trustworthy...

Just about every single guy has said the same thing. There hasn't been one person, in months, whose jumped out and made my heart flutter a little; apart from my date tonight.

I read on:

I'm looking to find a wife who can make my rotis! My favourite dishes are...

DELETE!

From his photos, he looks like he's just landed in the country from a small village back home. It's not far away from the truth. He is from Slough!

Mum and Dad can't figure out what it is I'm looking for in a man; they don't understand why I'm too picky.

The way I see it is though, you can't be too careful when it comes to finding your Mr Right. After all I'm not husband shopping for Christmas, with the intention of returning him in the January sales. This is for life. So absolutely everything has to be right.

I can make compromises and sacrifices for the right person; but when it comes to chemistry and physical attraction, there are no compromises. You've either got it or you haven't. You either feel it or you don't.

"Are you wearing that?!" Mum exclaims in a loud voice as I come down the stairs and into the kitchen.

For a brief moment I feel slightly self conscious that I may be revealing more flesh than I ought to be in front of her.

"Why, what's wrong with what I'm wearing?" I reply defensively, pulling up my top discretely so she doesn't notice my low cut.

"You've only got one sleeve on your top. Where's the other one?!"

"It's a one off shoulder top Mum; that's what it's supposed to look like - it's fashionable."

"It looks strange to me, are you sure?"

I bite my bottom lip to try and refrain from rolling my eyes at her.

"Where are you going again?" she asks in her usual, suspicious voice.

"I told you last week Mum, I'm going to Hayley's leaving do at, The Mustard Bar and Lounge in town. She's got a new job, down south in London so she's leaving."

"I don't remember you saying. Who is this Hayley? How many are going? Where's Mustard Bar?" she continues in the same breath.

"She works with me in the office," I sigh. "You don't know her; I have mentioned her before."

"I don't recall her name. Anyway, you're taking the car, right?"

"Yes."

"You're not drinking then, are you?" she says, in a tone that sounds more like she's telling me rather than asking me.

"Mum, I've just told you I'm taking the car, so why would I drink?"

"Just making sure. I know what it's like when you go out. You see your friends drinking, you get lost in the atmosphere and before you know it you've got a drink in your hand."

I can't help but laugh out loud at her, as if she was a serial party goer and socialite in her youth. "How would you know Mum? You don't drink, you don't have a social life and you never go out anywhere!"

She walks over to a kitchen drawer beside the cooker and pulls out a rolling pin, preparing to make chapatis for dinner this evening.

"Don't worry I won't be drinking and driving." I tell her reassuringly; feeling a tad guilty for my unintentional unkind words.

"You shouldn't be drinking anyway. What time are you going to be back?"

"I don't know. I haven't even walked out of the house yet."

"Still, you must have an idea?" she perseveres. "Didn't you say you're in work tomorrow?"

"Yes I am. It won't be late."

I glance at the kitchen clock above me, growing increasingly agitated at the twenty questions being fired my way. I was hoping to leave by seven, but it's now approaching nearly seven thirty; I'm already working to Indian timing.

In an attempt to make a sharp exit before being interrogated any further, I grab my jacket and walk into the hallway. Dad is hovering, pretending to fiddle with a set of keys hanging on the key rack. He casts me his customary sceptical look, which involves eyeing me up and down and pushing up his glasses above his nose so they rest on top of his head. Within seconds I find myself being quizzed again; repeating the same answers to the same questions asked only minutes earlier.

"I've told Mum that I won't be late, don't worry. I know I'm working early tomorrow."

"Just make sure you're home on time. I don't want to be ringing you..." His voice trails off in the distance as I slam the front door behind me, to deliberately avoid anymore trivial questions.

I'm not even around the corner, driving out of my estate when I ring him.

"Hi, I'm on my way," I say, already feeling exhausted at the evening ahead of me, but nonetheless excited.

It's only a white lie. Surely it can't be that bad? Potentially he could be the one, and then they wouldn't mind so much that I hid it from them. They'd be happy that I'd found someone who was not only Indian but Hindu Punjabi. That'd be the icing on the cake! He's already a potential winner based on their check list alone.

What about me though? Will he tick all the boxes on my checklist? Can he make my heart flutter? Get my heart beat racing? Make me weak at the knees? Can he make me laugh uncontrollably with his witty sense of humour? Most importantly, can he be my soul mate; that someone who's right there on my level?

My brow glistens with apprehension as I ponder over the newly formed thoughts processing through my brain.

I've been on a few dates before today, but none of them has made me feel quite so nervous like this time.

I smile at myself, remembering the shoe disaster on my first date from this site.

I was already feeling apprehensive about meeting the first Indian guy off it; but when I got to London to meet him, all my worries subsided because he was a real gent.

He opened and closed doors for me; even paid for lunch, refusing to take a penny off me. Well I suppose it was the least he could do since I'd travelled all the way to London to meet him. Normally I'd never have gone all that way to meet a complete stranger, but because Sarika had her own place in Canary Wharf I asked if I could stay there the night.

It was a bright summer's day and the weather was scorching hot. I wore a long, flowing white skirt and pink top with sandals. Puneet and I walked and talked for ages, taking in the scenery and sites. We ended up in Covent Gardens where he bought me an ice-cream. The conversations were flowing effortlessly and everything was going great, until I got up from a grassy area where we'd been sitting on. As we started to walk away suddenly my foot slipped and I tripped on to my side. I ended up on the floor on my back side with a broken shoe lying beside me.

I hoisted myself up as quickly as I could. I was mortified and tried to hide the embarrassment which was written all over my face.

Puneet was so sweet about it. My sandal broke in two and I couldn't walk a single step after that.

I ended up walking bare foot trying to find a shoe shop. We must have walked around for about thirty minutes before I came across a half decent looking shoe store. I paid an extortionate amount of money for what the sandals were worth but I wasn't bothered at the time. I wasn't about to worsen the embarrassment by pondering over the price of shoes.

Puneet found the funny side to it thankfully, but by the middle of our date, I'd already decided that although he was a lovely person, he just wasn't right for me. In person, the spark just wasn't there.

I ring Rohan's number and speak to him on loudspeaker, telling him I'm on my way.

"I was just about to ring you actually," he says. "Great timing."

"Really?" He hasn't clocked on that I'm working to Indian timing here.

"You're not cancelling on me are you?" I ask, sounding a little worried.

"No, not at all. In fact I was going to suggest something. Why don't you come to my house and we can go together?"

"Oh, erm..."

"That's if you want to. You don't have to come inside don't worry."

"No it's not that. I just thought we were going to meet up in the square. But if you want to go together, I don't have a problem with that."

"Yeah come over, we'll go from my house, the square is close by from my end."

"Ok, give me your address and I'll be there as soon as."

He sends me his address in a text message and I enter it into my sat nav. It's only a fifteen minute drive away.

As I approach the leafy suburbs of his home town I start to feel anxious. Foolishly, I've built up some sort of expectation in my head and desperately want him to meet it.

He is good looking (from the photos anyway) and sounds articulate on the phone in the few conversations we've had. He's a property developer, so financially he's extremely stable.

His house is signposted; leading me up a private path, set a few metres back from the main road. I arrive minutes later and sit in my car in awe. I'm parked outside the house which is fenced around a high electric gate. The house is stood about fifty feet from the entrance of the gates. I turn off the engine and text him telling him I'm outside.

A few minutes later he walks out of his house wearing jeans, a knee length coat and a hat of some sort. I pull down the window as he approaches my car.

"Hi," he says.

"Hello. Are you well?"

"Yes thanks, and you?"

"Yeah I'm good. So are we ready to go then?" I ask.

"I was thinking, shall we go in your car, rather than take two?"

I look puzzled. "I thought I was going to follow you from here, I thought that's why you said to come by yours?"

"Yeah I know, I just thought that since you told me yesterday you weren't going to be drinking, because you're in work early tomorrow, I thought maybe we could go in your car and I could have a few drinks. You don't mind do you?"

"Erm...." I don't know what to say. I'm not expecting this and I certainly don't feel comfortable with it. But I don't want to say no either, in case he thinks I'm being difficult.

"Well ok if you want. But I can't make it a long night."

"That's fine, don't worry about that. I just thought it made sense since you're not drinking."

He jumps into my car all too quickly, in case I change my mind. He leads the way and makes small talk as I drive.

It's only been a couple of minutes since I've met Rohan in the flesh and already I'm beginning to feel a little uneasy. In my mind, disappointment is already settling in. But I try not to show it on my face. It could be just first date nerves on both our part.

Just as we arrive on the square and walk towards the bar and restaurant he's chosen for us, he tells me it's one of the finest establishments around.

"You like your restaurants don't you? In your profile you mentioned you were a bit of a foodie," I ask.

"Yeah absolutely. In fact I've only just got back from Denmark after visiting a new five star Michelin restaurant that's just opened up. We were literally out there for one night, just to dine at this place. It was awesome."

"Oh wow," I say, trying to sound enthusiastic behind my fake smile. He proceeds to tell me step by step, in detail exactly what he ordered and ate during his starter, main meal and dessert; not forgetting to omit the endless wine tasting he managed to do.

I carry on pretending to look interested in what he is saying, but all I'm really thinking is, how much longer do I have to listen to his irritating voice for.

If you're so suave and sophisticated like you make yourself out to be then why are you sitting in this posh place looking all pretentious with a flat cap on your head? You're sat inside a restaurant with your hat on, you moron.

I begin to get angry at myself for wasting my time getting dressed up for him. On the phone he seemed different; interesting and fun. And he sounded interested in me and what I did too. But all he's done so far is talk about him the entire time, whilst knocking back fancy whiskies.

I definitely don't feel guilty about hiding this date from my parents.

It's not a potential partner this guy's after, it's a bit of company so that he can drink his whiskies and bore some poor soul with his fancy stories.

When I can no longer stand the sight of his annoying cap, which is covering half of his face, I politely ask him to take it off.

"It's difficult to talk to you properly Rohan because your cap is covering your eyes. How about you take your hat off? We are sitting inside a nice restaurant after all?"

"I don't want to take it off," he says, sounding annoyed that I've even suggested the idea.

"But I can't see what your hair looks like, how about you take it off for a second just so that I can see it?"

He shifts a little in his seat. "I don't want to take off the cap. I think it looks good on me."

"I'm not saying it doesn't look good on you," I lie. "I'm only asking you to take it off for a minute, but if you don't want to then that's fine, no big deal."

Rohan is grating on me in every possible way.

"If I asked you to take your make-up off, would you do that for me?"

I'm puzzled at his question, wondering where he can possibly be going with this. "Pardon?" I say.

"Well you wouldn't like it if I insisted on seeing you without your make up on, so similarly I don't want to take my cap off."

I laugh out loud in utter disbelief.

"That's a bit rude isn't it, saying that to a lady?"

He shrugs his shoulders in denial.

The food arrives seconds later and I'm thankful that I have a distraction for a short while. I don't want to be further insulted so remain quiet during dinner.

Surprisingly he's realised that the conversation is running dry, because he eventually decides to ask me a question. It's only taken him the best part of an hour to do so.

"Are your parents religious then?" he asks.

"They are kind of, yeah. My mum is probably more religious than my dad, but we all go to the Temple when we can for most religious functions. What about you? Do you go to the Temple?"

"Not really, no. My parents do, but I don't. I don't have time for religion."

Just when I think there is nothing else he can say to shock me, he proves me wrong.

"What do you mean you don't have *time* for religion? Do you need to make time to pray?"

"My priority is making money. I like to make lots of money so that's why I don't have the time to go to the Temple."

I'm speechless. No wonder this guy, who at thirty four isn't married yet. He might have the looks and the cash to flash, but there's nothing remotely intellectual or appealing about his personality. I'm disappointed at myself for not picking up on his character and traits before tonight. *It's one evening Anu, come on you're strong. Don't let him bring you down.*

I make my excuses and get up to use the ladies toilets, just so I don't have to breathe the same air as him for a few minutes. Five minutes later, after fighting the urge to punch him I return to the table.

"Shall we go on to another bar?" he asks. "I know a great beer place around here. They do the best beers."

"I'm not drinking, you know that."

"They do non-alcoholic beers too."

Why is he not getting the hint that he is the last person in the world I want to go anywhere with?

"Actually I'd better be going."

"But it's still early. You've still got a bit more time, surely?"

"I've got an early start; I did tell you I can't make it a late one. And I've yet to drive you back anyway; unless you wanted to stay out and get a taxi...?"

I could kick myself for stupidly agreeing to chauffer him. It's obvious that all he wants is a free taxi ride. I'm hoping he decides to make his own way home.

"No, no that's fine. Let's go then."

Damn!

On the drive back to his house I hardly speak.

"Did you like the restaurant?" he asks.

"Yeah it was nice."

"I love going to that restaurant, their food is awesome."

It's a Spanish restaurant for God's sake; all tapas food is the same. There wasn't anything special about that food other than the eye watering prices.

"It's one of my favourites," he says. I wonder how many other victims he's brought here and bored to death.

I pull up outside his house wearing my best smile. "Well it was nice meeting you Rohan. Thank you for a lovely dinner, I had a pleasant time."

"I'm glad you did because so did I. Maybe we can do this again some time. I know some great bars. We could do bit of a pub crawl if you like?"

Is this guy for real?

"I'll get in touch," I lie.

I make a quick getaway as soon as he steps out of my car; positively exhausted from my wearisome evening.

Everyone at home is in bed, other than Dad of course. He's still awake and waiting up for me.

I pop my head round his bedroom door on the way to my room. "How was your friend's party?" he asks. "It was good, yeah. I'm tired though now so I'm going to bed, I'll talk to you tomorrow. Goodnight."

"OK, good night."

I try to block out the last few hours of this evening. Physically and mentally I feel drained. This wasn't how I imagined the evening to pan out when I left the house. My phone pings. It's a text from Rohan:

Hi Anu, just wanted to let you know that I had a great time this evening. It was lovely getting to know you; going for drinks and grabbing some food. Let's do it again sometime soon. I know a great Thai restaurant.

I laugh out loudly for a second, forgetting that Sanya is asleep in her bed inches away from mine. She stirs.

"What's so funny?" she asks sleepily.

"Nothing. Never mind. I'll tell you all about it tomorrow."

An unwavering thought resides in my mind as I position myself in bed. If my existence was to be a lie, how could I ever feel content in life?

I couldn't.

No matter how long it takes, I'll always stay true to myself. I'll strive to remain the director of my life and my own destiny; and I'll live a life that I love and am happy with.

I will never crave for acceptance from anyone, but my heart.

10304713R00160

Printed in Great Britain
by Amazon.co.uk, Ltd.,
Marston Gate.